Spurred by the family name at an early age, A. M. Story harboured the ambition to be a writer and now lives in South Warwickshire writing novels, attending the theatre and enjoying rural pursuits.

ON A THIN STALK

At three in the morning by a disused airfield, jobbing farmer and local council-lor Amos Cotswold leaps for his life when Spitfires strafe the road. He lands in a ditch atop the corpse of a German prisoner of war. But it's 2006. Could this be a ghostly repetition? Or powerful interests opposed to the redevelopment of the adjacent army camp? Amos comes up against phantom aircraft, fine art, and a gangmaster's exploitation of immigrant labour. Hampered by his inherited obliga-tion to the wartime underground movement, Amos finally uncovers the dark reality of what the Second World War bequeathed the country.

Books by A. M. Story
Published by The House of Ulverscroft:

STRAWS UPON THE SURFACE

A. M. STORY

◆

ON A THIN STALK

Complete and Unabridged

CHARNWOOD
Leicester

First published in Great Britain in 2007 by
Robert Hale Limited
London

First Charnwood Edition
published 2010
by arrangement with
Robert Hale Limited
London

British Library CIP Data

Story, A. M.
    On a thin stalk.
    1. World War, 1939 – 1945- -Great Britain- -Influence- -
    Fiction. 2. Suspense fiction. 3. Large type books.
    I. Title
    823.9'2–dc22

    ISBN 978–1–84782–975–7

In loving memory of my parents,
Jim and Pegi Story.

Acknowledgements:

I wish to thank Christopher Farmer for his unwavering support and for keeping me fed with both food and information during the writing of this book; my friend, District and County Councillor Peter Barnes, whose fine example provided the inspiration for Amos Cotswold; and my friend and neighbour, Mike Woods, for his invaluable help on POWs in South Warwickshire during the second world war.

'You practise your pastoral music on a thin stalk.'

Virgil

1

Out of nowhere they came at him. He'd heard nothing, no approaching hum, no warning lights high above, no sudden rush of air. One minute silence, and the next that deep throb searing his soul.

The shots rang out — a barrage of bullets strafing the road, zinging off the metallic surface, whizzing past his ears like a scene from *War of the Worlds*, whipping up his thoughts, blinding, confusing — terrifying. How come he was still standing? Had he been hit? Was he already dead, looking on at his own demise?

Thus propelled, Amos leapt for the ditch and sank face down in the peat, his new hip groaning in its socket at the unwarranted exercise, his heart thumping, his mind in overdrive — continuously starting and restarting its diagnostic procedure, streaming sets of data through the dials, trying to make sense of what was happening.

The noise ended. No gradual retreat into the distance, no slow diminution of sound, no fading out. The engines had been abruptly cut. Had they landed and come looking for him on foot? The dials in his head stopped too. He had dreamt it all, must have. This was 2006 not 1943 . . . or 3050. And Spitfires had been ours, not enemy aircraft.

Nothing stirred in that awful silence, no burrowing badger, no screeching owl. Nothing. Amos's hands were trapped beneath him from where he'd tried to break his fall. In wriggling them free, his fingers closed on the twine that kept his jacket together. He played it through his hands, counting off the knots as though it were a rosary or worry beads. Anything to keep him occupied, stop him moving. And just in case, he waited. Waited for what seemed like hours, straining his ears and his hip, hardly daring to breathe let alone move — until he could bear it no longer.

Carefully, he extended a hand to lever himself into a sitting position. The sides of the ditch were steep, his weight had carried him through three or four feet — decades — of rotted vegetation. His face rested against something sharp, his cheek smarted from its lacerations. To prevent further wounds Amos propped himself upright with one arm and used the other to feel around, as he struggled to extricate himself from his opencast tomb.

He put his hand on a bunch of jagged sticks, maybe that's what had scratched him or . . . he examined a rounded shape, pointed in front but hard — with gaps in it. He shuffled further back down the trench. Maybe they were the bones of an old ewe who'd fallen in there and couldn't get out — though what a sheep would have been doing along here was a mystery.

Amos looked up, cracks of light were appearing low in the sky. A huge black shape loomed, silhouetted against this eerie dawn, grunting and whining and pawing the ground — panting hard from galloping. Distraught, Napoleon ran backwards and forwards along the edge looking for a way to reach his master, causing the ground above to thunder and earth to come tumbling down into the ditch. He was sweating profusely, Amos could smell him. Rarely had he looked so upset.

'Don't worry, old chap. I'm all right, you just calm down now.' Amos tried to prevent his pig from compounding their troubles by initiating a landslide.

That was it. Amos had been drinking in the melancholy smells of the autumn night while he waited for his pet pot-belly to do its business. The night had been impenetrably dark out here by the old airfield, so dark that in his mind's eye he'd likened it to a blackout curtain pulled taut across the sky and tucked in at the edges, admitting no light.

So, it had been easy to relive the emotion, imagine how it must have felt in this lonely landscape; conjure up the fire fighters driving down this very road to be on hand the moment the wheels hit grass, their teams standing where he had stood, drawing on shielded cigarettes, straining their eyes to catch a first glimpse of those who returned.

That's what must have triggered it. He'd gone to sleep standing up, like one of his cows.

He wasn't in any hurry, could do with a few more minutes in which to pull himself together. From whirring round inside their dials the numbers had stuck rigid, like hedgehogs in headlights. No amount of shaking his head would dislodge them. They'd seized up like his joints, refused to think . . . dared not think? What was it he didn't want to think about?

Scenes from that evening's Council meeting flickered across his internal screen — the site visit to the army camp and the heated argument, about whether or not to grant permission for turning the place into an industrial park, which had led to Bill Thomas's heart attack. Amos had gone with him in the ambulance, which was why poor old Napoleon had been bursting by the time

4

Amos had arrived back to pick up the Land Rover.

Think. Don't just give me a replay, think. Perhaps he was in shock . . . having been chased and shot at by Spitfires it would hardly be surprising. The cogs had unjammed, careful now, careful, they were dangerously close to spinning again. Go carefully, don't upset them. Where had he got to? Yes, the Spitfires. The unmistakable sound of the Merlin engine, devised by a wizard to instill fear in the enemy and pride in your allies — until they opened fire on you, that is. It must have been association, being in this area, by the airfield and the camp. He was tired, very tired.

Amos leant against the mud wall and for the first time since there'd been light, looked down at where he'd been lying. Curled up below him, in a parody of his own foetal position of the last hour, rested the remains of a man — bones, grisly pieces of flesh and hair, remnants of clothing; disturbed but recognizably a man. His skeletal face grinned up, teeth protruding, pouting to plant a second kiss on Amos's cheek. Was this whole thing a surreal nightmare, his weariness playing tricks on him? In a minute he'd wake in his own cottage, cold in his armchair by the fire, this icy feeling the draught on his neck from the open window.

Dislodged hip notwithstanding, he had to get out of this grave — now. Spurred by revulsion Amos managed to scramble up the steep sides and roll over the top at Napoleon's feet, gasping. He hobbled across to the Land Rover, its engine still running. Had that been the sound he'd imagined? Must have been, daft old fool. Look, no bullet marks denting the paintwork, what he could see of it anyway, no smashed glass. Depends which direction they'd come from, of course; if they'd crossed the road at right angles the vehicle might well have escaped injury. And the body? He hadn't imagined the body. That was no mirage — the illusion of a man desperate to be laid out in his own bed. That was real.

Amos snatched the mobile phone off the dashboard and wiped the muck off the Land Rover's clock with his sleeve. 6.30; Stephen Linklater might just be there. He struggled to keep his voice normal, unstressed, after all, it was an old corpse — if slain, the killer was likely dead himself by now. Nothing to get excited about.

'I've found a body, Stephen. There's no rush, I think he's been here a while.'

He couldn't desert the dead man. Now he'd been found someone had to keep a vigil, even if it was a touch late.

6

Linklater strode to the edge of the trench where Amos pointed, raised an eyebrow and waited. Amos explained why he'd been out so late, imagined he'd been shot at and leapt into the ditch for cover. Keen to get this over with — re-establish normality as soon as possible, escape from the extraordinary tricks his exhausted psyche had been playing on him — Amos looked straight at Linklater daring him to laugh. Or worse, send for a breathalyser kit. But he didn't.

The chief inspector cast around him at the surprisingly flat countryside for this part of Warwickshire, at the Ministry of Defence land which stretched as far as the now crimson horizon. 'Lonely spot out here, don't suppose many come this way?'

'Hardly anyone since the army pulled out. A few more have discovered the route recently, after they turned the airfield into a processing plant.'

'Any idea how long?' Linklater enquired of the pathologist now in the ditch beside the body.

'Could be anything up to sixty years or so. Going by his clothing, or what's left of it, I'd say he could have been a prisoner of war here. I think this is a German uniform.'

'A spy?' Amos suggested. 'Might explain why he was left here to rot.'

'Unlikely to have been wearing his German uniform, wouldn't you say?' muttered Linklater who evidently disdained civilian opinions at murder scenes, even from Amos.

'There are bullet holes,' the pathologist called to them.

Amos fought back the urge to enquire if the bullet holes were fresh. Of course they weren't. 'They kept POW's at the army camp. I think they were mainly on drainage gangs. The War Ministry helped the farmers keep the waterways clear by sending these POW's out to do the ditching,' he said instead.

'Perfect opportunity for them to hide a body then. Just drop it in today's ditch, cover it up and no one's going to find it for years if you're lucky,' Linklater surmised.

'Especially out here. There used to be barbed wire between the ditch and the road as well as beyond the ditch. When the army pulled out it fell into disrepair and the council eventually removed it.' Amos looked around him. 'This section borders the No Man's Land between the air ministry's land and the army's. It was doubly reinforced to stop the POW's getting onto the airfield which lies on both sides of the road.'

Linklater looked down at his immaculately

polished shoes as if to see his thoughts reflected in them. 'So, the prisoners found him there and decided not to say anything. If he had escaped they wouldn't want security being tightened up; much better to keep quiet and pretend he was still alive. But why the bullet holes? If he'd been shot escaping, the search party would have recovered the body, wouldn't they?'

Amos wandered back to his Land Rover, fatigue fast overwhelming him. He could leave it to the professionals now, they'd sort it out, nothing more he could do here. He wondered why he hadn't told Linklater about the Spitfires. Probably hadn't wanted to appear ridiculous. As if reading his mind Linklater came across the road.

'You said you were shot at.' He looked concerned. Linklater had seen Amos caught up in dangerous situations in the past and Amos realized he might be thinking this was another such. How to answer that without looking stupid or . . . Or what? Giving too much away?

'I said I imagined it. I was tired, OK?'

'Any idea who would do that?'

'No, of course not.'

Linklater patted Napoleon, his efforts at nonchalance failing to fool Amos. 'Who knew you'd be out here at that hour?'

'Bill Thomas, but he's in the hospital at Warwick. The ambulance men, the rest of the Council members, the taxi driver who brought me back — lots of people now I come to think about it.' Amos felt perversely comforted that there could be a logical, if unpleasant, explanation for what had happened; preferring a straightforward drive-past shooting to this weird experience.

Had someone really felt that strongly about the new development they'd waited all that time for him to return from the hospital — gone to those lengths to warn him off? He found it hard to believe his fellow councillors would have it in them . . . but the business concerns might. Except they were the ones who wanted the development as much as he did. So why pick on him? He dreaded to think someone had intentionally tried to kill or injure him. But if that had been the case surely they'd have come back and finished the job, wouldn't they?

And how had they known he'd have to stop and let Napoleon out of the Land Rover, or had that just been luck on their part? And why had Napoleon been running so hard — looking as terrified as Amos had felt? Napoleon couldn't have imagined it as well.

He shook himself. What was he delving into now? The whole thing had been the product of too little sleep and an overwrought evening. Bill had nearly died. Amos had been upset. Napoleon had been shut in the Land Rover for hours.

Linklater watched him wordlessly as Amos underlined his unwillingness to discuss the matter any further by heaving himself into the driving seat and setting off down the road. What was he really afraid of though? What was nagging away in the back of his mind? Why couldn't he tell Linklater? He couldn't remember, not now, but he would. Meanwhile, he needed to think — and to keep his own counsel.

Would whoever was gunning for him be watching as he left the police far behind? No one pulled out from side roads, no sign of bandits at six o'clock. Intoxicated with tiredness, he smiled wryly to himself. What a night. He wondered who the dead man had been.

2

Amos's housekeeper, Lindsay Martin, had come in to cook Amos's breakfast.

'What's happened? You look proper done in.'

Updating Lindsay would be much quicker than explaining to everyone else in turn, so he told her what he'd told Linklater — except for the part about being shot at.

'My, my. Well I never. Fancy that then.' Her brow furrowed. 'My Dad always said there were rum goings on over at that camp. Reckon he were right.'

'People often say things like that when they're kept out of somewhere? You know — 'What have they got to hide they don't want us seeing?' ' Amos answered.

Lindsay handed him his tea. 'Mind you, the POW's weren't allowed home right after the war neither.'

Amos looked at her. 'Come again?'

'They didn't go home, not for several years. Kept up in that camp they were. They let them go eventually, like. I remember Dad saying about the trains they put them on — liked trains, my Dad did. Anyway, the men

12

had written things all over the doors, drawn pictures and what not. It were all foreign he said but he could tell it weren't very nice.'

★　★　★

Amos called in at the Hathaway Arms to thank his friend for feeding the stock that morning, allowing him to snatch some sleep. He knew the penalty. Jack prided himself on having the best news service for miles around — his trade depended on it.

Jack Ashley held the glass he was polishing up to the light and removed an imaginary speck. 'Come on then, let's have it. What were you doing in a ditch out by the old airfield? Spying on the immigrants?'

'You could say that, I suppose, since the dead man probably was an immigrant and decidedly illegal.'

Jack put the glass down and leaned forward conspiratorially. 'Really? You mean one of those from the processing plant? I knew that lot were up to no good!'

'Neither were this lot, as you put it, up to any good — sixty years ago.' Amos enjoyed watching Jack's face as he struggled to assimilate the information. 'The police reckon the dead man was probably a POW from the last war — wearing a Luftwaffe uniform.'

'How come? I mean, why was he there, why was he never found? Wasn't he reported missing?'

'Apparently he has bullet holes in him.' Amos still wondered if they'd been rendered just last night, before he'd fallen on top of the man. 'I suggested he might have come out of an aircraft.'

'Ditched, you mean!' Jack took a minute to recover from his own witticism. 'I bet this is one of those cases where we'll never hear the end of the story. Not exactly going to be police priority, is he? And if the War Office get involved, or whatever they're called now, it'll all be hushed up anyway.' He resumed his polishing. 'Nah, we've heard the last of this one.'

'I hope you're right. Personally, I'd rather forget about it.'

For once Jack took the hint. 'You still think the army camp development should go ahead then?'

'We need those jobs for the local people.'

Jack gave a hollow laugh. 'Oh yes, like we did from the processing plant on the airfield?'

'Yes, like we did from the food processing. We weren't to know they'd import all the labour — and precious little we could have done about it if we had.' Amos felt guilty about that scheme. He had personally

14

campaigned for the old aircraft hangars to be converted into vegetable processing units so that the local farmers could take their produce there, instead of having to pay exorbitant transport costs to ferry their harvest to other plants. But he hadn't bargained for imported foreign labour and the conversion of the old airman's quarters into makeshift barracks. 'The difference this time is there will be many different enterprises needing various types of employees, not just one.'

'So what was the row about last night, then?' Jack persisted.

'Well, if the whole site is divided up into industrial units, the drag-racing guys suspect they won't be able to use the circuit there any more. Then there are traffic concerns, noise concerns, preservation of rural England concerns, you name it really. The way some of the councillors were carrying on they must be under considerable pressure from somewhere, is all I can say — someone is evidently intent on maintaining the status quo.'

Alan Tregorran came padding down the back corridor in his socks. Alan ran a large farm on the outskirts of Weston with his wife and three sons.

'I hear you've found a body, Amos?' Alan accepted the pint Jack forced between his

15

fingers. 'I must say, it makes a nice change from unexploded bombs.'

'What does Lindsay do? Put a placard up outside my cottage with today's headlines on it! What with her and you two I wonder a man can have any secrets in this place.' Amos smiled.

'Actually, it wasn't Lindsay. My Jacob was delivering some feed up that way and got talking to that new police lass. She told him. Said something about you being shot at too. So I thought I'd come and see if you were all right, like.'

Amos groaned. He'd hoped people would assume he'd simply come across the body, or that Napoleon had rooted it out. That he'd been in a ditch would be unremarkable — nothing could have been more common- place.

Jack stared at him, mouthing, 'Shot at?' in amazement.

'Well, I'm all right, aren't I?'

'You don't think it was those people who are against the army camp being developed, do you?'

'Jack, there was no sign of anyone! I'm OK. I was tired, I dreamt it. Now drop it will you.'

'I must say it's not every day you find a dead body though is it, I mean a human one.' Like Amos, Alan was miserably familiar with dead livestock. 'Perhaps it was meant to be. Never mind about how you came to find it — it was supposed to be found.'

'What 'planted' you mean?' Jack asked.

'But no one knew I'd be walking along that road, almost no one ever does — walk along that road, I mean.'

'Ah, but they will, won't they, once this industrial scheme gets the go-ahead. Maybe that was it, a sort of last ploy. No one likes the idea of a dead body on their doorstep. Maybe whoever planted it thought it might put people off opening up the old camp.' It was Jack's turn to be imagining things.

'What? For fear there might be mass graves and things?' Alan joined in.

'Do you think that's it?' Jack turned to Amos. 'Somebody fears the army camp being developed because they've something hidden there they don't want anyone to find?'

'More dead bodies?' Alan said.

'Not necessarily, could be anything. But yes, why not bodies?'

'Now, you two are being ridiculous. Stop blowing this up into some sensational story. There are plenty of old bodies in the churchyard, pretty near the surface some of them, why should you go embroidering things just because I found one in a ditch? If it was a murder it happened a long time ago. I for one don't think it's clever to put people off developing that site. We need it.'

⋆　⋆　⋆

Wired up in the hospital bed like an oversized marionette, Bill Thomas, Amos's friend and fellow councillor, looked seriously concerned.

'What's going on, Amos? I hear you've been shot at!'

'Rubbish. I was tired that's all . . . getting fanciful in my old age.'

'I was worried. After all, it was my fault. If I hadn't collapsed, you wouldn't have been out there so late and . . . '

Amos found a metal chair and sank gratefully onto it. 'I'm much more interested in why you're so against this development. You and I usually see eye to eye.' One glance at Bill's face and Amos realized, too late, that resurrecting the discussion could easily engender a repeat of last night. 'Hell, I'm sorry Bill, I didn't think.'

Bill held up a weak hand. 'No, I want to explain. Henry said . . . ' He stopped, his eyes half closed as if lacking the strength to stay open. Amos hobbled to the nursing station, hollering for help. The terrible paraphernalia of cardiac arrest whirled into action. White-coated staff in crêpe-soled lace-ups came

18

running with trolleys of tall white machines. Alarms sounded, screens were scrambled, everyone not directly involved melted away unseen like actors from a set, leaving the main character centre stage — spotlit, suspended.

Bill Thomas died ten minutes later.

3

What had Henry said? Henry who? Amos wondered as he drove along. Find that out and he might discover who'd attacked him — if indeed anyone had.

Back in Weston he threaded his way through the expensive motor cars abandoned round the green and pushed his way in through the armoured glass doors cunningly concealed behind the oak ones which once had sufficed.

The ground floor of the old house on the corner had been transformed into a series of open-plan areas each tastefully, if minimally, appointed with occasional furniture and objets d'art: the well-placed bronze figurine, the regency card table, the vase of glazed bulrushes. Enough to take the edge off emptiness but insufficient to detract from the centre of attraction — the paintings — hung one to a wall on a background of vermillion. No vulgar over-crowding here.

Throngs of well-heeled art lovers from the surrounding shires stood carefully posed at a strategic distance from each exhibit, champagne glass in one hand, canape in the other, engrossed, critical, admiring. Amos smiled inwardly — good. He'd worked hard to round them all up, get them to come and support this new venture. Weston Hathaway hadn't previously been known for its culture so a little advertising had been justified — words dropped in the right ears, gentle reminders of the need for countryside diversity. If this morning's turn-out was anything to go by, his efforts had paid off handsomely.

Declining the champagne but balancing an incongruous bonne bouche in each hand, munching as he went, Amos meandered into the first room. Old friend and one-time fellow councillor, Lord Gray — christened Alec Fitzsimmons before he inherited the title — gallantly held two champagne flutes while his wife fumbled in her bag for her glassses. He smiled warmly at the sight of Amos.

'I must say, this chap Fishbroke's done a first class job of renovating the place.'

Amos swallowed quickly. 'Thanks for coming, Alec, I really appreciate it.' He looked around. 'And for bringing your friends.'

Alec's face clouded over. Handing his wife back her glass, he took Amos's arm and moved him away from the group who had now gathered beside them. 'I was shocked to hear about Bill Thomas.'

Amos scratched his head. 'To tell you the truth, Alec, I don't understand it. It wasn't like Bill to get het up, but he was that night — wanted the army camp development stopped. Yet he'd always been very pro anything which would help the diversification programme.'

'Somebody else pulling the strings?' Alec asked.

Before he could answer Amos looked up to see a beaming Henry Fishbroke bearing down on them. A big man in every dimension, he wore a tan linen suit, fashionably creased, and sported a huge red-and-white spotted silk handkerchief cascading artistically from his top pocket.

'Do you have a particular preference, Lord Gray?' Henry asked.

'Let's say, I'm not a modernist. Give me a nice Gainsborough or a Stubbs any day.'

'I'm afraid I haven't either of those today, but give me time.'

'You've certainly amassed a large stock here, something for everyone eh, catering for all tastes,' Amos remarked. 'Must have cost you a fortune! With this range of art they'll come from all over the country. You'll put Weston Hathaway well and truly on the map.'

Amos escaped the rarefied atmosphere into

22

the outdoors, a milieu more suited to his homespun tastes, and lowered himself onto the wrought-iron chair in the garden. Henry followed him out and sat down beside Amos, surprisingly agile for a man of his size, but then Amos was at least fifteen years older than him, he reckoned.

'How well did you know Bill Thomas, Henry?'

'Not very. Just from Rotary.'

Amos knew he had to tread carefully. The last thing he wanted to do was offend Henry but he was painfully curious to understand what Bill had wanted to tell him before he died, especially if it had any bearing on what had happened out near the airfield.

'It's just that Bill mentioned you moments before his final seizure.'

'Me?' Henry looked genuinely taken aback. 'You must be mistaken, Amos. What did he say?'

'Said he wanted to explain his position on the army camp development. His very words were: 'Henry said . . . ' '

'Said what?'

'That's what I'm trying to find out.'

'What army camp?'

Amos looked at Henry, could he really have been in these parts for the best part of six months or more without hearing about the

23

army camp? It was difficult to believe, but then again . . . Amos caught sight of the cars which still littered the lane. Henry lived in a different world. 'Oh, one the other side of Lower Farthing they want to turn into industrial units.'

Henry clapped a hand on Amos's back. 'Search me, dear boy, must have meant another Henry. Fellow councillor perhaps?'

As far as Amos was aware there weren't any councillors called Henry, or any other Henrys whom Amos and Bill had both known — other than Henry Fishbroke. He'd been trying to think of one all morning. Henry strode off to join his lunch guests at the Hathaway Arms.

Chief Inspector Linklater purposefully weaved his way between the cars towards Amos, jacket buttoned, one hand in his trouser pocket, shoes perennially undimmed.

'Well, we don't know much yet, but the pathologist was correct. The man was wearing some items of German Luftwaffe uniform and he had been shot, several times.'

'What with?' Amos asked, thinking the information might help him decide whether the shots had entered the body sixty years ago or more recently.

Linklater looked mildly surprised at the question. 'We're not sure yet. There is something curious though.'

Here we go, they were recent shots, he knew it. He hadn't dreamt it, the man had taken those bullets instead of Amos.

'We've found a drawing. In his inside coat pocket.'

Amos sat back down on the seat, Linklater beside him. 'You've just missed the man you need for that — Henry Fishbroke. He's gone for lunch.'

'I'm told it's a man's head and shoulders — a portrait.'

'Fascinating. Is it valuable do you think?'

'We might need your Mr Fishbroke to tell us that. Who knows, perhaps it comes under treasure trove and you've found yourself a fortune! Forensics are busy doing their research. I just thought you'd like to know.' Linklater stood up. 'It might turn out it was planted there long after the man was killed, but I can't see why and anyway, that would suggest someone knew he was there.'

'Might it also suggest a motive for his murder?'

'There you go again, Amos, trying to do my job for me. Yes, of course it might . . . but again, once they'd killed him why didn't they take what they were after?' He held up a hand. 'I know, they were disturbed. So why didn't they come back later?'

'Could the coat have been put on the man after he was shot?'

'What for? That wouldn't make any sense at all — it's not as though a corpse is a good hiding place, is it?'

'No, I mean perhaps he was wounded but not dead and someone with him gave him the coat to keep him warm, before they left him.'

'And the attackers pursued the friend who got away, thinking he had the drawing, when it was with the injured man all along. I like it Amos. But it doesn't tell us much for the moment except that our man may not have been alone when he was shot.'

'No records of other bodies being found I suppose?'

'Where do you want to start? Sixty years ago, war time? Yes, quite a few I'd say.'

Linklater was becoming irritable. Amos daren't ask how far around the ditch the police had searched. Probably not far, not much point looking for a murder weapon at this late date.

'His papers were still on him. His name was Franz Schumann. We'll try and trace him through the German police when we've time, but a lot of their records were destroyed, so I don't hold out much hope — it's a fairly common name.'

★ ★ ★

'Do you think he realizes what he's got coming?' Jack laughed as he and Amos drove away from the Hathaway Arms at 6.30 — making an early start in order to move the cows across the Stratford Road before the morning traffic.

The entrance to Horace's field was in a hollow on the right. From Weston Hathaway the road approached down a long hill into the dip then sloped upwards and ran straight until the bend at Lower Farthing, over a mile away. So they could see the traffic from both directions and, more importantly, the traffic could see them.

Halfway down the hill from Weston, Amos pulled over and parked up on the left-hand verge, outside the gate to the cows' field. He scrambled out grabbing a stout cane and an empty feed bag and set off down the road as quietly as he could for fear of attracting Horace's unwanted attention.

As long as the bull wasn't at the entrance to begin with, Amos could stand in the middle of the road to turn the first cows, then move across, rattling the bag to keep them from straying while he opened the gate, and the rest of the cows would follow. Horace couldn't get out whilst they were coming in

. . . and why would he want to?

He was nowhere in sight. 'OK' he bellowed up the road to Jack. 'Let them out.' Looking over his shoulder in the hope Horace would first digest the noise before he acted, Amos moved into the road.

A long way off he heard the truck coming from the direction of Lower Farthing. Too late to hold back now. Jack had already opened the gate and the cows were stepping out into the road, their hooves ringing on the metal, jostling, skipping, their great bellies bumping into one another, heading down towards Amos — curious, hungry, high-spirited. Whoever it was coming down the road would have to wait a few minutes. It always happened.

Here came the tricky part. Attracted by the feed bag Amos was rustling, the cows gathered momentum down the hill. He glanced sideways. Hell, there was Horace now, lumbering up over the rise but still about fifty yards from the gate. Though he daren't take his attention off the cows or Horace long enough to look round, Amos could hear the truck accelerating down the straight from Lower Farthing. It would slow in a minute; he just prayed it wouldn't sound its horn.

Encouraged by the incline and the promise

of food the cows broke into a trot. Amos stood his ground to ensure they turned and didn't overshoot to cannon into the vehicle coming up behind him. Jack started yelling. What was he thinking? The cows were eager enough, they'd be stampeding at this rate and then he'd have real trouble getting the gate open, Horace or no Horace.

In the excitement and the clatter of hooves, he'd tuned out the noise of the truck engine, but now he could hear it above everything, roaring down the hill. What the hell did they think they were doing?

4

In the moment when he realized it wasn't slowing, Amos half turned to see a dilapidated open-backed truck crammed with terrified people. In front of him Jack was hurtling down the road yelling and gesticulating.

Amos leapt aside, fell backwards into the nearest beast, and instinctively curled up like a fallen jockey to protect his head from the hooves as the truck careered into the herd — smashing and slicing their flesh.

The screams of the livestock lying butchered alive on the road joined the screams of the two dozen occupants who'd been catapulted into the carnage. Finally, the truck tipped head first into the ditch, its engine straining to connect with the wheels which spun feet above the ground, cruelly mimicking the downed cattle struggling desperately to right themselves.

The cows which had escaped being hit tore off down the road in terror. Amos struggled to sit up, feeling only disbelief and horror as he took in the scene, for now oblivious to the clouts to his head. On the verge he could see men staggering to right themselves, then clustering round the cab of the truck. He watched as they prised open the door and immediately recoiled — turning away, mumbling, in words Amos couldn't decipher. Miraculously, the passengers were all at least walking . . . and to his amazement, began to run as best they could back down the road whence they'd come.

Around him two cows lay motionless, one calf could only move its head and cry for its mother, another cow kept trying uselessly to get up on a leg bent at right angles to her heavy body. Three others had gaping wounds in their sides gushing gore and milk into the gravel. Another had half its head ripped away where in panic it had caught its horns in one of its fellows. The smell of death hung in a pall, the morning poisoned.

Jack reached into the truck and turned the engine off without lingering. Amos saw the phone in his hand. 'Ring Alan, quickly. Tell him to bring his gun, he'll be quicker than the vet. And his boys — to round up the rest of those cows before there's another accident. Then get the vet.' The tarmac rose up to meet him as his world went dark.

★   ★   ★

The road was closed all day. Alan Tregorran, his sons, Lindsay's husband, old Sid and several others all came to tend the livestock and take Amos back down to the village away from the distressing scene. Jack stayed up there long enough to hand over the whole sorry mess to the authorities.

Later, back at his cottage, Amos asked, 'What happened, Jack? You could see better than me.'

'Couldn't you hear it coming? I couldn't believe it when you just carried on, I thought they were going to mow into you!'

'I heard it back in Lower Farthing, yes, but not after that. Not with all that clattering going on, not until right at the last second, and probably only then because I could see you yelling and finally realized something was wrong.'

'It just gathered more and more speed. It was weaving all over the road but I don't know why the driver didn't aim for the fields rather than plough straight into the herd. It was as if the brakes didn't work . . . or he didn't know where they were.'

Sergeant Wilson tapped at the open door of the cottage. 'We picked some of them up on the roadside outside Lower Farthing, those who'd been hurt and couldn't run so well. They'd come from the old airfield, from the processing plant there.'

Amos's heart sank. It was the scheme he himself had promoted.

'They were pretty shaken. We tried to take two or three to the hospital but they were too scared, refused to move, thought we were going to lock them up, I think. It was difficult to get them to understand, their English isn't too good.

'From what we can piece together they were due to be apple picking the other side of Stratford, only their driver didn't turn up.' Sergeant Wilson displayed the resignation of a man whose job was a constant round of dealing with the less fortunate. 'These poor sods don't get paid if they don't show up so one of them decided to drive. No licence, no insurance . . . and it doesn't look as though he knew how.'

'Far Eastern chap, I'd say. Impaled his head on the spike which held the map to the sun visor.' Jack volunteered, shuddering in sympathy. 'He's paid for it now, poor bugger, but he could have killed us and the rest of his passengers and God knows how many other people in the villages! Can't you prosecute whoever's in charge, someone has to be to blame?'

The sergeant looked at his feet. 'There's not much we can do, sir. We don't go after foreign drivers.'

Jack looked fit to explode. Amos levered himself out of his armchair and said very quietly, 'What about the gang master then — or is he foreign too?'

Looking relieved to be on safer ground Sergeant Wilson answered with a sigh. 'No, as it happens he's not, he's English . . . but he wasn't driving.' He turned to Jack who already had his mouth open to protest. 'We will of course caution him about allowing his workers to transport themselves in an open truck. I can tell you what he'll say now: 'I tell them not to, that's all I can do.' But it's the only vehicle he gives them.' The sergeant shrugged. 'What are they supposed to do, wait for the twice-weekly bus?'

'This gang master, what's his name? Is he based at the airfield?' Amos asked. If the police were unwilling to act, then maybe he could do something himself.

'I don't know where he's based, slippery customer — which won't surprise you. They call him Karloff, as in Boris I imagine, you know, the horror-film man. His real name is Carlton.'

'Not Graham Carlton?'

'Yes, councillor. Know him do you?'

'Only of him, Sergeant. His father was in and out of prison until he legged it altogether. The boy was always a cocky bastard.

Importing illegal labour and treating them worse than slaves sounds just like him.' Amos paused. 'But surely there's a manager, someone in charge of the processing plant. What's he say about it?'

'Yes, there is, but he says the barracks are let so they're nothing to do with him — he outsources the recruitment and management of the labour. Technically his company employs no one.' Sergeant Wilson grimaced. 'And Karloff would swear he never had half the people who we know were here. If they all went off a cliff tomorrow in that rust-heap of a truck no one would be any the wiser. These people are less than nothing to him, and officially they don't exist.'

Sergeant Wilson's footsteps had barely died away when Amos reached for his keys.

'Where the hell do you think you're going?' Jack looked aghast, guessing.

'To make sure this doesn't happen again. Coming?'

5

He hadn't been near the airfield since that night. It looked very different in daylight, still bleak, but much less evocative. Tawdry more than sinister. They turned in at the main entrance through eight-feet-high wire fencing and an empty guard post — remnants of its former days. Far over to their right were the rows of old barrack huts and to the left in the distance were the hangars. Closer, new temporary sheds and offices littered the parade ground haphazardly underlining the change from order to chaos. The place looked deserted. Perhaps they'd all finished early because of what had happened to the driver. Somehow Amos doubted that. Expecting a visit from the police more like.

They left the Land Rover and moved towards the nearest building, some sort of site office. Amos hauled himself up three rickety wooden steps by the handrail and kicked on the door with his boot. No answer. He tried the handle, locked. Beside the temporary building lay a scrubland of tall thistles and nettles, the bindweed and ivy making light work of hiding the abandoned pallets.

'Do you get that feeling we're being watched?' Down below, Jack looked about him apprehensively.

Twenty yards away the undergrowth parted as if by some invisible hand and a figure emerged. Jack visibly jumped. The newcomer had a jaunty air of laboured innocence, like Billy Bunter caught stealing the cakes, though he looked to be over fifty. He put a hand out to steady the field glasses round his neck as he bounced along.

'Don't think he's in if you're looking for the manager,' the man volunteered whilst still several yards away. 'I expect I can guess what brings you out here, Councillor Cotswold.' Amos failed to recognize the speaker but Jack knew him.

'It's George isn't it? From the caravans?'

'George Churchman, at your service.' He turned to Amos. 'I'm sorry about your cattle Mr Cotswold, dreadful thing to happen, a wonder you weren't killed.' How George had heard so quickly wasn't surprising when Alan Tregorran owned the field on which George parked his van.

'Do you know these people then?'

The cheerful bonhomie departed. 'Not really. Always coming and going, must be hundreds here sometimes, leastwise it seems like it.'

Nodding towards the binoculars Amos had to ask. 'Spying were you?'

There was a moment's pause followed by embarrassed laughter. 'Oh you mean these? Bird watching, I'm a bird watcher.'

Surprising them all, a four by four raced in through the gate like a charging bull, klaxon speakers mounted on top in place of horns. The occupant yelled through the open window. 'What the f — are you lot doing here! I've told you before, Churchman, f — off.'

Careful not to get too close, George yelled: 'And you'll watch your tongue, you young . . . Who do you think you're talking to? This isn't your land.'

The young man got out of his truck, his baseball cap backwards atop his head. 'Look, Granddad, I'll have you thrown off if you don't get out of here. See!' He jabbed a finger at Churchman as he sneered; 'And take your friends with you.'

'It's Graham Carlton, isn't it?' Amos said. They all turned to look at him. 'I knew your father.' Inwardly he thought, well that much is true. Had a hand in having him put away actually.

'Oh yeah? Well you won't find him round here. Now f — off,' Carlton sniffed in emphasis. Where he came from, thinking was probably frowned upon, a quick comeback was what mattered; nevertheless, Amos thought he detected a flicker of curiosity if not interest.

'You killed my cattle this morning. You owe me.'

Amos saw Jack take a sharp breath, George Churchman looked delighted. They waited for Carlton's reaction which wasn't so quick in coming this time. 'You can't prove nothing,' he muttered finally.

'I don't need to prove it. You need to pay.'

'Oh yeah?' Carlton gave a small laugh and sniffed again, now patently much less sure of his ground. The mention of his father had been inspired. Carlton clearly hadn't a clue who Amos was and having had time in which to think, probably thought him part of that world which extracts its own justice. By the look on his face it was a world he recognized . . . and through experience, feared.

'Ask him what happened to the usual driver,' George Churchman urged, hopping from foot to foot, seizing his opportunity whilst support was on hand. 'Go on, ask him.' Gathering courage he volunteered the answer himself. 'He's buggered off, hasn't he! He was an illegal immigrant. You brought him in, didn't you? Now he's gone off to richer pickings! Ha ha, that's good, richer pickings!'

39

Was Churchman always such an idiot, Amos wondered, or was it because he was nervous. 'Is this true, Carlton?' he asked.

'None of your effin business, mister.' As though for the first time, he took in Amos's ragged clothes, the string which held up the several sizes too big trousers bought at the Scouts' jumble sale, the threadbare jacket covered in dried mud. 'Bloody old tramp coming here questioning me about my business.'

Amos looked around. 'Little visit from the Inland Revenue will do for starters, more effective than sending the boys, don't you think, Jack?' With the morning's slaughter still stinking in his nostrils it was all he could do to stop himself punching this no-good. 'What the hell do you think you're playing at, letting people career around the country like that? Do it again and you'll wish you hadn't, sonny,' he finished, menacingly.

Amos turned on his heel and got into the Land Rover taking Jack with him. George Churchman scuttled in beside them, obviously afraid to be left there alone.

'It's right what I said you know, the driver disappeared over a week ago, he was a Romanian. I spoke to him once or twice. You know Carlton's bringing in illegals, don't you?' It seemed George Churchman had a real bee in his hood over these people.

'I thought it was legal to use Eastern European labour these days, since they all gained membership of the EEC?' Amos asked, confused.

'No, they're not all legal. Not all European countries were given membership and I've seen Chinese, Vietnamese, Taiwanese, Filipinos, you name it, all here too. It's criminal, I tell you!'

George Churchman alighted at the entrance to Alan Tregorran's farm. When he'd gone Jack remarked, 'Funny sort of cove. Comes here regularly, you know. Worked up about those immigrants, isn't he?'

Amos was quiet for a while before he answered. 'Didn't look much like a bird watcher.'

'Oh, I don't know, field glasses, anorak . . . looked the part to me.' Then Jack realized. 'You mean, he looked *too* much like one?'

'Struck me as phoney, that's all.'

'Oh, I think he was just nervous because he was trespassing. I don't blame him, I'd be nervous of that Carlton lout,' Jack replied.

Amos was sharply aware they'd achieved nothing by their visit. What had he expected? If the police couldn't stop these people what did he think he could do?

Could he have known all this when he'd advocated the airfield's change of use? Should he have realized? More practically, what on earth could he do about it now? Maybe Bill had worked it out — had looked at the airfield and realized the army camp was likely to go a similar way. Was that it? Was that why Bill had got it right and Amos hadn't? Maybe he'd been about to explain how all developers weren't like Henry, not all new enterprises necessarily advantageous. Maybe he'd been about to explain why Amos should be more discerning, more selective in his support.

Amos parked the Land Rover back outside his cottage and he and Jack walked round the corner and headed up the lane towards Jack's place. On the opposite side of the road Henry was backing carefully out of his front door, locking it. They could hear the alarm finish its setting sequence and saw Henry's shoulders lower in relief.

'Still having trouble mastering the technology Henry?' called Jack across the lane.

Henry jumped. 'Oh, good heavens.' Then he beamed. 'No, my assistant is so impressed with my prowess she's left me to lock up. There's confidence for you.' He clutched his top pocket, felt round his neck, patted his other pockets. 'Damn and blast, left my glasses inside, haven't I. You go on, I'll catch you up.'

But they waited on the kerbside while he painstakingly reversed the alarm process. 'Beats me how he affords all this,' Jack muttered waving a hand over the smart Regency property into which Henry had vanished. 'He's so disorganized, I find it hard to believe anyone like that can run a successful business.'

'Oh, I don't know,' Amos smiled. 'I've met plenty of completely hopeless businessmen who are enormously successful. And some who pretend they're useless when underneath they're more capable and cunning than a forest-full of our forefathers. It's probably all an act to stop you feeling inadequate. You're just jealous, Jack.'

Harry Fields, the local butcher, passed behind them on his way to the shop. Overhearing their conversation he grumbled, 'He ain't paid my bill for last month yet.' He lowered his voice. 'And I know for a fact he ain't paid the painter nor the carpenter.' Harry walked off.

Amos shrugged and picked up the conversation where he'd left it. 'Anyway, Henry managed all that restoration, did a wonderful job.'

'You must be joking. The architects

managed everything. You sure have a short memory, Amos. Henry wasn't even here most of that time.'

Now Henry was backing out of his building again, only noticeably faster this time.

'No harm in that. Whatever he did he's good for this village. Look at the trade he's brought you already and he's only just opened the place.'

Turning, Henry seemed surprised to see them still there but quickly recovered.

As the three of them made their way towards Jack's place, Amos said, 'I hope you don't mind, Henry, but I've volunteered your services to the police should they need an expert opinion. They've found a sketch on that skeleton I discovered.'

'What sort of sketch?' Understandably interested, Henry's eyes bulged.

'They're working on that but from what I could gather, a man's head.'

'I expect it's in pretty poor condition after all this time,' Jack said as they reached the Hathaway Arms.

'No, apparently it was properly wrapped. Curious isn't it?'

'Had it been there long?' Henry asked, now deep in thought.

'I don't think they know that much yet.

Why do you ask? Have you lost something from your place?'

Henry didn't answer. Instead he asked abruptly, 'Do you think those people this morning had something to do with it?' News had travelled fast.

'You've lost me. The immigrants, you mean? Why should they?'

Henry shook himself. 'No reason at all, dear boy. Old train lines crossing over in my brain that's all. Junctions fall apart, get all jumbled up, then I reconnect them up on the wrong tracks. Happens when they're short of lubrication.' They hastened their steps up the lane.

6

'Come in.' Busy feeding Napoleon in the kitchen, Amos had heard the smart rap of knuckles on his front door.

Abandoning his dinner, an almost unprecedented act, Napoleon whirled and stood growling at the visitor, teeth bared. Embarrassed, Amos pushed past him into the sitting-room and closed the door before the visitor could witness the pig's hostility. It was rare for Napoleon to take against anyone like that.

Without needing to duck his head under the lintel, the caller crossed the threshold and very deliberately lined up his feet at the edge of the rug, not a centimetre beyond the fringe.

'I'm Eric Stanton. I've come about the 'change of use', Councillor Cotswold. I understand I need a representation from you as District Councillor.' His wasn't exactly a lisp, more an affectation — a toss of the chin upwards as he spoke as if something were stuck to his palate. Like a cat with fur adhered to its tongue.

Amos surveyed his visitor. Dapper, dressed

in jeans with pressed creases down the front, loden jacket and check shirt. An outsider, but he'd seen him about in the last few months, rented one of those posh camper van things on the mobile home park near Stratford.

'What change of use would that be, Mr Stanton?'

'I'm renovating the old rolling stock at the army camp. Been doing it on and off for a while but now I've retired I can spend most of my time here.' Stanton went on. 'Most of the original track is still serviceable but I need to test and clean the equipment and I'm told I need a change of use licence for using one of the sheds there.'

As seen from the road, Amos was familiar with the rows of engines, carriages and freight wagons in a multitude of faded colours and liveries, which stood on the army camp site — as if in some great marshalling yard for dying trains. Had they been old cars they'd have been piled in a heap, but because they were trains they stood in linear correctness on their track, queuing for their final destination. In daylight it was an eerie sight, abandoned, silent — no shunting or whistling, no clanking or clamour. At night it was more like a film set from a horror movie.

Amos stroked his stubbled chin. 'And what do you need from me?'

'Apparently the Countryside Commission want to be sure of the benefit to the local area.' Stanton spoke as though such benefit were self-evident to all but the moronic.

Privately Amos thought removal of the eyesore would be the best outcome but he knew some considered that rendezvous of rolling stock to be romantic in a melancholy way; a stationary tribute to a moving memory.

'And will it be?' Amos was unafraid to look simple in the cause of discovery. 'What are you going to do with it when you've renovated it?' He was aware some of the stock and the track were in working order because now and again various buffs had permission from the ministry to come and run up the engines, do some repairs, have some fun. He assumed Eric Stanton wanted to go one step further. 'Are you going to reopen the steam railway, like they have between Stratford and Birmingham? They run it for folks on Sundays — I hear it's always fully booked.'

'It's early days for that at present, we'll have to see.' There it was again, the arrogance, the toss of the head as if there were a nasty smell under his nose.

Reluctant to prolong the conversation, Amos decided to ignore the point but had he been interested in trains he'd have been mildly puzzled. He knew the line was functional, so why was Stanton making such a big deal about the work involved?

'I'll support your application, Mr Stanton. Just send me the form.'

Two minutes after Stanton had left, Jack came through the door. 'What did that weirdo want?'

'My support for his change of use application. Odd isn't it?' Amos mused. 'The army camp sits there, unused, unloved, deserted by all except the odd train club, for what? At least thirty years. Then suddenly everything seems to point in that direction — or to the airfield next door.'

'Who knows, pr'aps a lot goes on there we don't know about; after all no one was allowed in there for decades.' Jack replied, echoing Lindsay's father. 'Just think what it would have been like if it had been us who lost that war?'

'I don't think many of us would have survived that.' Amos remembered what he'd been told. Carefully, he added: 'The men would have had to go underground.'

'Thinking of becoming a subversive, Amos?' Chief Inspector Linklater put his head around the door. Amos jumped. 'Heard about your accident, came to see if you're all right.'

Recovering himself quickly, Amos replied, 'No thanks to the police, Stephen. It seems this rabble can drive around killing animals and people while we get nicked for having dirty number plates.'

To demonstrate the falseness of this exaggeration, Linklater looked out towards Amos's mud-covered vehicle and raised an eyebrow.

'Don't get funny with me, either. You know what I mean.' Why was he picking on Linklater, why distance himself from him? Surely the time when he might have had to do that was long gone.

Linklater cleared his throat. 'We've been doing some more work on your man — the dead German. I thought you might be interested.'

Amos sank back into his armchair and Jack and Linklater took the two dining chairs from the table and turned them round to face him.

'We've confirmed he died around 1945, which is part circumstantial admittedly, because of where he was found, how he was dressed, and the fact he has obviously been dead for some considerable time.'

'Can you tell *how* he died?' Amos asked, sitting up straight. At least now he'd be able to put an end to his concerns about the other night, prove he had dreamt the attack.

'Oh, he died from the gunshot wounds, we're certain of that.'

Amos breathed out, so they weren't new. Why had he had that crazy idea?

'Actually, it puzzled us for a bit because the angle of the bullets is strange, as though he'd been lying down when he was shot — which he could have been, of course, sheltering, hiding, having a sleep. And why so many shots? There must have been a dozen or so, he was riddled with them.'

'Then we realized how slow we'd been. It's our belief he was shot by an aircraft — a fighter plane, possibly a Spitfire or something similar. We're checking now but we think they would have had the same ammunition as other weapons at that time.' He looked apologetic. 'Our chaps don't see many of these cases.' Linklater's voice faded into the background.

Amos couldn't move, his throat constricted. He didn't believe in ghosts. Yet it seemed that poor devil had indeed been shot by a fighter plane, as he walked along that road . . . and exactly the same thing had very nearly happened to him the other night. What had it been? He searched frantically for a logical explanation, any interpretation which would close this chasm which had just opened up. Could it really have been a replay after all those years? Was the man haunting the road, re-enacting the tragedy whenever the circumstances triggered it? Wanting people to remember, not resting until his body was found? And what were those circumstances — did it have to be a certain time of year? Did there have to be a solitary walker? Did it have to be night-time?

'Amos?' By his tone, Linklater feared he'd lost his audience. 'I was just saying, the No Man's Land there, running between the airfield and the army camp, probably explains why he lay undiscovered all these years. That and the fact that both Ministries pulled out long ago. No one ever went there.'

'Have you looked around?' Amos asked abruptly.

Linklater's face bore that exasperated expression it always wore when Amos tried to teach him his job.

'I mean, did you find any new bullets on the road or the grass? Were all those bullets in the body old, or have your people just assumed they're all the same?'

7

Amos desperately needed the answer to be yes. The other night he'd wanted to think he'd dreamt it. Now he wanted to know it was real, tangibly real — if necessary, frighteningly real. The alternative was too unspeakable; that somehow he was caught up in something which had happened in the past . . . or been made to re-enact it. He held his breath, for one horror-bound second wondering if he himself had once been the dead man. Linklater had admitted that the determination of the date of death had not been entirely scientific . . . they'd deduced the POW had died in 1945. Amos had been born at the end of the previous year.

Linklater was on his feet towering over Amos. 'You told me you imagined being shot at. Now it sounds as if you believe it. Which is it, Amos?'

'I just need to be sure, that's all.'

Linklater opened his mouth, obviously thought better of it and sat down again instead.

Jack had no such reservation. 'I told you I didn't believe you'd imagined it when you first told me, but you wouldn't have it — told me to give it a rest. Now you agree with me!' Doubtless driven by righteous indignation, Jack demanded, 'What is it you're not telling us?' only to quickly subside, belatedly aware from his reluctant involvement in some of Amos's previous escapades, that his friend may not wish to reveal whatever secret he had in front of Linklater — the representative of legal authority.

'If you'd told me the whole truth it might have helped,' Linklater added, scathingly.

Even if he'd wanted to, Amos couldn't have explained about the noises he'd heard. When he thought back, the Spitfire engine drowned out any other memory; that and the gunfire — his brain was incapable of separating them. Plus, he had the overwhelming feeling he should keep from the police whatever was scudding about in the back of his mind. He was unsure why; wouldn't know until he'd grasped what this was all about.

He pulled himself into a more upright position to signify a change of mood to himself as much as to the others. As nonchalantly as possible, as if nostalgic for the past, he enquired, 'A Spitfire, you reckon? I don't suppose there are many of those left these days?'

Jack obliged. 'I think there's about thirty

still flying. The biggest collection of restored ones is at Duxford in Cambridgeshire, at the RAF museum.'

Amos wished there had been hangars-full, to make it more likely to have been a prankster having a lark — but it sounded unlikely. 'They haven't resurrected them for old times' sake then, like Volkswagens and Roberts radios?'

★ ★ ★

Back at the Hathaway Arms after the weekly parish meeting, Jack enquired: 'I hear our friend Stanton's been stirring up the villagers — telling them how the traffic will increase exponentially if the army camp project goes ahead. Can't see why he should care about that. He doesn't even live here.'

Amos felt mollified by Jack's equal bewilderment. 'All I can think is he reckons the old railway will be destroyed in the development.'

Jack's face cleared, he straightened up. 'Yes, that's it, isn't it? That makes sense. Can't blame him really if he's that keen on old trains.'

'Except . . . ' Amos was having difficulty pinpointing the problem. 'You'd think if that were the case he'd start a campaign to save

55

the railway, encourage local enthusiasts to have the line reopened on Sundays or something. It'd be easier than trying to get the whole army camp project stopped, surely.' Amos sat up straight, more confident he'd grasped the non-sequitur. 'That's what's strange, don't you see? I asked Stanton whether he intended reopening the steam railway for folks,' Amos slowed his speech. 'And he said: 'We'll have to see', Doesn't that strike you as odd from a man who's trying to preserve something that might get destroyed through public disinterest?'

'I grant you it's not how I'd go about it.' Jack leaned forward over the bar and dropped his voice. 'You said yourself there seem to be covert influences involved in this army camp project — powerful interests who for some reason don't want it to happen. Who knows, maybe they suggested he should stir the locals up against the extra traffic?' He straightened. 'So, what are you going to do?'

'Stall . . . until I find out what the hell all this is about. I've told the village we need to start by determining the current traffic levels. I've already asked County to install their measuring kit.'

Jack looked over Amos's shoulder to the door where people were still streaming in

56

from the meeting. 'Look out, here's another queer one.'

'Councillor Cotswold, Mr Ashley, glad I caught you.' George Churchman pulled up a bar stool next to Amos. 'A busy evening tonight I see, something special is it?'

'Oh no, our parish council meetings usually play to packed houses, Mr Churchman,' Jack muttered.

'George, call me George.' He ordered his drink and turned to Amos. 'You know he's still doing it, don't you?'

'Doing what, Mr . . . George?' Amos felt uncomfortable with this man. Whereas Stanton seemed cold and precise, George Churchman was nosey, pushy.

'The gang master, Karloff whatshisname. Using unqualified drivers.'

'Surely that's a matter for the police.'

'Ah, but the question is *why* is he?' He settled in his seat and took tiny sips from his half pint of real ale. 'I'll tell you.' Amos had feared he would. 'Because the drivers are here for a short time then off they go, it's their way of getting into this country.'

Amos twisted on his stool to face Churchman. 'Why does this concern you so much, George?'

Churchman gulped a bigger mouthful and coughed and spluttered, whether by mistake or to hide his consternation at the direct question was hard to tell. Amos cared little either way. 'It doesn't really.'

'I still think it's a matter for the police.' Amos didn't want to hear about the airfield or anything to do with it right now, and least of all from this twitcher. He slid off his stool and picked up his beer to move away. Churchman touched his sleeve.

'Actually, Councillor, I wondered if I might have a word.' He must have caught the look on Amos's face because he added hurriedly, 'About something else.'

Amos replaced his mug on the counter but declined to resume his seat. He had no intention of spending any longer in George Churchman's company than was essential.

'These trains up at the old army camp . . .' Churchman began. 'I understand there's a chap who's started doing them up, restoring them, mending the track and so on.'

'You mean Eric Stanton? I can't see that can harm anyone, George.'

'I've never been able to catch him long enough to have a proper chat, always seems to be driving away whenever I've tried.' Amos's opinion of Eric Stanton rose several notches. 'You see, I'm keen on trains, so when I heard what he was doing I thought maybe he could use some help over there. I was hoping you might put in a word for me.'

This time Amos was determined to escape. 'I'll mention it if I come across him, I should think he could do with some help.' Amos heard himself say the last phrase and wondered why he was bothering to encourage Churchman. He shrugged inwardly. It was true, that's why; Stanton was going to need plenty of warm bodies to stand a chance of properly resurrecting that old system.

Jack caught up with him in the next bar. 'What did 'call me George' want?'

When Amos told him Jack grinned mischievously. 'It's obvious,' he said, answering the question Amos hadn't asked. 'All the birds have flown so he needs some other ruse to keep from going home to his wife. What better excuse than a dilapidated railway in need of restoration? Perfect!'

'I hope it's that simple, Jack, but he's far too interested in that processing plant for my liking. Do you ever hear him talk about swallows or cuckoos? No, but he never misses an opportunity to lead off about foreign labour.'

'So what do you think he's up to?' Jack's brow furrowed. 'I'll bet he's one of those Empire Loyalist wallahs or whatever they call themselves these days; Britain for the British. He's got a point.'

'It would fit, wouldn't it — explain why he's spying on them. I think you're on to something there, Jack.' Amos cheered up, one less mystery to worry about.

Back home, he poured himself a scotch and sank into his armchair. Why was his mind dwelling on the war in which Britain had very nearly been invaded, for the first time in close on a thousand years?

What was it Lindsay had said, that the prisoners of war had been kept there long after the war ended? Why? Probably because we'd desperately needed the labour. How different now. The country no longer needed overseas workmen, yet this time it was foreign labour which was using us for its own ends. Was this indeed the invasion they'd all feared?

A distant memory flitted across his thoughts like a ghost across a chamber; so ephemeral he couldn't catch it. Was it something to do with that dead POW? He didn't know. What had he been thinking about just then — invasion?

When he'd become ward member for Weston Hathaway and Lower Farthing, eighteen years ago, Amos had inherited responsibilities he'd never before heard of — few people had. Some of these stemmed from the Second World War and Churchill's plans in the event of full-scale invasion.

Unlike the French who'd found themselves forming their underground network whilst under occupation, Churchill had wanted England to be prepared in advance.

Amos tried to ignore the sirens far in the distance, one, two, wailing their clarion call. He shook his head and Napoleon stood up. Not the Merlin engine this time, not an air raid warning either — not more living movies, not tonight. Surely he'd imagined them, dozed off without realizing. Is this how it had been? Every night wondering if this was it, the night they'd have to act.

He glanced at the clock on the mantelpiece. It was nearly midnight. Napoleon twitched his ears and padded surprisingly lightly across the room as the front door was pushed open — cautiously.

8

Napoleon snorted and trotted back to the fire. Amos eyed the visitor.

'Thought you might just be awake but I didn't want to disturb you if you weren't.' Chief Inspector Linklater pushed the door fully open with one hand and came into the room, his mobile phone clutched in the other.

'Disturb me?' Amos said in a low voice which belied the words. 'You damn near gave me a heart attack.' He levered himself out of the chair. 'Smell scotch at half a mile you can.'

'Not right now Amos, thanks.'

More awake now Amos shivered, piecing together the sirens and the unexpected appearance of Linklater at this hour. 'What's up? I thought I'd been dreaming but I heard sirens.'

Linklater's phone crackled, obviously still connected to an open line. 'Yes?' A pause, then, 'OK, I'll be right there.' He turned to Amos. 'Fancy a ride?'

Amos followed Linklater down the path to his car. 'What's all this about, Stephen? It's way past my bed time.'

Linklater slid behind the wheel and started the engine. 'There's been a road accident.' He paused as he pulled away up the road. 'In almost exactly the same place where you fell in the ditch.'

'Corner of the airfield and the army camp?' Amos digested this. 'What the hell was anyone doing out there at this hour?' Here it was again, the previously uninhabited space which kept haunting him. 'And why is it so special they send a chief inspector?' He thought again. 'And what do you want *me* for?'

'As far as I understand it a courting couple from Alcester were coming back from wherever they'd been and ended up smashing their car into the ditch.'

'Must happen every day,' muttered Amos, relieved but now missing his bed.

'I daresay. The difference is they say they were being shot at.' Linklater glanced quickly at Amos as he drove. 'I thought you might like to see it while it's still fresh, so to speak.'

Linklater was no fool. He'd obviously been puzzled about what had really happened the other week and now it had apparently happened again. 'Are they all right? The couple?'

'Yes, that's what the call was about. I'd like you to talk to them out there rather than in

63

my office — more likely to jog both your memories.'

In many ways Amos felt better. So he hadn't been reincarnated or made the unconscious instrument of a dead man. Nor had he imagined what happened, and neither was he any longer alone in this experience. It sounded as though there was a maniac around taking pot shots at people — much more explicable. In comparison, it was almost acceptable.

The road had been closed. Lights whirled in the darkness, their beams washing blue waves across the anxious faces of the blanketed victims whose car lay nose down in the ditch, only yards beyond the police tape which still defined where the POW had been found.

Linklater and Amos were introduced to the couple by a police sergeant in charge at the scene. 'Mr Cotswold had a similar experience here a week or two ago and we thought it might help if you could tell him what you saw.'

The man was about thirty but young faced, obviously in shock. His girlfriend looked about the same age — quiet, bewildered.

'We didn't actually see anything,' the young man said. 'Did we Amy?' The girl shook her head. 'But we heard this firing.'

'Could you tell where it came from?' Linklater asked.

Amos looked around him, although the victims were sitting just inside the ambulance, Amos, Linklater and the sergeant were exposed on the road. If someone really was firing at random targets then surely . . . The police appeared not to share his concern. His anxiety growing, Amos turned to Linklater and mumbled quietly, 'What if he's still out there?' He moved round the side of the ambulance, away from the airfield. Linklater followed. 'You don't believe they were shot at?'

'There were no bullets, no spent cartridge cases, no obvious chips out of the road . . . ' Linklater explained as he watched Amos's face.

The young man came out of the ambulance to join them. 'I don't know if this helps and I know it sounds crazy but . . . ' He hesitated, Amos held his breath. 'It was like from an aeroplane. Like it was raining bullets — from above.'

'Might it have been a very localized hail-storm?' Linklater suggested. The man shook his head.

'Did they have lights?'

The young man thought hard; was he wondering why he'd thought of aircraft? 'No.

I don't know. I had mine on, of course. There was an engine, the noise of an engine.'

Amos sat down where he was, in the road. The ambulancemen came running but he waved them away. Linklater and the sergeant crouched beside him. 'You OK, Councillor?'

Amos held his head in his hands. So he hadn't imagined it, or if he had he and this young man had more in common than was immediately apparent. But it couldn't possibly be an aeroplane strafing the road so what the hell was it? Some sort of hallucination? Caused by what?

★ ★ ★

A bracing north-east wind, that would sort him out. For the express reason of blowing fantasy away, at first light he collected a grumbling Jack and drove up to the field he rented on the hill beyond the old manor. On the way he told Jack what had happened the night before.

'And that's what you never told us — that it was an aeroplane which shot at you.'

'Can you blame me?' To his credit Jack kept a straight face but that was probably because it was so early in the morning. Amos still didn't mention the Spitfires . . . he daren't think about that, dismissed it as fantasy on his part.

They struggled for ten minutes, moving the cattle hoop onto new grass to give the churned quagmire where it had been a chance to regrow, each content with his own thoughts.

'How about it's the ghost of an airman who used to patrol the perimeter to keep people away from the airfield?' Jack finally suggested, chuckling. 'He's probably been patrolling out there for years but you said yourself, no one ever used that road until this talk of redeveloping the army camp. Now the world and his wife seem to have rediscovered its usefulness.' More thoughtfully, he added, 'Who knows, p'raps they all thought they weren't allowed to use it before — like those roads over Salisbury Plain where the army do their practising.'

'Are you saying it's the army or the air force — practising?' Amos clutched at the first real possibility. That might explain why the police appeared unmoved by it. But surely they wouldn't be allowed to do that where they might kill someone? Amos found that notion incredible, refused to believe Linklater knew. 'Linklater denied any physical sign of shooting whatsoever.'

'Maybe they're practising with dummy bullets,' Jack was thinking now. 'Which would explain why they're being allowed to do it.'

'And the police know you mean?' Amos's mind was whirling. 'But are worried about us knowing! That's the problem, this is meant to be a secret for some reason.' It didn't explain why Linklater had fetched him out to the scene last night.

For the next few nights, busy with council meetings, Amos had no time to dwell on the subject. But on the Friday night, as he drew into the car park of the Hathaway Arms ready for the pint he'd been contemplating for the last five miles, his mobile phone rang.

'It's happened again, on that same stretch of road,' Linklater said.

'Another one? In the same place! I don't believe it. Are they all right?'

'Oh yes. Two men this time, on their way home from playing indoor bowls at Chipping, thought they'd short cut through there. Seems that route's on the map these days. They heard aeroplanes and thought they were being fired at. Difference was these two put their foot down and hightailed it to the nearest police station.'

From Linklater's tone, Amos detected there was more. 'What aren't you telling me?'

'Not on the mobile, Amos, I'll come over.'

'I'm at Jack's.'

Amos clambered unsteadily out of the

Land Rover and leaned against it. Why was Linklater telling him this? He pushed himself upright, he'd find out soon enough.

Jack took one look at his face, pulled him through into the kitchen away from the Friday-night crowd and thrust a medicinal scotch bottle under his nose. 'What's happened to you? You look as though you've seen a ghost.'

Amos told him about Linklater's call.

'They've been practising again, you mean? If these men definitely heard aircraft . . . ' Jack reached for another glass off the dresser behind him and sat down, excited. 'You know, I've been wondering what this reminded me of and I've suddenly remembered.' He poured himself a tot while Amos regarded him through glazed eyes. 'Where I grew up, in the Home Counties, there was a series of accidents, serious ones. I remember a motorcyclist was killed and several carloads of people injured. They all happened at night, on exactly the same lonely stretch of road, I mean within a few feet, and those reported in the paper happened within weeks of one another — and they weren't the only ones.'

Jack had Amos's full attention. The similarities were remarkable. So Jack had had the answer all along. 'So, what was it?'

Jack shuffled closer in his seat, his face

went pale as he remembered. 'Well, they tried all sorts of explanations of course — camber of the road was wrong, an icy stream ran across under certain weather conditions . . . '

'Jack, I'm warning you!'

'I'm coming to it, I hardly know how to say it but you can look it up in the old newspapers if you don't believe me — early 1960s it would have been, '63 or '64. I remember because I was driving by then and I never went down that road at night, ever again.'

A soft tap at the back door heralded Linklater's arrival. He declined Jack's offer of scotch, settled for coffee and sat down with them at the table.

Amos was ready for some straight answers. 'So, what's the big secret?'

'As I told you on the phone, the two men heard aeroplanes and shooting. Apparently it came out of nowhere, one minute they were cruising along, happy with their evening's sport and the next this crazy aeroplane starts firing at them.'

Amos nodded in recognition. 'Did they actually see it?'

'No, but I don't think they were craning their necks up through the windscreen, they were too frightened; more bothered about getting out of there fast, I gather.'

Amos looked directly at Linklater and waited several seconds before actually speaking. 'Are the Forces — or any other group — practising there at night, Stephen? Is that what you don't want us to know?'

Linklater stared straight back without blinking. 'Amos, if they are, they sure as hell haven't told me about it! They'll kill someone soon if they carry on like this.'

Amos grunted, satisfied that Linklater at least was as ignorant of the facts as they were, except . . . 'So what was it you couldn't tell me on the phone just now?'

Linklater held his coffee with both hands, head bent towards it as if drinking in the aroma. 'Only because I don't want the press getting hold of it, that's all. The last thing we need is people flocking out there to be scared witless and driven off the road. Until I get to the bottom of this I don't want word of it getting out. I told those two guys to keep it to themselves.' Linklater glared meaningfully at Jack. Amos wondered if this policy of silence was wise, surely folks ought to be warned.

Linklater looked up. 'The men tonight recognized the engine sound — they were adamant about it. Insisted it was a Merlin engine. You know, the one they put in the Spitfire.'

71

9

Amos dropped his scotch glass. From being convinced there was a rational if underhand explanation for all this, he was right back in unreality. Up until now he'd succeeded in discounting the familiar noise he'd heard on the basis of where he'd been and what he'd been thinking of at the time — put it down to auto-suggestion, his tiredness playing tricks on his mind. He could no longer do that, now he had to face the truth. Whatever they might be up to, present day armed forces would not be practising in Spitfires.

'That's what you heard too, isn't it?' Linklater demanded. Amos nodded. 'I guessed as much when I heard those men tonight. No wonder you were reluctant to tell anyone, they'd have thought you'd been snorting something.'

Amos didn't reply, what could he say?

Linklater went on. 'And before you ask, yes we've checked. The only airworthy Spitfires in the country are safely tucked up in their hangars fast asleep, have been for weeks. You couldn't scramble one inside a morning if Hitler himself were coming.'

Jack looked stunned. His tale, suspended when Linklater arrived — the accidents he'd been describing which had occurred all those years ago in another place — had seemingly begun to resemble more and more what was happening here now. Amos explained to Linklater about the multiple accidents in the town where Jack had grown up.

Jack began to speak as if mesmerized. 'You see, the road where it all happened ran along the side of the cemetery.' He shivered. 'And every one of the survivors told a similar story.' Jack looked from Amos to Linklater. 'They said it had been foggy, and out of the gloom a coach and four horses had reared up in front of them, huge black horses at full stretch, straining at their traces, racing towards them on their side of the road. The drivers had done the only thing they could which was swerve violently out of its path.' He gulped. 'One or two who'd been able to look back said they saw them gallop in through the cemetery gates and vanish.'

Nobody uttered a word, each presumably struggling with their own sense of reason. Nonsensically, all Amos kept thinking was, 'Why can't the ghost rest now the body has been found?' If the ghost was indeed a Spitfire pilot sent to apprehend runaway POW's, now that they'd found the body surely he should stop. Amos stood up to break the spell. What were three grown men doing sitting round a table telling ghost stories!

'Thanks Jack,' he said, aware of sounding unnecessarily short. He opened the door to go. 'Sounds to me you had a damned good yarn-spinner on your local newspaper.' He turned to Linklater. 'I quite see why you don't want the press getting hold of our little mystery.' He stomped over to the Land Rover muttering to himself, now perversely comforted by the news that all the victims on the perimeter road had heard an aeroplane, heard the sound. You didn't hear ghosts.

Linklater strode across the yard after him. Amos turned. 'If it's all the same to you, I've had enough talk of phantoms for one night, Stephen.'

Linklater put a hand against the driver's door, preventing Amos from opening it. 'Thought you'd like to know, we've found out some more about your dead POW.' He dropped his voice as a group of Jack's customers cut behind them in the car park.

How could he resist? If he didn't find out now he'd toss and turn all night wondering. He looked around, starting to feel the cold. This was no place for a private conversation.

Amos put the kettle on while Linklater warmed his seat in front of Amos's fire. 'It seems the sketch we found on our friend is a Dürer, self portrait of the artist I'm told.'

Amos peered round the door from the passage. 'A real one?' He knew little of art but he'd vaguely heard of Dürer. 'A self portrait, you say? Was this Dürer a relative of the dead man, do you think?' Amos relaxed. Profoundly unwilling to contemplate wartime aircraft, inexplicable shootings or unexplained apparitions, he found art infinitely more appealing.

Linklater chuckled. 'Sounds as though you know as much about art as I do, Amos. I suppose he could be a relative, or rather a descendant — Albrecht Dürer lived in the fifteenth century.'

Amos hovered the bottle over the mug of coffee and raised an eyebrow. Linklater looked at his watch.

'Just a drop.'

'If it wasn't a family portrait then I guess the only reason he'd be carrying it would be because it's valuable?' Amos sat down in his armchair, nursing his mug and blowing on it.

'If it's the genuine article, yes . . . probably priceless.'

'What!' Amos almost spilled his toddy. What on earth was a runaway POW doing with a priceless sketch? And why had he and the sketch lain undisturbed and undiscovered in a Warwickshire ditch for the last sixty years? He dismissed the idea as preposterous. 'You did say he was shot?' he asked. 'Full of bulletholes.'

Linklater looked momentarily nonplussed at this seeming change of tack. 'Oh, yes . . . yes. He was shot all right, and we're pretty sure it was from an aircraft.'

'Then, doesn't it strike you as odd that a man is shot, but then lies where he died with a valuable picture on him? Surely whoever shot him would have come back for the loot?'

'Only if they knew he had it.'

'Why shoot him otherwise?'

'To stop him escaping, of course. He was a prisoner. Nothing too unusual in that.'

Amos still wanted to know why the man had been left by the wayside but more pressing in his mind was another question. 'How come he had the picture in the first place?'

Linklater settled himself by the table. 'We're trying to figure that out now.' He sipped his drink. 'The favourite theory is he probably stole it from somewhere local, maybe from one of the estates where the prisoners were sent to work on the farms.'

'But what if he'd had it on him when he baled out, and had had the presence of mind to bury it as soon as he landed?' Amos leaned forward, excited he might have the answer. 'And when he went back for it he got shot because they thought he was trying to escape? Which he may or may not have been.' He grinned, triumphant.

'Ah, but that presupposes he was originally captured near here. Odds are he certainly wasn't. These people were shipped into here from all over the country — from wherever they were apprehended.'

Amos sank back into his chair, deflated. 'Well, you're the detective, you tell me.'

'I can't, we don't know. We're still trying to find out who he was precisely, this Franz Schumann.'

'No luck with the German authorities then?'

'Not so far — it's even less of a priority for them.'

'Be useful to know whether the drawing belonged to him though, wouldn't it?' Amos mused.

'Thinking of your reward are you, Amos?' Linklater chuckled. 'More likely he wrenched it from some poor Jewish devil whose family had owned it for centuries.'

They were both quiet for a moment. Strangely, Amos found it hard to think of that abandoned body as a villain rather than the victim he'd become. Strange because, unlike with the living, he'd no way of judging the man's character by his facial expression or his actions or by what he said; all he had to go on was a skeleton's visage. Still, he felt sorry for him.

'Actually that's the other theory we have. That it was part of one of these wartime art hauls you read about.'

'You mean that he had lots more paintings, not just the one?' Amos found it hard to believe.

'It's possible; much of the art which was either stolen by invading forces or, conversely, hidden to evade its capture by invaders, was never found, you know. Mind you, I daresay much of it got destroyed anyway, the way it must have been mishandled.'

Especially in the early years when it had been touch and go whether Hitler would invade, thought Amos. Funny, just the other night he'd been talking to Jack about that and thinking about what Churchill had set up. Now he remembered the rest of it. 'But how . . . ?'

'How did matey come by the sketch?' Linklater shrugged. 'Found the cache and helped himself? Or was part of a gang who moved the pictures one by one to sell on?'

'And how did they get them all here in the first place . . . if they weren't English?'

'Who knows, but don't forget this was a RAF base, and the Americans were also here later on. Some of them could have discovered the haul in war-torn Europe and transported the lot over here, hidden it somewhere until they could dispose of it.'

'And you think Schumann found the store and that's why he was killed?' Amos answered automatically, his mind elsewhere.

'Maybe, but like you said, it's surprising they left the picture on him. Or he could have been an art expert who told them where to find the cache on the Continent — in return for a share of the haul, one Dürer sketch he knew to be worth a small fortune.'

'Then they shot him anyway?' Like I'd have to you, thought Amos.

'What?' It must have been something in Amos's tone which made Linklater look at him curiously. 'No, then he was shot as an escaping POW . . . by a squadron who knew nothing about the pictures.'

Amos had finally realized why he kept associating Linklater with what he, Amos Cotswold, would have to do in case of invasion. As in many rural parts of England, as instructed, the local men who weren't for whatever reason in the Forces — those who were too old, farmers and those in other reserved occupations — had been formed into guerilla cells. Many of the operational bunkers, OB's as they'd been called, still existed — secret meeting places dug out in woods — and the orders still held.

He didn't even know exactly where the local hide-out had been. He'd never given it much thought before . . . except for one appalling instruction. Apparently the first thing an invading force would do would be to round up all the local men and take over the police force. Therefore, Amos had read in the orders he'd inherited as a councillor, in order to safeguard vital information it would be his duty to shoot the top three senior ranking policemen in the district.

He looked across at the intelligent, dedicated face of Stephen Linklater. He couldn't possibly do it. But what if there were an invasion now, or next year? Was it so unlikely? Had they left the old hiding places, the old instructions, in place simply because they'd forgotten about them, or was there a more sinister interpretation — as a fail-safe, just in case. Was the idea of forces practising out there on the airfield quite so far-fetched? They wouldn't have told the police during the war because the police would be taken over by the invading authorities . . . so why would they tell them now? He realized that, even today, duty prevented him from sharing this knowledge with Linklater.

Ah, but why weren't they telling him then — as a councillor? Was he to be bracketed together with the police on this? Nonsense! So it couldn't be that after all, thank goodness. Whatever was going on was much more likely to be criminal activity than some ridiculous counter-invasion strategy.

'. . . caused his death.'

'What?'

'I thought you'd gone to sleep the way you were looking at me through half-closed eyes. Either that or I'd suddenly grown horns. I was saying, we've been trying to establish the cause of death.'

Amos rubbed his eyes. 'We're still talking about Schumann, the POW I found? You said he'd been shot — riddled with bullets in fact.'

'Yes, but there may have been other contributory factors.'

'You mean he could have been lying there asleep and got shot accidentally?'

'Yup. Or he was being chased and couldn't run because of his condition. Although, as you can imagine, there are bound to be pieces missing after so long — our people don't think he was in very good shape when he died.'

Amos jumped to the defence of the POW camp. 'Nothing like the shape some of our poor buggers were in when they came back from Burma.'

'No one's accusing the authorities of ill treatment. Maybe he'd been injured when his plane crashed, who knows.' Linklater stood up. 'Anyway, I thought you'd like an update.'

'What happens now?'

'We'll put it in the papers — about finding the body, and the Dürer sketch. It'll be free publicity for you, Councillor. Apart from hundreds of would-be owners claiming it as their long lost aunt's, you never know, we might just get some sort of lead on it. We've nothing to lose at any rate. Don't worry, we won't say where the body was found.'

'You think it's genuine then?'

'That's one of the things I came to ask. You mentioned Henry Fishbroke last time we spoke about the drawing. Do you think he'd authenticate it for us? The chief superintendent seems to think he's the best hereabouts.'

Amos reached for the phone and dialled Henry's number. Henry had a flat on the top floor of his renovated gallery. The phone rang and rang in those vast empty rooms. He wasn't surprised. 'Too late for Henry, you can rarely get hold of him after dark. You'll have to wait until the morning.'

10

Windy Nook, an aptly named pastureland on this grey October day when even the cattle loured and the clouds raced so near his head Amos could have reached up and squeezed the rain out of them. Jack was balancing windmill-style on the edges of the deep ruts the cattle had carved near the margins of the river.

'It wasn't a tale you know, Amos.' Jack battled back up the hill, gasping for breath as he laboured to make his point. 'About the coach and four by the cemetery. I grant you it sounds ghoulish but . . . ' He stopped. 'Have you never been in one of those places that feels wrong, cold, eerie, however you want to describe it, but you're uncomfortable, as if something dark happened there?'

'And you think that's what your cemetery road was like, and you think that's what explains the sound of Spitfires strafing the road out by the airfield?' Amos asked.

'In the absence of a better . . . ' Jack looked up to where several kites circled slowly above them brushing their wings on the clouds, distant gliders describing a wide circle, riding the air currents. 'Were you ever into those remote-controlled aeroplanes? My friend was dead keen, used to go up on the local plain every Sunday with all the other enthusiasts and stand there craning his neck clutching his black control box. It's a wonder none of them ever fell off the ridge.' Jack and Amos stared at one another. 'You don't think . . . ?'

'Why not?' Amos said. 'It would fit. Don't they use them for films and things?' He sat down on the nearest tuft, oblivious of the damp and the dirt and the wind streaming past him, recalling Linklater's words: 'The only airworthy Spitfires were all tucked up in their beds. But what if they'd been models?'

'Of course! They had them for war films, quarter-size Spitfires and Hurricanes complete with dummy pilots in goggles and flying jackets. I remember seeing them in one of those documentaries about how they made those movies!' Jack cried.

'But what about the sound, Jack? They could just dub the soundtrack on to the film, couldn't they, but out here . . . what about the sound?'

'Well, if the model's big enough I imagine you could strap on a miniature tape player to provide a soundtrack, whatever you want really, and operate it remotely.'

'Why didn't we think of this before?' Amos

was amazed at his own slowness.

'Because to begin with you omitted to mention being shot at by aircraft, let alone the Spitfire sound you heard.'

Amos was thinking hard, turning this technological revelation around 360 degrees in his head to see if it worked. He quickly decided to take technology for granted . . . which left motive. Someone was going to elaborate lengths to safeguard the army camp.

'I admit at first I thought I'd imagined the Merlin engine in the atmosphere of it all.' Amos turned to Jack. 'Like you said this morning, there are places that have vibes — and you're right there. That airfield perimeter late at night has vibes all right. Imagining Spitfire engines would be easy.' He sneaked a look at Jack who seemed to be taking this confession with a straight face. 'Even for me. But when those other men told Linklater the same thing, well, I for one don't think we all imagined it.'

'Hadn't we better tell the chief inspector?'

'I'm surprised he hasn't worked it out for himself by now. But if no one's actually being shot at then he may not consider it worth pursuing. Road hazards aren't exactly his province, are they?' Frankly he could see no harm in telling Linklater their theory now but there remained that niggle in the back of his mind, and until he really understood who was doing this and why, he'd rather keep it quiet — just in case. 'Tell him if you like but I don't think I'll bother.'

'You're not planning on going out there looking for it are you?' Jack asked, clearly worried.

Amos had every intention of finding out why these attacks were happening but reasoned he'd learn little by attempting to track a remote-control operator miles across a lonely airfield.

⋆ ⋆ ⋆

It was only now, on his way to speak to Henry, that it struck him as odd; he realized Henry hadn't enquired about the sketch they'd found on the dead POW since Amos had first mentioned it. He'd seemed so interested at the time; for some strange reason he'd seemed to think it may have been put there recently.

Linklater was waiting outside, flanked by two other plain clothes policemen. Amos had the disturbing impression that all three were probably armed. If the drawing did turn out to be genuine then they couldn't afford to take any chances, not that anyone other than Henry who was expecting them, and Amos himself, would have had any idea what Linklater was carrying in his briefcase. Neither did Amos really need to be there but Linklater had asked for the introduction, probably to be courteous. After all, it was Amos who'd discovered the body on which the sketch had been found.

The two bodyguards remained outside. The oak doors stood open and as Amos and Linklater approached, Henry's assistant triggered the switch and the glass doors slid noiselessly back. 'You could do worse than keep that drawing here,' Amos remarked as they entered. 'It's like Fort Knox.'

Henry strode across the entrance hall to greet them and they followed him through to a gracious office at the rear furnished with what appeared, to Amos's untrained eye, to be expensive Italian style furniture. Pale watercolours adorned cream walls and tasteful bronzes stood on marble-topped tables.

Amos tried to read Henry's demeanour, but he always seemed much the same — outwardly expansive and garrulous, keen to please, besotted by the beauty of art, infectious about it. He wondered how often Henry had handled the objects others saw only in books or museums. Had he started in one of the big auction houses perhaps, or did he come from a stately home which had crumbled from death duties and black watch beetle forcing the young Henry to make his own way? For one so approachable, it was surprising that Amos knew so little about him.

'The chief superintendent has asked if you will take a look at a drawing we've found — see if you can tell us anything about it,' Linklater said.

'By all means, Chief Inspector, anything I can do to help.' Henry's eyes shone with delight.

Linklater placed the briefcase flat on the desk, fiddled with the combination and flipped it open. He extracted a plain manilla envelope and closed the lid. All three of them remained standing, not daring to breathe, as he took the slim oilskin package from the envelope and placed it in front of Henry. 'We found it like that in a metal cylinder.'

Henry's long artistic fingers carefully undressed the picture. Pushing back the final cover he gasped — just once, as if shocked. Or bowled over?

It was a small sketch, perhaps six inches by eight in grey and brown colouring on a darkish background yet, even upside down as it first appeared to him, Amos would never forget the hand. It was as Linklater had first described it, a head and shoulders portrait of a Renaissance man with his right hand resting lightly on the crossed arm in front of him. The hand was so lifelike, had such character, Amos felt it could stretch out at any moment and touch him. He moved around the table to stand at Henry's shoulder so he could see the face. It was the face of Jesus. Bearded, angelic, prophetic, wise, benign, all those images he'd imagined or been conditioned with.

'I thought you said it was a self portrait of the artist,' Amos whispered to Linklater, fearful of disrupting the moment or disturbing Henry.

Henry straightened, serious. 'And so it is. Albrecht Dürer, 1471 to 1528, painter and engraver. He painted a number of self portraits like this when he was in his twenties, portraits which made his appearance look supernatural . . . metamorphosed into Christ.' Henry turned to Amos. 'To understand it you have to understand what the Renaissance was about. Dürer here was a humanist, he believed in the advancement of humanity by its own efforts, that man is the centre of the universe. This philosophy emerged from studying the classics — hence the huge resurgence of classical art, design, proportion, philosophy, all those things during this period.'

'He saw himself as God?' Amos asked, incredulous.

'Not exactly . . . but perhaps he liked to imagine himself in the role. The Renaissance Humanists didn't reject Christianity but they liked to concentrate on human achievements particularly in the arts and sciences.' Henry stepped back. 'He was without doubt the greatest German artist of the Renaissance, but the irony was it was the German hordes who'd destroyed the ancient culture in the first place.'

Amos breathed out. What a parallel there was here with the Second World War . . . and a second irony: for the Dürer to be found on the body of a dead German prisoner.

'And that's not the only irony,' Henry said, as if reading Amos's thoughts. 'Dürer came from, of all places, Nuremberg — where the annual Nazi rallies were held in the '30s, home of the anti-semitic decrees in 1935.' He paused, distracted for a second. 'And of course, where the Nazi leaders were eventually tried for their crimes after the war.'

'Is that where this came from then, do you think? Brought over by our pilots during the war?' Amos was hooked.

Henry didn't answer immediately. Instead he lifted the sketch, turned it over, produced a powerful-looking magnifying glass from a drawer and studied the back. Finally he held it up to the light and twisted it round slowly.

'You know, Dürer became rich by realizing early on that it's much more lucrative to sell a picture several times over rather than just once. So he set himself up as an engraver — virtually invented etching — and turned out prints which he engaged an agent to sell on his behalf all over Europe. Of course prints can't be sold for as much as an original but the benefit is in the volume . . . in reusing the asset as it were.'

Linklater spoke for the first time since he'd produced the painting. 'Can you confirm this sketch is genuine then and if possible who it might belong to?'

Henry stepped back. 'Oh, there's no doubt about it, dear boy, no need to go through all those fancy tests they can do nowadays analysing the materials and so on. It's a fake. A good one, but a fake.'

Amos's spirits plummeted, disappointment set in. He could hardly credit it. He stared and stared at the drawing, a work so real, so lifelike, so compelling. Whoever had done this must have been very, very good. Still, at least he'd had the privilege of seeing a wonderfully powerful picture close up, even if it wasn't the original.

Henry went on. 'It's one of Dürer's

drawings all right, but it's a copy. Probably done in the nineteenth century I'd say or even later. A very good copy like this might fetch a few thousand, but not millions.'

Amos looked across at Linklater, if anything he looked relieved. As far as he was concerned it must be one less worry.

'Any idea where it could have come from?' Linklater asked.

'None, dear boy. Sorry.'

Amos couldn't stop looking at it, the drawing had a mesmerizing effect. Remembering Henry's question on first hearing of the find, he asked, 'You wondered if the sketch had been put there recently, Henry . . . when I first told you about it. Were you thinking of an art theft you'd heard about?'

Henry looked blankly at Amos. 'I don't remember that. But no, I don't think I was.'

Amos sensed there was something there but decided against probing further. He knew little of art but understood there were private collectors who preferred to remain totally anonymous for all sorts of reasons he could only guess at. Did Henry suspect that one of his clients had lost this picture but daren't say so for fear of betraying the man's confidence? And Henry had asked if the immigrants had had a hand in this, and neither Jack nor Amos had been able to see the relationship between

93

the two subjects at the time. There was an obvious one of course, that the picture had recently come from abroad.

Henry turned to Linklater. 'What happens if you can't find the owner, Chief Inspector? Some of them are very shy, you know. Will it be auctioned?' Amos couldn't blame Henry for wanting the picture.

Linklater smiled. 'I think we've a lot of work to do before we get to that stage, Mr Fishbroke. If it was stolen during the war then we've a great many archives to sift through.'

11

Amos settled himself on the bank above the weir while Napoleon snuffled around under the elders. Here, far away from airfields and army camps, he sought to restore his sense of proportion. He often came down here when he wanted to think, gazing as now at the fast-flowing river washing the stones clean, carrying away the debris, liberating the life force, preventing the water course from choking. And that's what it did for him.

His mind kept returning to the dead POW. In order to erase this uncomfortable notion of anti-invasion activity from his mind, he had to dispel Alan's theory of the body having been recently planted in that ditch. Which meant he must satisfy himself that there was a rational reason why the body had not surfaced earlier.

One reason had to be its location. But surely whoever had ordered those Spitfires, and the pilots who had flown them, must have known something . . . or had they in their turn been killed? Maybe that was it. And if there had been an alert over an escaped prisoner, then wouldn't the man in charge have wanted to know what had happened? Or had he been all too happy to accept there had been no escape? After all, it would look none too good on his record if he'd let his POW's get away. Then Amos remembered a film he'd once seen and realized that too might provide the answer. If the pilots had brought back a dead POW then there could easily have been reprisals extracted from British POW's held in Germany. Far better to leave the body where it was. And that commandant would have known the remaining POW's would cover for the missing man, to give him a head start.

Granted, the man may well have been missed but it wasn't in anyone's interest to call attention to his absence from the camp. His family would have been a long way away in a war-torn foreign land. It could have been years before they realized he was actually missing and they'd simply have put it down to the exigencies of war.

So it was feasible the body had been there since the war — through an unwitting conspiracy of circumstances. Where could it have sprung from otherwise? Dug up out of a cemetery? Amos shuddered.

Napoleon's ears went up and Amos turned to see Lord Gray striding towards him.

'I came to see how you were. Not only shot

at but very nearly run over, I hear.' He looked at Amos keenly. 'What's going on, Amos?'

Amos wished Alec hadn't said that. It was one thing to privately feel persecuted or unlucky but to hear the same implication voiced by someone else meant he had to take it seriously, and he didn't want to.

'Coincidence, Alec, just coincidence. No one could have known I'd be in either place at the time so don't go reading some dastardly plan into it.'

'That's not what I heard.' Alec Fitzsimmons knocked a stray piece of mud off his toecap with his cane and continued to study his feet. 'Just about everyone on that site visit knew you'd gone with Bill in the ambulance and would have to come back for your Land Rover. All they had to do was wait.' He looked up at Amos. 'And I daresay people hereabouts knew you and Jack would be on the Stratford to Lower Farthing road the other morning. Knowing Jack his whole bar would have been aware.'

Amos didn't want to hear this. 'If you think any of these people or my fellow councillors would . . . ' He stopped. 'And besides, the poor devil driving the truck couldn't possibly have cannoned into us purposely — it cost him his life, for heaven's sake.' Then again, if they'd offered the man a few hundred pounds to arrange a little accident, enough to feed his family back in China for years . . . it was just feasible.

Alec held up his hand. 'I'm telling you to be careful, that's all. I have no idea what's going on either but I'm hearing rumblings.'

Amos grinned despite himself. 'Not you as well?' Alec looked puzzled. 'Haven't you heard? There have been two more car accidents up near the airfield since I came a cropper and they both heard shooting — aircraft strafing the road. Spitfires, you know, the Merlin engine job.'

Alec looked up quickly, his mouth ready to laugh. 'You're serious?'

'It's all right, those bangs on the head from the cattle haven't undone the final screws. Jack and I reckon it's some kind of remote-controlled aircraft. The real question is why.'

Alec began to pace in front of Amos. 'Something to do with the proposed development of the army camp?'

'Fits time-wise. Why, have you heard something?'

'Oh, only the usual. There are always those who don't want progress, aren't there?'

Here was another group who could have planted the body. Amos shifted on the log he was sitting on. 'Everyone knows I'm for the development despite the airfield project misfiring.' He looked curiously at Alec. 'Surely the powerful concerns, those with money, are the ones who want this project to go ahead?'

'Not if there's another proposal on the table — for a site the other side of Warwick.'

Amos slumped, this was news. 'But surely there's enough business for two new parks?'

'If I'd sunk a lot of investment into one of them, I'm not sure I'd want to bank on that. The economy is growing only slowly, will there be so much demand for these units? And what about price? The developers will have to reduce their rents if there's competition.'

'Well, surely these big businesses do their sums before they start these schemes?'

'Look, I don't want to add to the speculation but it simply occurred to me that what's been happening to you wasn't exactly accidental. You're a key man, Amos, people follow you, lots of the other councillors look to you. If you say it's OK then they tend to think it is too.' He paused for breath. 'Nobble you and it would make a big dent in the pro-campaign for the army camp development.'

Amos ignored the compliment. They both sat listening to the river and watching Napoleon.

'I told you Bill Thomas spoke against it, didn't I? Do you think he'd been influenced by these people you're talking about? Are they the ones pulling the strings, do you think?' Amos suddenly realized. 'It's in his county ward, isn't it, this other development? I represent this area on the county council but his is, was, Leamington.' Well thank heavens that's finally explained, thought Amos. Except for who the hell was the Henry he mentioned before he died?

'It wouldn't be the first time something like this has happened, would it?' Alec said, sadly.

'No, I suppose not. I was more comfortable with the theory that someone was keen not to have the army camp excavated for fear of what we'd discover.'

'What did you think might be buried there?' Alec asked.

'Apart from the operational bunker, you mean?' Amos knew that Alec as one-time county councillor had been privy to the same instructions as himself, albeit for a different area. Amos shot him a sideways look, reluctant to give voice to his concern. 'You haven't heard any re-mobilization rumours have you, Alec?' He tried to say it lightly ... as a joke. 'You don't think it's the old underground groups who are doing this?'

Acknowledging the humour, Alec smiled

fleetingly but offered no reply. Maybe he didn't think it needed one — couldn't believe it was a serious question.

Amos changed the subject. 'Alan Tregorran thought there might be a mass grave over there. After all, no one hereabouts has ever known that much about the place. They employed some civilian labour after the war but I think their movements were pretty restricted. They used to pick workers up from the villages by bus, drop them at the gates and then transport them to their place of work by train within the site. Security was tight, they didn't go wandering around on their own.'

'I can't believe they were hiding anything bad. It's more likely to be a chest full of gold or a cave full of priceless paintings,' Alec said.

'You've heard about the Dürer, then?'

Lord Gray nodded.

'Interesting isn't it? I mean what would a dead POW be doing with a very good fake Dürer? Tell me that.' Although Amos had given plenty of thought to how the POW had come to have the drawing, could rumours of an art cache have been part of a clever deception? 'Do you think they were trying to convince people they did have some sort of art haul brought out of Europe during the war . . . so that people would accept the fakes

101

more easily? I mean, they'd be expecting to see the real thing, their natural scepticism would have been allayed by the stories.' Amos went on.

'The fake was very convincing, Alec, a work of art in its own right even if the composition wasn't original. Henry says it's worth a few thousand because of that.'

'So you think any rumours of an art haul are just that, rumours? And always have been, except . . . you're saying they were started deliberately.' Alec looked thoughtful.

'Well, it has only just occurred to me. Trouble is you'd need one hell of a good faker somewhere. You should have seen that drawing, Alec.'

'I can imagine, amazing isn't it? I'll never forget that chap who was jailed in the seventies for faking Constables, I think it was. He's a magnificent artist.'

'But if there is no hoard buried at the army camp, what is there to hide?' Amos scratched his head. 'Oh no, you're not suggesting the fakers want the camp to remain sealed because otherwise people will find out there is no hoard of masterpieces!' They both laughed.

'There is a more realistic possibility.' Alec looked enquiringly at Amos. 'I don't know if you've considered the processing plant at the airfield?' Amos bristled as Alec went on. 'Maybe those people don't want any other activity near them. It's much more likely to be them who have something to hide.'

From what he'd seen and knew of Carlton and what he'd heard from other people, Amos had to admit that was likely. And who was it who had nearly run him over. 'Well, they won't win if that's their little game.'

'All the same, I'd be careful if I were you, Amos.'

12

Henry was sitting on the seat outside his gallery as Amos and Lord Gray walked back. He beckoned them in. 'I think I've got something which might interest you,' he said mysteriously, addressing his remark more to Lord Gray than Amos. He led them through the viewing-rooms and into his office, fiddled with two alarm dials and then locked the door behind them. From a room at the rear he extracted a large canvas draped in a sheet, propped it on an easel already set beside the desk and uncovered it.

Lord Gray took two or three paces back from the painting. 'It's a Gainsborough, isn't it?' he said softly.

'I say, well done. Yes, very dirty but undeniably by Thomas Gainsborough. You've just recognized what many before you have failed to, hence its reprehensible state.'

The picture depicted two young girls, richly dressed but as if in mourning, arrayed in drab greys and muted mauves. The centre of the picture was so dark Amos couldn't make it out. Contrary to his usual views on cleaning, he wanted to rub the grubby window with his sleeve; remove the film which tantalizingly prevented the picture from coming alive.

'Been hung over an open fireplace for a century or two, that's the problem. But it'll clean up well, you mark my words.'

'Will you do it here?' Amos asked.

'Oh no, for one thing it's not mine.' Henry's face took on a conspiratorial slant. 'I asked if I could borrow it for a day or two. The insurance company came up specially to check the security here before they would allow it.'

'Are you selling it then?'

'Not exactly.' Henry waved them into a seat, propping his own ample form on the edge of the desk. He leaned forward and spoke in a hushed tone even though there was evidently no one else around to overhear. 'Most of them are in private hands, so it's rare for one to turn up unannounced, so to speak, but it can happen.' He gazed at the painting then went on.

'You can see how dirty it is, no one paid it much attention, thought it was Great Auntie Alice, or Maud and her sister as girls.' He slid off the desk and moved beside the easel, facing them.

'In 1759 Gainsborough painted a picture of his daughters with a cat. It hangs in the

National Gallery, you've probably seen it.' Neither Amos nor Lord Gray moved. 'Like several of his portraits it wasn't carefully finished. It was done the year he moved to Bath seeking a fashionable clientele amongst which to set up as a portrait painter. And he became very successful. So it's long been thought he'd been short of time — which I'm sure was true.' He turned to peer at the painting. 'But if this turns out to be what I think it is then we may have proved a different theory.'

He wiped his brow with a large silk handkerchief, more for effect than any practical reason, Amos reckoned. He had to hand it to Henry, he was a good showman. Amos knew nothing about painting but even he was sitting on the edge of his seat. Now he could see Henry was indeed sweating a bit, a big man struggling to contain his excitement. Amos had to help. 'Isn't it sufficient that it's a Gainsborough, Henry?'

Henry beamed. 'Yes, Amos, but I think this one is the finished painting. I think he hurried over the other because he'd changed his mind, or his daughters did, but rather than scrap it at that stage he skimped it and went on . . . to paint this.' He reached for the magnifying glass which lay on his desk and scrutinized the middle of the painting with it.

'I think that's what he did with a lot of his portraits; we've always thought them roughly finished but in a sense they were meant to be, that way he could still sell them — easily. It was much better than scrapping them and after a certain point, easier than changing them — but he didn't want to spend over long on something he didn't have a commission for, such as pictures of his daughters.'

'And then he painted the finished article, you mean?' asked Lord Gray.

'Precisely. Just think how many times some of these sitters must have changed their minds — particularly ladies. They'd want a different dress, or a different hat . . . or, as in this case, a different pet. Of course, sometimes you get similar paintings with a changed detail or two so that the artist could reuse a popular composition whilst each client still received an original.' He turned and offered the magnifying glass to Lord Gray. 'Look in the centre there, what do you see?'

Alec did as asked. Peered, stepped back, peered again.

Amos, who had twisted in his seat to position himself at a different angle to the light, answered for him. 'It's a dog, you can see it is. Come and look from here.'

'I see it now, looks like some kind of spaniel.' Alec turned to Amos. 'Funny how you can see something once you know what you're looking for, isn't it?' He handed the glass back to Henry. 'So what's the story, Mr Fishbroke?'

Henry brought his own chair out from behind his desk to join them and mopped his brow again. 'The painting belongs to an elderly lady.' He looked directly at Alec. 'You'll understand why I can't tell you her name but she's a titled lady who needs money in a hurry.' He looked at his feet. 'I don't know this for sure but I suspect she's ill, perhaps she needs expensive medical treatment,' he shrugged apologetically. 'I'm speculating.' He cleared his throat. 'As you can imagine she doesn't want any of this bandied about so she's reluctant to put it up for auction or anything like that until she's ready. Sotheby's would be far too public — all her friends go there regularly and would start gossiping about why she was selling the family silver so to speak. And then her nieces and nephews would start bullying her about selling their inheritance.' He raised his hands imploringly. 'I'm sure you get the picture, if you'll excuse the pun.'

Alec and Amos made sympathetic murmurings. Amos could well see why the lady would want anonymity. For one thing she might have several more where this came from and would be reluctant to advertise for burglars.

'My client wants to sell the painting quickly . . . and discreetly, knowing it'll mean getting less for it.' He rose and went over to his desk, searched amongst the papers. 'I've seen the provenance, someone in the family was related to the Gainsboroughs and the lady herself still lives in Wiltshire.' He selected a thick cream sheet of paper and handed it to Alec.

Alec looked at it and let out a low whistle. 'It's insured for four million.'

'Which is why it's been kept in the insurance company's vault ever since they insured it. That's another reason why she's chosen this particular painting — she can't enjoy it anyway.'

'So, how do you come into this, Henry?' Amos was wondering where this was leading. He felt out of his depth with expensive portraits; hardly dare look at the picture and daren't get any closer to it, not something worth that much.

'The lady approached me, asked if I could help,' Henry looked at Alec carefully. 'My client wants two million,' he held up his hand as Alec looked aghast. 'No, I know, but that's what she says. She knows it wants cleaning but that'll take time, which she hasn't got. So she'll take two now.'

'I'm sorry Mr Fishbroke but, attractive as this proposition undoubtedly is, I couldn't put my hands on that sort of money,' Alec said openly.

'It'll be auctioned as soon as it's cleaned. In today's market I wouldn't be surprised if it made more than six. And if I'm right and this is the real picture of his daughters, the one that was finished properly, then we could have all sorts of people after it, including the National Gallery. Today they have the original but that one would become the working drawing, whereas this is the finished article.' Henry paused. 'Do you know anyone who might be interested in investing in a share of the picture?'

Amos saw Alec relax. 'You mean like a racehorse, own part of it?'

'Exactly, only it would have to be on the strict understanding that the picture was to be sold once it had been cleaned, otherwise everyone will be falling out over whether to keep it or sell it,' he smiled. 'By then, you see, it'll be too late for the lady's family to intervene.'

'Ah well, that's a different proposition, I might be interested in a share. What had you in mind?'

'I have to tell you I'm down for half a million myself so we need another one and a half. I don't think it matters whether the shares are all the same size or not, obviously the profit will be divided up pro rata.'

'How long have we got?' Alec was very interested now.

'A week or two.' Henry smiled ruefully. 'I'll have to let the insurers have this back after tomorrow but anyone who's interested can go and look at it down at their place, it's just not so convenient that's all.'

Alec looked at Amos. 'I should think Bengy Pargetter might want in don't you Amos? And my cousin's husband,' he turned to Henry. 'Don't worry, neither of them will want to see it, Mr Fishbroke, they're businessmen not art connoisseurs. If they know I've bought in that'll be enough for them.' He grinned. 'They'd probably give me hell if I didn't give them the chance.' Alec looked searchingly at Henry. 'Are you sure she only wants two million? I wouldn't want to think we'd . . . '

'I know, that's why I made a point of telling you up front. I didn't want you finding out what it's really worth when we auction it and then accusing me of diddling the lady.' He wiped his brow again. 'She's adamant the figure is two million.'

All this was way out of Amos's league. He

got up and stretched, assuming Henry had only invited him in because he happened to be with Lord Gray at the time and it would have been rude not to.

'Interesting,' Amos said, after he and Alec had left.

'He's certainly very knowledgeable. I'm not so sure about his business acumen, mind. I daresay he could make a lot more out of that painting if he went about it differently.' Jack had been the first to doubt Henry's entrepreneurial capacity, now Alec had remarked on it too.

'Isn't that what makes him so likeable though, he's so obviously not out to make the last penny all the time, is he? Not like a few others I fear we're going to get.' Amos chuckled. 'I can't see him trying to frighten people away from developing the army camp, can you?' Amos stopped still. 'I was just thinking about Bill Thomas and then about what you said, about that other development over in his County ward, the one near Leamington. You don't think Henry's involved in that, do you?'

'That's an odd question, Amos, even for you. Why should he be? As you say, even if he were I'm certain he wouldn't be indulging in dirty tricks. What makes you ask?'

'Only that when Bill died he was trying to

tell me why he'd so unusually voted against the development at the army camp and all he managed to say before he collapsed was 'Henry said . . . ''

'There must be several Henry's you both knew,' Alec said. They'd arrived at Alec's car. Barred from the gallery, Napoleon had been keeping it company — slumped against the rear wheel like an oversized wheel clamp.

'Who am I to blame him if he is investing in that development? Henry told me he knew nothing about any army camp, and I've no reason to disbelieve him, so I daresay he simply told Bill he'd invested in the Leamington project and that's what Bill had been about to tell me . . . perhaps by way of explaining to me about the other site and its potential. He and Bill were in Rotary together, it was only natural Henry might have confided in him, knowing the scheme was in his ward.'

'It's probably something far simpler,' Alec said. 'We know why Bill did what he did, I should stop worrying about it if I were you.'

13

Amos had sat on his backside over this whole affair for far too long; must be getting old, he mused. What was he thinking about, letting Leamington beat them to a development which might well mean the difference between prosperity and a slow lingering death for Weston Hathaway? He was damned if he was going to let some grotesque scare tactics stop him from doing what was right.

He knew most of the villagers would welcome the extra trade and the fillip it would provide for their remaining amenities; but how easily they'd succumbed to Eric Stanton's tales of hugely increased traffic. The answer was glaring at him — use the old railway for what it was intended.

Next stop, Mr Stanton. Just what was that man up to? Unless he was being coy for some misguided reason, he certainly hadn't seemed eager to open a steam service. Could it be he had ambitions to open the commercial line? Amos pulled over on to the verge and turned off the engine. But if so, why had he been sowing dissension over the army camp development? That wouldn't help him. No industrial park, no need for a goods railway.

Clever, the man was clever. He had pointed out the increased traffic — that was the villagers' complaint, increased traffic; what better way to initiate a clamouring to reinstate the commercial railway? He could leave it to the industrialists to fight for the development itself. Stanton was ensuring that when the go-ahead was given it had the proviso of the railway indelibly scheduled in with it. Which meant he and Amos were on the same side.

Amos decided to track Stanton down at the army camp — see if together they could determine the best way of promoting the railway.

The gates stood open. Inside, the camp lay sleeping, like a giant open air museum, preserved in concrete. Rolling stock brought in by the Railway Preservation Society was parked on one of two branch lines near the airfield side of the camp, beside the road and adjacent to the No Man's Land which separated the two.

Amos glanced across to the rows of rusting wagons and carriages then wandered along the nearest track. This must be the restored section. Here engines gleamed with the application of love and fresh paint, their tenders brimming with coal, their couplings oiled — ready for duty. Amos even recognized one or two of them from his school days. Stanton certainly seemed to be doing a good job.

In the silence he caught the sound of a machine, some sort of tool — not a saw, a drill maybe — which appeared to emanate from the direction of the No Man's Land scrub. Curious, he followed the sound to a break in the chain-link fence, which had once housed a high gate, to which only its posts now bore testimony. The undergrowth had been recently cleared for a foot or so either side of the path which led through it. Amos followed the path, emerging beside a long brick-built single-storey shed.

He felt uneasy in here, the vegetation crowded in on him, doom-laden, scene of unhappy memories. He was becoming like Jack in sensing bad vibes; if anywhere felt like that, this did. What was this place? Why was it hidden away between the airfield and the army camp and who was using it now? Sensing how largely unchanged the area was since last occupied by the Forces, he half expected to pass a couple of squaddies in army fatigues coming the other way, laughing and smoking.

The noise grew louder. Shortly, a well-swept flat-roofed concrete porch came into

116

view housing a pair of army issue green metal doors. Amos tried the handle but found the door locked. He battered on the metal with the flat of his hand until the drilling noise ceased.

Footsteps approached, a key turned and Eric Stanton opened the door and peered out cautiously. He seemed neither pleased nor annoyed, more as if he'd been disturbed in the middle of a good film — vacant, engrossed.

Amos followed him inside, his uneasiness growing. Here the hut consisted mainly of one long barrack-like room, fifty feet wide by about a hundred and fifty feet long. The part they were in was well lit and laid out, presumably by Stanton, as a jobbing machine shop. Each machining station stood neat and tidy, the swarf cleared away, the parts gleaming. Stanton barred his path, his body language unmistakeably unwelcoming.

The man had wasted no time had he? He'd probably been working here for months only bothering to apply for change of use permission when attention had focused on the army camp.

Amos looked around. 'Impressive set-up you've got here, Mr Stanton. Tucked away though. I'd have thought you'd have used one of the sheds in the marshalling yard.'

'This one already had the electricity laid on.'

That was possible, stuck out here away from the main buildings it could have had a direct link to the grid, one which no one had remembered to disconnect. Idly Amos wondered who was getting the bills.

'Come to check me out, Councillor?' There it was again, that affected upward tip of the chin.

'On the contrary, Mr Stanton, I think we are on the same side.' Since he obviously wasn't going to be invited any further inside, nor offered a seat . . . or tea, Amos rested against the nearest machine. 'I've come to see how you'd feel about the old railway being opened up on a commercial basis, for freight. As you know, it would solve the traffic problem the villagers are . . . ' he trailed off as he watched Stanton's expression turn from arrogance to anger.

'It's the very last thing I would want to see happen. What a desecration that would be, all my hard work for nothing!'

'I thought it was what you wanted, I thought that's what you were trying to interest the villagers in.' Amos felt genuinely nonplussed.

'Commercial use? You're joking. Hoards of people who don't appreciate railways, all

118

these beautiful old carriages being turfed out. No! This is a sanctuary and must remain so.'

So that was it, Stanton wanted his own private railway. Again, it was obvious now. Thinking about it afresh, Amos realized that had Stanton wanted it recommissioned he'd have been more likely to simply march into the council offices demanding they reopen it rather than cajole the villagers into campaigning for it. No. He'd had to resort to manipulation to stop the army camp project altogether because he refused to see the railway disturbed.

Stanton had found his Shangri-La, a deserted army camp full of discarded rolling stock — heaven on wheels. Though how he thought it would stay that way for ever, just so he could gratify his childhood's desire but without actually owning the place, was a mystery to Amos. Maybe he'd wrongly assumed it had remained mothballed all these years out of neglect rather than the more prosaic truth that the Ministry had thought they may one day need to reactivate it.

Amos looked around, the place made his skin crawl, or was it Stanton who had that effect on him? And what was that strange smell he couldn't quite identify — some sort of cleaning fluid? There was little point in antagonizing the man any further. Stanton couldn't stand in the way of progress if the Council decided to reopen the line but it would have been nice to have had an ally, useful too with Stanton's expertise.

Remembering George Churchman, he had the odd idea these two obnoxious individuals might just hit it off and Churchman had been so keen to come and work here; perhaps he was the one who could talk Stanton round.

'It looks as though you could do with some more foot soldiers out here.' Amos tried to sound helpful. 'I know another man staying in Weston who's mad keen on trains like you; I'm sure he'd love to come and lend you a hand. Name's George Churchman.'

Stanton replied silently with a steely glare, his fists clenched, chin lifted, visibly seething.

'Suit yourself.' Amos shrugged. If Stanton wanted to carry on being a bloody fool then let him, he'd done his best. Trouble was he'd banked on Stanton's support which he wasn't going to get.

14

'What's the traffic contraption saying then, Amos?' Trust Jack to want to be ahead of the news.

After Stanton had worried the village about the traffic increases to be expected if the army camp development went ahead, Amos had arranged for County to install their measuring kit — to determine the current levels in Weston Hathaway.

'So far, much as I suspected, the traffic through here isn't as bad as people make out. In fact the volume per hour is the same as it was five years ago. Though it has shown up one or two oddities.'

Jack leaned across the bar eager for information. 'Oddities?'

'Traffic at funny hours, such as the middle of the night . . . and no, it wasn't me nor Alan either and it's not the lambing season so it isn't any of the other usual suspects disturbing the peace in the early hours. Something comes through here at over a hundred miles an hour roughly twice a week.'

'That's what people are talking about then. They hear that and convince themselves it's happening all the time now because of the increased activity all this army camp discussion has caused. You know what they're like.'

'Yes I know,' Amos said. 'Which is why I intend to find out what it is tonight.' If he couldn't persuade Stanton to help reopen the railway, he needed to understand how real this traffic concern was.

'Top up?' Jack asked, reaching for Amos's glass.

'No thanks, Jack, I need to be awake tonight. Can't have you saying it was the drink when I tell you I saw the phantom horseman speeding through here like Dick Turpin outrunning the revenue man, now can I?'

★　★　★

His boots were shiny with moisture although it hadn't been raining. He turned the collar up on the check jacket to deflect the wind which whistled round his neck. This felt like one of those interminable watches for an unknown predator when night after night something had been attacking the flock — biting the faces off the ewes as they struggled to defend their young, literally tearing the little ones apart, piece by red woolly piece, dissecting them where they lay twitching. Why should he feel like that tonight? Why should his blackest thoughts surface now, not half a mile from his cottage . . . with only a few hours left before daylight? It was the waiting, what was he waiting for?

Amos stood deep in shadow in the lee of the hedge a few hundred yards up the road to Lower Farthing, motionless, picking up the rustlings and sniffings of the nightlife. Far off he heard it as it rounded the corner from the next village, where the accoustics were known to change. He was coming, the culprit. Amos was about to reap the reward for his vigilance.

The bike was well silenced, its rider silhouetted against the moonlight as he raced past, a streak of silver and black, streamlined paniers encasing the rear bullet shape, man and machine indistinguishable from each other, concentration palpable at that speed.

So, it was a bike rider. Weston's Dick Turpin was a biker. Amos wondered if he would stop in Weston, was the village his destination? Was this a local man using the only possible time of night to live out his fantasy . . . or someone passing through with the same intent . . . or was it someone with a purpose and if so, what? If he was local he'd kept that bike a well-garaged secret, Amos would certainly have remembered seeing it.

There was no danger the biker would hear his footsteps and he wanted to know whether it would continue on through the village or stop somewhere. About to step into the road he picked up the sound of another vehicle coming from the same direction and decided to remain hidden. The new sound obliterated the first so he could no longer tell what the bike was doing anyway.

As the four-track sped past him he recognized the klaxon horns mounted on the top — Karloff. What was he doing out at this hour and in a tearing hurry by the look of him? Were he and the bike connected? They hadn't been far apart, though at his speed the biker was widening the gap with every mile. Was that why he was moving so fast — to outrun Karloff? He could hardly be a runaway immigrant with a bike like that, more like a courier. He was certainly no amateur rider. Amos smiled to himself over his earlier analogy, nor was Karloff like any revenue man Amos had known.

What was the biker carrying in such an all-fired hurry then? No one would come this way normally, if speed were important they'd go down the motorway. So, whatever the night-rider had been carrying it had either originated from or was destined for some-where local.

Amos thought about those paniers — something about those expensive-looking holdalls definitely screamed courier, despatch rider. Big, sleek, roomy, capable of carrying much more than you might suppose; could it be paintings, rolled up like the Dürer had been? Pity he hadn't managed to get the licence number, not that he'd have had any more success had he tried to read the ear tag on a galloping ram, but it would have been handy — he could have twisted Linklater's arm to check out the company, see who the client was that night.

He admitted to natural curiosity, but this was more. Why did it feel so sinister? Who would transport things at night when they could do it perfectly well in normal hours? Were they smugglers, was that it, modern smugglers? And how coincidental was Karloff's appearance seconds later — were they in the same racket?

Almost back home, as he turned out of the Stratford road to cross over he glanced up the street towards the village shop and Henry's gallery and noticed the light still on in the penthouse. Another burner of late night fuel it seemed. Amos shrugged. Weston Hathaway was fast becoming the village that never slept.

Thinking he'd seen everything he was likely to see for one night, he sauntered across to his cottage, where a familiar black shape was detaching itself from the gatepost to follow him lugubriously up the path, when above Napoleon's snorting and snuffling Amos thought he heard the sound of a third vehicle approaching much more cautiously — a small car, judging by the sound of the engine. He slipped behind the oak tree, hidden from the headlights which swept his garden as the car turned right then left towards Alan's place, going slowly and quietly, not wishing to disturb . . . or be seen? In the reflection Amos recognized George Churchman.

Dozing off, the night's events mingling his conscious and subconscious thoughts, Amos saw those klaxons again, kept seeing them. Could those car horns of Karloff's also be set up as independent loudspeakers? Was that what he was doing? Who said it had to be an aircraft? No one had seen it, including Amos. Was Karloff's vehicle the phantom remote controlled aircraft patrolling inside the airfield perimeter, scaring away any would-be interlopers with the terrifying other-wordly sound of the Spitfire fighters? But why?

Amos was wide awake now, sitting up in bed in the dark, shadows of clouds crossing the ceiling, the night air cold on his face from the open window. What difference did it make to Karloff and his pals what happened at the army camp? Why should they care when they had more than enough room at the airfield for their requirements? Or were they illegally using the army camp for something else? What might they be hiding? His brain was racing now. Is that what Churchman knew? Churchman and his obsession with immigrants. Unbeknownst to anyone else were there thousands of them illegally housed in the army camp?

Thinking back, Karloff hadn't seemed that bothered the afternoon he'd caught Amos and Jack snooping round the processing plant. Irritated yes, angry even, but not scared. Is that because his secret lay in the army camp, not the airfield?

It should be easy enough to find out. Amos looked at the clock. Too late, it would soon be light. He'd start with Churchman in the morning, try and find out what he really knew without appearing too curious.

Why was he taking this on, why not hand it over to Linklater and his colleagues, let the police do their job? Because he knew they wouldn't. The police had mixed orders about immigrants; with more than enough to do already, they'd be only too pleased to sidestep this one. Besides, daft as it sounded, even to Amos, he didn't want the police carrying out intensive searches in the army camp and happening upon the old operational bunker. Maybe it was crazy, but he wasn't going to jeopardize those secrets for the sake of an unfounded suspicion. First he had to find out for himself what, if anything, was going on up there.

★ ★ ★

Churchman was cooking his breakfast. When Amos rapped on his van door, the rancid smell of old cooking fat wafted out with that of bacon and fried bread.

'Thought I'd come and tell you I put a word in for you with Eric Stanton,' Amos started. Churchman's face brightened as he deftly scooped the contents of the frying pan on to his plate. 'But before you get excited I'm afraid it's no-go at the moment.' Amos had wanted to begin with Churchman in his debt, win him over, hoping then he might be all the more forthcoming with what he knew. And it was true, he had tried to intercede for him with Stanton.

'Oh, why's that then?' Churchman looked miffed.

'He seems to want to keep it all to himself. Matter of fact that's what I came to see you about.' Once inside, Amos perched on the edge of the bed, which looked rumpled but felt cold and unslept in, while Churchman lounged against the cooker, eating his breakfast.

'You know, it would be a really good thing for these villages if the army camp development went ahead, but some people are worried about the extra traffic it would cause. Well, one way to stop it would be to open up the old commercial line, and insist as a condition of the planning permission that all goods are moved by rail.' Amos beamed, pleased with his solution and knowing Churchman was bound to like it. 'But I put the idea to Eric Stanton yesterday, thinking he'd be over the moon about it, in fact believing that was his game anyway . . . and you won't credit this, but he was dead against it.'

'Then so am I. The last thing I want is that army camp given over to developers. It will go exactly the same way as the airfield, you mark my words. If it hasn't already.' Churchman gesticulated at Amos with his fork to emphasize his point. 'I'm with Mr Stanton, I think you should leave it alone.'

'What do you mean, if it hasn't already? What's going on up there?'

'Nothing,' Churchman said a little too quickly, Amos thought. 'I just meant, well . . . you know how these things happen,

Councillor . . . I . . . er, wouldn't be surprised if the powers that be hadn't already done a deal over it, that's all.'

Amos fell silent, realizing he might have put his foot in it. Judging by the way he'd phrased his reply, Churchman was siding with Stanton in order to ingratiate himself with the man. But there was more — he was definitely hiding something. Amos had been knocked off balance. 'But I thought you were keen on the railway?'

'So I am, but I'm not trading it for more immigrants. Not on your nelly.'

'It's not a question of trading anything.'

Churchman brandished his fork aloft and mumbled with his mouth full, 'Councillor, I'm sure Mr Stanton knows best.'

There was little to be gained by prolonging the conversation. Was Churchman genuinely afraid the army camp development would attract even more illegal immigrants into the country? And was he right? Amos eyed the man as he threw his dirty plate into the sink. Churchman could be playing a part, there had been something false about him all along. Was he from some far right organization dedicated to stamping out the use of foreign labour? Or could he be from the Ministry of Defence, who'd been told to shed the land but who had secrets to protect there, even now. Was Churchman a military man trying to hide his normally neat habits?

Whichever it was, the chat had not gone the way Amos had planned; he was back where he'd started, only this time wondering what he'd missed.

15

Harry Field kept a box outside the back door of his butcher's shop especially for Napoleon. A fair queue had formed in Harry's this morning as his usual helper was away at a funeral so, while he waited, Amos wandered idly around the side to watch Napoleon munch happily through five pounds of Bramley fallers.

Amos leaned against the wall in the October sunshine, one eye on Napoleon and one on the people leaving the shop. Idly he glanced into the side window where Harry kept his groceries, in time to catch a hand select a tin of soup then disappear. He thought nothing of it, everybody served themselves with groceries at Harry's, presenting them for payment when their turn came. But as he watched, the hand came again and again. He watched, fascinated. It was a female hand — small, brown and dirty. Still only passing the time, he levered himself off the wall in order to get a better look and saw that the hand put each item into a scruffy carrier bag. Nothing surprising about that. No one could have balanced that lot until they reached the till.

The crush in the shop prevented him getting a clear view of the hand's owner. He'd had a glimpse of lank dark hair as she stretched back and forth between the other shoppers, part of a jeaned leg — if that belonged to her, he couldn't be sure. The hand kept going. She must be in a hurry or lacked transport; most folk bought that sort of volume at the local supermarket. Harry would be pleased.

No sooner had the hand stopped than a woman pushed through the crowd which moved aside good naturedly to let her through, obviously presuming she simply could wait no longer, would come back later.

Amos felt sick, instantly wishing he hadn't seen what he'd seen. Why couldn't he have stayed watching Napoleon? Why couldn't he just ignore it, pretend he wasn't there? Because Harry was his friend and didn't deserve to be robbed. Amos stepped away from the wall as the woman hurried out. Feeling he might be missing something, Napoleon chose that very moment to desert his box and gallop into the street. The woman lost her balance, dropped the bag whose contents spilled out into the lane at their feet. She would have fallen had Amos not grabbed her; more to steady her fall than apprehend her. She looked petrified.

'Let me go, let me go,' was all he could make out, interspersed with much more in a different language.

People began to notice the disturbance outside. A thin little girl ran out and started putting the groceries back in the bag, looking as frightened as her mother. What should he do? Yes, she'd been shoplifting, he was sure, but he'd rarely witnessed fear like hers. Without loosing his grip he helped them gather up the rest of the goods.

'It's all right Mrs Smith, Edna, she's all right,' he told those who came to help. 'Tell Harry I'm going to borrow his kitchen for a few minutes, will you?'

Amos held firmly to the thin arm with one hand and hefted the heavy bag in the other as he marched the woman round the corner and in through the side door of the small kitchen-cum-store room at the back of Harry's shop. He looked across to the phone, he ought to call the police.

Silent since her first outburst of shock, the woman looked up at Amos and, registering his working clothes, relaxed slightly. He stared back, unblinking. The child started to snuffle. Still he said nothing, partly because he didn't know what to do. A young woman with a child stealing food and obviously distraught hardly constituted a hardened

134

criminal, more like someone in need. Get Lindsay, Lindsay would be the best bet, this needed a woman's touch. He moved towards the phone.

'Don't do that, mister,' she said very quietly, looking up at him from beneath her eyelashes. Oh Lord, was she about to start bargaining with the only thing she had? The sooner he fetched Lindsay the better.

'I'm going to call a friend, all right, not the police.' He dialled, praying she'd be in. No answer. He sat down at the table. 'You're from over at the processing plant aren't you . . . the food place beyond Lower Farthing?' Here was his chance to find out what was going on with the immigrants . . . and what, if any, connection they had with the army camp.

She looked down at her feet encased in trainers so old and worn their original colour was indeterminable. Had she walked all the way from the airfield this morning? Probably.

'Stephan make sure we paid . . . but he go.'

'Who's Stephan? Did he go home?'

'Dunno.' Her lips tightened in a line which belied that one word denial.

Amos leaned towards her, then saw the fear and moved back again. 'Tell me about it.'

The woman looked around the cramped kitchen, looked towards the door from the

shop through which Harry Field would walk
when he'd finished serving and demand she
be handed over to the police. Looked at the
child. Amos followed her gaze.

'Don't worry about Harry, I'll tell him you
were just stepping outside to get a better view
of something you wanted in his window . . . '
Her face brightened. ' . . . If you tell me
what's going on up there.'

She looked at her feet again, obviously
considering her options.

'Where are you from? Originally, I mean.'

'Romania.' She cleared her throat and sat
up in the chair. 'He say he pay two pounds an
hour. We no have money for lorry but he say
he take care of that and the papers. All we
have do is get on lorry one night. Easy.' She
swallowed. 'Until we here, then we prisoners.
He say we must pay, what you call it,
National Insurance, to your government, so it
come out of our money, so we only get one
pound an hour. Someone say it good because
if we sick then government pay but when
some of them sick Karloff he say we no right
be here so if we go to the town for money we
go jail.' The child sniffed. 'So you see we no
escape, no do anything. Then he no pay us
but Stephan he stand up to him, say he going
to report Karloff for not paying the insurance
to the authorities. I no understand but we

136

given money. Then Stephan go. Now sometimes we no paid again.'

'Where did this Stephan go? Didn't you report him missing?' The minute he'd said it Amos realized he was applying the normal actions of a British citizen to someone who thought she had no rights, someone who lived in a separate society, a feudal set-up ruled by a gang master in the shape of Graham Carlton.

'He not alone. Many go missing.' She paused and looked at him. 'We hope they escape.' Of course, why would they want to report their compatriots, their friends? They hoped they could do the same given half a chance.

'Didn't Karloff report the people who escaped?'

'He no like Stephan, Stephan make trouble for him.' Surely all the more reason to report him then, hope the authorities pick him up. She'd gone tight-lipped again. Amos took a guess.

'You think something happened to Stephan, don't you? Was it Karloff . . . ?'

The sound of voices came from outside then a tap and Lindsay, with her beaming genial face, stepped over the threshold bringing wholesomeness and common sense into this dark conversation. Close on her heels came George Churchman.

'I met Mr Churchman down the lane as Edna and Mrs Smith were telling me Napoleon had knocked over a young woman. Thought you might need some help.'

'Heard you were in here with an immigrant woman,' Churchman boomed from behind Lindsay.

The woman leapt up and turned her back on him, gathering her child to her. 'That creep, he always coming around,' she muttered.

Luckily Amos was prevented from saying anything by Lindsay who barred the door with her bulk and said over her shoulder: 'This is no place for men, Mr Churchman. I'll deal with this.' She winked at Amos who rose to his feet and whispered to her on his way out: 'Take them home and give them a good meal, Lindsay. Oh, and take the stuff, I'll pay Harry later.'

It was a pity the woman had been so frightened, though how much she knew was doubtless limited; they sounded pretty much incarcerated up there.

16

Amos needed to fetch some more feed, stock up for the coming Winter. As he approached the traffic island where the airfield spur rejoined the main highway he glanced to his left attracted by the bright colour in the field, a complete contrast with the surrounding mile after mile of barren earth. Row after row of huge orange globes perched on the ground, gourds without a tree, balls without a beach, incongruous, unbelievable. The pumpkin park he called it.

At the road end of the field stood the trailer, but instead of the workers beavering away like black ants against the low sun, harvesting and loading the fruit, they were gathered together in a knot. Instinctively he realized something was wrong, the scene was too tense for a tea break. He drove back the way he'd come and in by the field gate, bumping over the rough terrain.

Several men detached themselves from the group and came running towards him, concern in their faces. Maybe they thought he was their driver. They pointed to where a man lay clutching his stomach and rolling from side to side in agony. 'He not good yesterday, we tell him no come but he need money,' one tried to explain. Amos looked round. They'd been left out here without transport, the trailer unhooked for them to load on to, a gerry can of water standing against it, presumably for drinking. No phone of course.

The man's eyes were staring in horror, as if someone were knifing him; Amos could see he wasn't going to last long without proper help. He reached for his phone then remembered they were only a few miles from Evesham hospital. He turned to the two nearest. 'Can you load him into my truck, you'll find some old blankets there, lie him on those and stay with him.' They were Napoleon's blankets but he was sure he wouldn't mind in the circumstances.

It felt like hours but took just five minutes for Amos to drive the short distance to the hospital. Porters came, loaded the man gently on a trolley and wheeled him away. Amos and the other two men sat in reception, silent, their heads in their hands. Presently a nurse appeared requiring the usual details which the men tried to supply. Next of kin? Yes, the man on Amos's right was his brother. Contact telephone? Amos gave his mobile number. She addressed Amos, probably because he spoke the best English. 'He has a ruptured appendix. The doctors will operate straightaway.'

Amos drove the other two back to the pumpkin field and took the opportunity of quizzing them. 'Do you know a man called Stephan?'

Both men looked at him, clearly uncertain whether or how to respond. Was it a glimmer of excitement he detected? 'He send you?'

'No, I heard he disappeared.'

Nevertheless the name Stephan seemed to be the password to their being more forthcoming. 'Stephan crazy, him believe paintings hidden.'

What a day this was turning out to be. Amos didn't know which question to ask first. What paintings? Where? What gave him that idea? Any of which might give the impression he was too eager, might want to find the paintings himself.

'Can't think why around here, can you?'

'From war. Somebody tell him.'

'What, someone back home? Is that why he came here?'

'Don't know, but think he find them.'

Careful Amos, don't frighten them off. Keep the interest light.

'Did he tell you that? I expect he was boasting.'

'He not only one.'

Where had he heard that before, only hours earlier? Only that time Amos had had the impression that the woman stealing from Harry thought Stephan had been threatened by Karloff, or worse.

'Others talk, say lots of paintings hidden near here. They go look . . . at night.'

'And you think they found them.'

'They no come back.' The man shrugged as though it were the logical conclusion.

'I would think a lot of your friends simply decided to leave, didn't they.'

'Where they go, no money? Find paintings — have money.'

Amos wasn't so sure about that. And had no idea whether or how any of this related to the army camp and the Spitfire attacks, unless there really were valuable paintings stashed around the place which someone was trying to protect. Neither would he have the faintest idea how to go about selling a valuable painting. But he knew someone who would.

⋆　⋆　⋆

'Hoped I'd catch you before you shut up shop. Send the Gainsborough back safely, did you?'

Henry turned, surprised. 'Oh, it's you,

Amos, didn't hear you come in. Yes, yes, can't be too careful, can you?'

Amos was wondering how to handle this. The last thing he wanted to do was to start or lend credence to any rumours about an art haul. It had been one thing for him to surmise about it as a possible explanation for the Dürer being found on the dead POW, but quite another to bring it into the realm of today's reality. If nothing else it could turn lots more people against the army camp development while they all had a shot at finding this fool's gold. Not that Henry would be party to anything so silly.

'I've been thinking about the Dürer. I can't understand what that POW thought he was going to do with it,' Amos scratched his head to emphasize his perplexity. 'Was it different then? I mean you couldn't just sell it on a market stall, or in a car boot sale or through the small ads column in the *Stratford Gazette* could you?'

'You don't think he wanted to keep it?'

Amos hadn't thought of that. 'Well, I can't speak for the poor blighter I found can I . . . but hypothetically, today I mean, people who steal paintings are going to be doing it for the money aren't they?' He knew that of the immigrants for certain.

'Not necessarily. Some stolen paintings are

never seen again, either for the very reason you mention, they're too obvious, too well known, hence too difficult to sell without the thief being apprehended . . . or they were stolen to order.'

Was Henry being purposely obtuse or was it simply that his world was so very different from that of village life? 'Yes I see,' Amos said, dismissing from his calculations the timely accident of happening upon a rich art lover when one needed one. 'But what if someone did have a valuable painting, let's say that it was reasonably well known but not so famous everybody knows it like the *Mona Lisa* or something . . . and he needed the money? What would he do?'

Henry fished out his handkerchief and dabbed at his forehead while he thought. 'Well, I'm not sure, Amos — find a crooked art dealer, I suppose. The thing is he's not going to get anything approaching its real value because people will assume it's a fake. No one would be trying to sell a stolen original on the open market now would they? Too likely to get caught.'

'So it would be very difficult.' Amos thought again. 'What if he didn't know much about art and therefore had no idea of the picture's real value. If you have nothing then a few thousand would seem like a small

144

fortune.' Amos was thinking of Stephan and the other immigrants.

'Mmm, can't say, Amos, it hasn't happened to me I'm sorry to say. That fellow was carrying a fake Dürer. How someone like that would sell a valuable original without copper-bottomed proof of ownership I've no idea. P'raps, as you say, these things were easier during the war.'

Henry had reverted to the initial example, the Dürer, and Amos didn't want to arouse suspicion by bringing him back to a present day example. But he'd confirmed Amos's view that had Stephan or any of the other immigrants tried to sell an interesting painting or two then a man like Henry would soon have known about it. News like that must leak out very fast in the art world . . . and Henry would surely have mentioned it in passing. As it was he seemed remarkably uninterested, apparently finding the whole supposition too bizarre to contemplate.

The hospital rang while he was with Henry. The patient would live, they'd operated just in time. Amos had no choice but to deliver the good news in person. He drove up to the airfield — the third time that day he'd been in the area. Seemed he couldn't keep away. The trailer of pumpkins stood unhitched just inside the gate and as he pulled in, a second truck carrying the pickers came from the opposite direction. Damn, he'd have liked the excuse for a scout around.

'He's OK. We got him there in time.'

'You do, mister, you do!' The brother hugged Amos like a saviour. 'Lydia say you're councillor, important man.' For the first time Amos noticed the woman from Harry's, she must have joined them out there this afternoon.

'I knew it you when they describe you,' she said shyly. 'Mrs Martin tell me all about you. I tell them you all right, give us food.'

He drove back along the same road, past where he'd discovered the body. It was quite dark over on this side but not late. Not late enough for a recurrence of the Spitfire phenomenon.

He glanced across the road to the army camp. He was going round in circles with this, though the answer was simple. All he had to do was go up there unexpectedly one night, and he'd probably find a lot of frightened immigrants bedded down in the old barracks. Which would prove it was Karloff and his cohorts who were trying to stop the army camp development. But then what was he going to do? Explain to his fellow councillors and expect they would all magically change their minds?

No, because Lord Gray was probably right. The real antagonists were the Leamington site investors. So his grand exposure would only make life more difficult for these poor sods without guaranteeing the development would go ahead.

Deep in thought he failed to see the figure in the middle of the road until almost too late. Braking in panic and bathed in adrenalin he wrenched the steering wheel hard over, praying the Land Rover would respond in time.

17

The vehicle rocked ominously as it fought to bend itself around the obstacle, cutting an unnatural curve on what should have been a straight path. Rubber smeared across the tarmac as the wheels skewed sideways, the metal framework creaked and groaned like a sailing ship caught broadside to the wind. Wrestling with the forward motion of the Land Rover it was seconds before Amos could glance back. He hadn't felt a crunch but would he necessarily have heard the impact? He knew he hadn't run over him, but he might have hit him. Amos pulled up the vehicle and crawled out, shaking.

Ten yards up the road the figure remained where he'd first seen it, a dark sentinel near the crown of the road, unmoving. As he made his way towards it a wave of apprehension gripped Amos, not because he feared what he may have done but because the figure might not be real. What was it about this stretch of road, and him? Was this another illusion which had very nearly caused him to crash his vehicle — or worse?

Leaving the glare of the Land Rover lights

behind, his eyes grew more accustomed to the dark. It looked like a man, a man turned sideways to him gazing into the airfield. As Amos reached him he turned slowly as if in a trance. Amos stretched out his hand to touch the man's sleeve. He hadn't knocked him over, he was alive, and he was real — had a face, an elderly face.

Once he realized the man was all right, the repressed anger welled up. Anger forged from relief that he hadn't killed him and anger that he himself might have been killed through this man's stupidity. 'What the hell . . . '

But he couldn't be angry, the man looked to be in shock. Amos led him to the side of the road, noticing his pronounced limp. Had he been hit after all?

'I can't find where . . . I'm not sure now. It's been so long.' He turned and looked at Amos, fear in his eyes. He straightened, struggling to pull himself together mentally as well as physically. 'They said it was here.' His English was perfect except for the slight foreign accent. All sorts of questions scudded through Amos's mind, not the least of which was how uneasy, how vulnerable he felt standing out on this road. Was the old man a decoy — of his own accord or set up? Would the firing start again at any moment? The man's fear was infectious. And if he was in shock, he should get him home.

'Where do you live, how did you get here?'

'I walked from Lower Farthing, got the bus there. I live in Stratford.' He might be thin but he must be tougher than he looked to do all that.

'Come on then, I'll give you a lift. Are you all right, can you manage?' Amos and the stranger climbed into the Land Rover. 'I live in Weston Hathaway. Cotswold, I'm Amos Cotswold.'

The stranger turned very slowly in his seat. 'You're the man who found him, aren't you? They said so.' Then he remembered himself and added, 'I'm Karl Weiner.'

'Are you talking about the prisoner of war, the dead body?' Amos asked.

'Yes, Franz Schumann. He was my friend.'

What a surprise . . . and what a coincidence that Amos had happened along at that moment, except of course he'd been around here a lot in the last eight hours. Judging by his reaction when he heard the name Cotswold, Weiner obviously thought so too. Linklater had said he would put it in the local press in case someone had some information on the man and what may have happened. It had worked — better than they could possibly have hoped. Fancy, Schumann's friend still being alive . . . and living locally.

Now Amos could find out what had happened all those years ago, both to Schumann and the paintings — and in the process lay his own more recent ghosts to rest.

'Have you told the police this? They know his name from his papers but they've been trying to find out who he was.'

'No.' Weiner bristled. 'I don't talk to the police.'

Amos put it down to those years as a prisoner, no wonder the chap had an antipathy to authority, who wouldn't have. Amos said nothing, he could tell the police whatever Weiner had to say without breaking any confidences.

'All these years . . . ' Weiner mused, as if talking to himself. 'All these years and I never knew.' He said it hesitantly, as if searching for the right words. Amos knocked the keys against the steering column and the man jumped. Was he always this edgy? What had he really been doing out here, miles from anywhere — trying to find the exact spot where his friend had died? Why? Was it the same impulse that drove people to put flowers at the scene of road accidents, or was there more to it than that? What did he know? They sat side by side in the dark cab, on the corner by the No Man's Land, staring out at the airfield and the ditch.

Weiner went on. 'It was the picture, the Dürer. I recognized it immediately.'

Amos held his breath. So Weiner knew about the fake Dürer. Here was the man who could enlighten them, explain all these rumours about paintings.

'It had been in his family for centuries. We were at school together, I saw it in their home every day.'

'What?' Suddenly the conversation had taken a totally unexpected turn. From being about to hear how Schumann had acquired the sketch and whether or not he had been a trickster — which was why Amos felt Weiner had seemed a bit cautious, not unnaturally reluctant to speak ill of his dead friend — the dimension had changed completely. Amos was having difficulty assimilating the change. 'Are you saying it's real?' Amos stammered. 'The Dürer's not a fake? Oh, but of course it still could be. Hadn't Henry said it had probably been done in the nineteenth century?'

'The one Franz had was real. His ancestors were descendants of the man who taught Dürer engraving. They had old documents which explained it all, he showed them to me once.'

'But . . . ' No, he couldn't tell Weiner about

Henry Fishbroke, no need to anyway. Anyone can be wrong, it was just strange that Henry had been so adamant. Then again, in Henry's line of work, where so much depended on trust, Amos realized you had to exude confidence. He didn't want to consider the alternative — that Henry had lied. Henry wouldn't have done that, he'd know he'd be found out sooner or later anyway, he wouldn't have risked his reputation. Like Amos in his role as Councillor, reputation was everything, lose that and well . . . it didn't bear thinking about. No, Henry had simply made a mistake. Amos thought back. Henry had mentioned the tests they could do, date the materials, things like that . . . so he'd probably assumed they'd be bound to do those too. His had been a preliminary estimate, that was all.

'Did he have any more? Paintings? Here in England?' Amos asked.

'Franz was delighted when we were caught by the British.' Weiner turned towards Amos, he was speaking very softly. 'You see, he was half Jewish and lived in constant fear that the German authorities would find out.' Almost inaudibly now Weiner added, 'Or that he'd be ordered to slaughter his own people . . . as we'd had to slaughter those Romanian dissidents.'

For the first time, Amos realized that some POW's had deliberately set out to be captured by the British. And some had never wished to return either. 'So what happened to Schumann . . . and to you, then?'

'Franz wasn't very well,' Weiner paused as if about to say something else but then changed his mind. 'He was scared.'

It seemed stupid to ask why a man in Weiner's position would be afraid, even once he was here, so Amos didn't. Obviously had any of his German compatriots discovered his Jewish blood then he wouldn't have been safe; especially since they'd been brainwashed into believing that Germany would still win the war and they'd all be liberated by a victorious Hitler marching across Britain, imposing his pogroms.

It must have been good for Schumann to be captured by the British, given a respite for a few months, a year or two, but he must have known that sooner or later he'd have to return to the German Luftwaffe and the nightmare would start again. No, for him capture by the British could be only the first step in his escape plan.

'I think he thought if he could get to some remote part, like the north of Scotland, to some of those islands up there, that he could stay there undisturbed, no one would care. As

154

long as he could survive physically he'd be all right.'

'So he ran away?'

'Yes, I helped him.'

He said it matter of factly. Sixty years ago he'd been party to the escape of a fellow prisoner. Something in the way he said it suggested there'd been more to it than that, had they killed someone else? But again Amos didn't want to push him, what business was it of Amos's anyway, what would he have done in that situation? And now of course, after all these years Weiner had finally discovered what had really happened that night. Having thought his friend free and happy, the truth had now confronted him. No wonder he looked dazed. Weiner must feel guilty, he'd helped his friend to his death.

'You never heard what had happened to him?'

'No. The sound of aircraft fire was common here, this airfield was the training station as well as an active base. I didn't expect a postcard.' Weiner had obviously been in England a long time, long enough to acquire the wry sense of humour. 'We always covered for anyone who was missing.'

'You didn't try and find him after the war?'

'Where would I have begun? No.'

There was something very final in that 'no'

which precluded further questions. Weiner had probably had his own hands full. Had he escaped himself? So what about the paintings? Why come out of the woodwork now ... or perhaps he hadn't? If Amos hadn't nearly run over him he may never have discovered his existence and in five minutes Weiner had provided a veritable treasure chest of useful information.

Amos's curiosity was overcoming his sense. 'There have been tales of a hidden art haul, which could date back to those times. Did you ever hear anything about that?' he asked as casually as he could.

'No.'

'You don't think . . . I mean, Franz having this valuable painting, was that what started the rumours?'

'I don't know, I never heard them.'

'Well, I've only heard it recently, not from local people but from the people they bring in to work at the food processing plant on the airfield over there.' In the dark, Amos pointed towards the far side of the site.

'What sort of people?' Weiner asked warily.

Amos scratched his head thinking about Lydia and the man with appendicitis and what he'd heard about Stephan. 'I don't know, the east Europeans not the Chinese. Why do you ask?' Amos turned to look at

Weiner, who'd gone white and was visibly shaking.

'I didn't realize, I didn't realize,' Weiner mumbled. 'Why now, after all this time? Is that who really killed Franz?'

Amos was lost. 'Franz was killed during the war, Mr Weiner.' He wondered whether to add 'shot by aircraft fire' but thought better of it. Weiner was rambling, poor old boy. He started the Land Rover, fearful the shock would take further hold of Weiner before he could get him home. He'd be glad to get out of here anyway, the place held far too many unpleasant memories.

As they drove along in silence Amos remembered the mention of Romanians. What had Weiner said? Something about Schumann fearing he'd be made to slaughter Jews 'as we'd had to slaughter those Romanian dissidents'. Romania had provided military support for the Germans in the Second World War so that would fit, if some of their people had objected to it. But he didn't see what it had to do with all this. He shrugged. Trying to put himself in Weiner's place, he supposed he too might jump at shadows if he'd gone through what this man had, even after sixty years.

'Tell me some more about Franz Schumann. Was he married? What happened to his family?' The police would need some help if they were to trace the rightful owner of the Dürer today.

'No, he wasn't married. We were still at school — hoping to go to the university — when we were drafted into the Luftwaffe. The war wasn't going so well, Herr Hitler needed more and more pilots.'

'Where did you live?'

'Nuremberg.'

There it was, that Dürer connection. Amos was becoming more and more convinced that Weiner was right, the Dürer was an original.

Why was he so fearful? What was Weiner hiding? Had he and Franz Schumann stolen the Dürer from the Romanians? It sounded unlikely. And if, as he appeared to think, Romanian dissidents had killed his friend, they wouldn't have left the drawing, would they? That was easy to test surely, all Linklater had to do was find out if the Dürer had been owned by the Schumann family in Nuremberg before the war — simple.

And how had Weiner managed to remain here after the war? How had that worked? Had ex-POW's been allowed to stay if they wanted, no questions asked? Amos doubted that exactly but maybe it hadn't been too difficult.

'You didn't go back then? After the war?'

They were on the outskirts of Stratford now.

'I live in the old town, Mr Cotswold, right here, then second left. Anywhere here.' Much calmer now he turned to Amos. 'I'm most grateful to you. I had to go and say goodbye, do you see?'

Amos wasn't sure he did. He watched as Weiner clambered down and limped along the pavement, disappearing into a neat terrraced cottage. A trade sign hung on a post in the garden, swinging gently back and forth in the wind. It read:

Weiner's
Radio Controlled Models
Trains, Cars, Planes.

18

Amos was stunned. One part of him wanted to run after Weiner, ask him what it meant, ask him what the hell he was up to — until he realized he was just an elderly man. And the remote-controlled plane theory was only a suspicion anyway, one of Jack's ideas, if he recalled correctly. The other part of him wanted to get the hell out of there fast — he'd had enough for one day.

What did it mean? Why had Weiner been out near that ditch? More importantly, had it been accidental? Surely he could have had absolutely no idea that Amos would come driving along that road. No idea, none. Or could he? Had someone seen Amos drive that way to deliver the message from the hospital? And how could they have got Weiner out there in time . . . or had Weiner already been there when Amos drove out and realized he was almost certain to return the same way.

Or had Henry told him? Amos had been with Henry when the message had come through from the hospital, he may have told Henry about the man with appendicitis — he couldn't remember, but he may have. What was he thinking about, how could this possibly involve Henry of all people?

It was just about possible Weiner had been there purposely, knowing Amos would come along. It was stretching credibility but isn't that what coincidences did? The question then was why? And if Weiner was the phantom Spitfire controller why hadn't he been doing that when Amos found him? There'd been no noise at all. But Weiner could have disposed of the controller by throwing it in the ditch as Amos struggled to control the swerving Land Rover, and yes, maybe he'd been intending to give Amos another dose of strafing music and the equipment had failed, hence the silence. But for pity's sake, why had Weiner been standing in the middle of the road? And why would Weiner let Amos see his house . . . and that sign, if he were trying to hurt him? None of it made sense.

Unless — Amos kept coming back to it — there were other paintings and those other paintings were still buried somewhere near where the body had been?

The Dürer! He swung the Land Rover round again and headed back towards the police station. The sooner he told Linklater the Dürer might be the original the better. Even as a fake the police were aware it still had value. Nonetheless, Amos suffered nightmare visions of the drawing being used as a dart board in the canteen, or a wanted poster with whiskers crudely drawn on.

Linklater was in his office and the Dürer was not in evidence — bewhiskered or otherwise. Amos slumped into a chair. 'I think you'd better get a second opinion on that painting you found on the POW, I have it on good authority it is in fact the genuine article.' He enjoyed watching Linklater's face turn from surprise at seeing him there, to amazement at what he'd just said. Without a word Linklater picked up the phone.

'Get me the National Gallery. I know it's six o'clock but they'll still be there, I'm sure.' Seconds later the phone rang and Linklater arranged for the drawing to be re-authenticated the following day.

He looked enquiringly at Amos inviting an explanation, which Amos duly provided. He told him about Karl Weiner, where he'd found him, his friendship with Schumann and his family and hence his knowledge of the Dürer's provenance, that Schumann hadn't been married, and why Schumann had tried to escape. He told him of Weiner's fear of the Romanians and about his business. 'He said he doesn't talk to the police.'

Ignoring that last remark Linklater asked,

'You think the fact he deals in radio-controlled models is significant?'

'Don't you?' Linklater had not been party to Amos and Jack's conversation on the topic. Amos had purposely not told him, fearful of his inherited obligations, wanting to keep distance between himself and the police — just in case. But now he'd have to explain in order for Linklater to understand the connection. 'It's the only rational explanation for the sound of Spitfire engines and strafing that caused those accidents out there.'

Linklater was quiet while he thought. 'Why? Why would someone go to all that trouble?'

'Well, I did think it was something to do with the investors who plan to develop a big industrial park outside Leamington. Lord Gray told me about it.' The idea seemed lame now he was voicing it to Linklater. 'They won't be keen to see another development in the area reducing their rents, reducing their chances of letting all their units. So they were trying to frighten people off our site, make them think it was jinxed or haunted or something.' Amos purposely omitted any mention of anti-invasion measures — that the perpetrators could just possibly be Amos's fellow countrymen, keen to protect the whereabouts of their hidden bunker. And for the same reason was still reluctant to engender a police search for immigrants at the camp, so he left that out too. Linklater looked sceptical.

'But now I think it could be our friend Weiner, frightening people away from where that body was found in case they find what he's looking for — the other paintings Schumann had on him.'

'But remember, you only found the body that night because of those sounds. That's why you leapt for the ditch. That would mean he knew where the body was before you found it.'

'No, he couldn't have — otherwise we're back where we've been before, why leave the Dürer there? He must have known roughly where it was but hadn't yet found it. That's it, and that's why he didn't want anyone snooping around there.'

'Sorry, Amos, but that makes less sense than your first theory. If you don't want people snooping why draw attention to the place with intriguing noises? And why use aeroplane strafing which is guaranteed to get people leaping for the ditch.' He paused for breath. 'And why now? Why would he do it now . . . why not donkey's years ago? No. The only way that Weiner's models could be implicated is if he uses that area to test them out, when he figures no one else is around to steal his prototype ideas . . . or be frightened.'

'But what about Schumann and the paintings then?' Amos kept hold of his hunch.

'The irony is that his testing resulted in your finding the body of his old friend. Did he tell you Schumann had more paintings?' Amos shook his head. 'Well then, it's pure supposition. The old boy was just out there to pay his last respects.'

Amos struggled out of the seat. 'You'll get on to Nuremberg then? Find out if there are any Schumanns left who'd like their Dürer back?'

He could see Linklater counting to ten. 'Yes, Amos. And if you're very good I'll let you come and hear what the expert has to say tomorrow.' He looked up at Amos. 'Why do you think Henry got it wrong — if he has?'

'Probably because it was so unlikely to be the real one that he simply couldn't believe it.'

'You don't think he was trying to pull a fast one then, telling us it was a fake in the hope of buying it from us cheaply later?'

'Certainly not. He's got a reputation to worry about. And anyway, he would assume you'd find its rightful owners sooner or later.' Though to be truthful, Amos himself hadn't rated the chances of that very highly either, that is until he'd, almost literally, bumped into Karl Weiner.

★ ★ ★

Before, if anybody had shown excitement at the prospect of seeing a particular piece of art for a second time, he wouldn't have understood them. He did now. He could still see that hand as though it could move, feel, reach out.

The man from the National Gallery had already arrived — of medium height, greying hair, nondescript — the world expert in European Renaissance drawings, particularly those of Albrecht Dürer. He and Amos were shown down into what Amos assumed was still the most secure part of the police station, an old cell under the courthouse, where the only daylight was admitted through iron bars. Linklater acknowledged Amos with a nod. The oilskin package was produced from a safe and laid on a table in front of the expert.

Amos held his breath as the treasure was unwrapped. He'd known all along it was real, regardless of what Alec said about artists being capable of reproducing brilliant copies. How could anything as good as this be a copy? He gazed at that ethereal face, the wisdom, the kindness, the authority, the

166

humility radiating from it. That's what they should do to get people back in the churches — show them this, show them what the Son of God looks like.

'Hmm,' said the man examining the drawing carefully. He carried it over to the light and examined it again. He looked puzzled. Perhaps he wasn't sure, thought Amos, unsurprised. After all if Henry could make a mistake, and it still remained to be proved he had, then this Dürer was obviously a difficult subject to authenticate.

No one dared breathe for fear of disturbing the man's concentration. After what seemed like half an hour, he straightened and addressed Linklater. 'Yes, it's the original drawing, there's no doubt.'

The rest of those present all looked again at the drawing in amazement, dumbfounded that something so old and so rare and so beautiful should be lying on a table in a humble police cell, right here in front of them.

'You say it was found on the corpse of a wartime POW who'd been shot trying to escape? And that the drawing had been in his family for centuries . . . in Nuremberg?'

'Yes, that's right,' Linklater said. 'Well, that's certainly where we found it. The rest we were told yesterday by the man's friend.

Why? Would where we found it, and who we believe it belonged to, have altered your opinion?' There were no flies on Stephen Linklater.

'It could sometimes, but not in this case. Whatever you'd told me I'd have said the same. This is the original.' He looked at Linklater then shifted his gaze to Amos and the other two policemen in the room. A consummate professional, he asked, 'Can I speak freely?'

Linklater nodded, curious.

'Although I didn't see it myself, I have to tell you that the original was reported stolen from a Mr and Mrs Jeremiah near Winchester . . . two years ago.'

Amos gasped out loud, he couldn't help himself. Now what? 'You mean this wasn't Schumann's, it was planted on his body later? But why would anyone do that?'

'The only time I've come across this sort of thing is where thieves have taken something they fail to sell, I think the expression is when it's too 'hot'.' He smiled for the first time. 'If they have any morality, they realize they're holding a priceless work of art and want it to be found — with no risk to their anonymity. We've had paintings left on the doorstep, sent through the post, in luggage lockers. It does happen. As for whether it was at one time

Schumann's . . . well, it could have been. So much was lost during the war we're still trying to pick up the threads.'

'But why plant something on a body? And who knew the body was there?' But of course, Amos knew the answer. Linklater was watching him.

'Precisely, the body could have been moved from somewhere else. Used for the purpose.' Linklater held his hands up to deflect the impending question. 'I know, I know. I've no idea why anyone would do that.'

Neither had Amos. That the body might have been planted as part of an elaborate warning to keep people away from developing the army camp had been one thing but for housing a drawing . . . was quite another.

Back in his office after the expert had left, Linklater was explaining what forensics could do. 'It didn't occur to us that the body might have been moved. I mean, in the ordinary way of things, why should it have been? It was found where you might expect such a body to be found. We can get them to check the soil on him to see if all of it corresponds with the terrain up by the two camps. And they can check the pollen content. Did you know that every area has its own distinctive pollen fingerprint?'

'How sure are your people about when

169

Schumann died?' Amos asked. Nothing was as it seemed, so now he was questioning everything. 'Could it have been much more recently? Could Schumann have escaped as planned then come back? Was that it? Had he left the Dürer with friends for safe keeping, in case he was recaptured, then years later had to steal it back, either from them or whomever they'd sold it on to — possibly in good faith, believing him dead?'

'Well, it wasn't two years ago if you're thinking he got the picture back, then mysteriously bought it one night while out walking by his old prison camp, shot by his old friend Weiner's model aircraft — carrying live ammunition. Now that would have been ironic.'

'Or deliberate. Recreating the original scene even down to him having the painting on him? Then someone comes along, me, and Weiner can't get the Dürer back in time.'

'Stop right there Amos.' These amateur suppositions were clearly affecting Linklater's patience. He continued loudly. 'No, we don't have an exact time of death but it was approximately 1945. So yes, he could have escaped to Scotland or wherever then come back later and been shot. Yes, he could — but not this year. You can't fake the age of a corpse like you can a painting you know. He's been dead sixty years.'

Undeterred, Amos said, 'You weren't there but when I first told Henry you'd found a drawing on the body do you know what he asked? 'How long has it been there?' ' He'd got Linklater's attention. 'Not, for instance, how big was it, or who by but . . . how long had it been there? In other words he didn't assume as we did that it had been there all along. Now why do you suppose that was?'

'Because his first thought was that a valuable drawing would never be left to rot on a body, ergo it can't have been there long? Who knows.'

'I expect you're right,' Amos said, genuinely relieved. He didn't want to think ill of Henry. 'Will you be telling him you've had the drawing re-authenticated? He's not going to take it very well, is he?'

'I like that, Amos Cotswold. It was you who suggested him in the first place, and again, you who came and said you'd got reason to believe he'd been wrong. And you were right. So don't blame me. If you value that friendship I would go and tell him before he finds out from someone else, if I were you.' Linklater grinned. 'And watch your step. I don't want to hear about any more accidents with airfields or immigrants.'

Immigrants, immigrants, that's what Henry

171

had said. Instead of answering Amos's question about losing anything from his gallery, he'd asked if the painting had been connected with the immigrants.

19

He peered through the letter box, rang the bell incessantly and wandered around to the small walled garden at the back and the open garage where Henry kept his Jaguar. No car, no Henry and no assistant either. Still, if Henry wasn't around he was unlikely to discover there'd been a second authentication until he returned; the man from the National Gallery hadn't struck Amos as a gossip, not in the trade he was in. If the Gallery were to stand a chance of acquiring the Dürer for the nation then the fewer people who knew of its existence the better.

He was no further forward this morning than he had been days ago when he'd set out to build support for the army camp development. Stanton wouldn't help him, neither it seemed would George Churchman. He was pretty sure Karloff and his people were using the site illegally anyway so they wouldn't want it developed, and he still thought some powerful business interests must be orchestrating the accidents out on the perimeter road to dissuade folks, but if so — who on earth were they?

Added to which he'd found this strange elderly man wandering out on that same road where the corpse had been found, a man who may or may not be responsible for the Spitfire strafing. But if not, it was a damned funny coincidence that Weiner just happened to be a specialist in radio-controlled model aircraft.

And now Henry wasn't all he'd seemed. There, he'd said it, admitted his suspicion. But that wasn't fair, Henry had done his best. After all he'd not had the benefit of knowing the painting's provenance as Amos and Linklater now did. The question was, had Henry done it deliberately? Had he wittingly pronounced the Dürer a fake so he could stand a chance of acquiring it? Yes that was it. If, as Alec had said, some fakes were really so good the experts had difficulty in distinguishing between them and the real thing — and even the National Gallery man had taken his time — then since it could easily have been either, Henry had come down on the side which might do him the most good. Not a laudable approach but nonetheless understandable. After all, with something that rare the odds must always be that the one in question is a copy, the law of averages dictated that.

On the other hand, Henry may well have been aware that the same drawing had been stolen a couple of years ago. But, if he'd taken it to be the stolen one, and that had to be the most logical conclusion no matter that it had been found on a long-dead corpse, that meant he knew it was the genuine article. So why pronounce it a fake? He must have known that the police would eventually check their missing paintings list and hey presto there it would be — stolen two years ago from a couple in Hampshire, a two hour car journey away — one genuine Dürer drawing. So again, why say it was a fake? There were only two explanations: either Henry hadn't associated it with the stolen painting, hadn't remembered — which Amos thought unlikely, surely one sight of that drawing would have jogged his memory, as indeed it had that of the Renaissance art specialist — or he'd dismissed the idea believing the stolen drawing couldn't possibly have been placed deep under peat on a body sixty years dead. In which case, if this was not the stolen drawing then in Henry's eyes it must therefore be a copy. Thank goodness, that was all right then.

There was one other possibility which Amos was reluctant to consider. That Henry had indeed remembered about the stolen drawing and knew it was the same one; after all, corpse or no corpse, the same piece of art turning up two years later in the same

175

country was in itself a huge coincidence. Perhaps Henry had known the Hampshire drawing was not actually the original?

Amos's brain was doing cartwheels at a speed likely to create sparks. True he was intrigued, but he especially didn't want folks to think ill of Henry; the diversification effort would suffer if one of its leading role models was seen to be less than upright. He had to clear Henry's name. And anyway, he had a lot of questions of his own to ask the Jeremiahs which were nothing to do with Henry's authentication. They couldn't be too hard to find.

★   ★   ★

Once over the county border near Newbury, he raided the first public telephone box he could find for its directory. Not knowing the initial he had two possibilities to choose from — one at 9, Terrace Gardens, Basingstoke and the other at Alderton Manor, Sparsholt, near Winchester. No contest.

He drove down the ancient lane where gnarled oaks constricted the passage, hoping nothing would come the other way — passing places were rationed. After a mile, the lane opened out unexpectedly into a clearing before continuing on as narrow as ever. On

176

his left stood a set of businesslike wrought-iron gates soaring twelve feet above ground with a box on the outside mounted at driver level and a microphone. He wondered idly whether these had been installed before or since the robbery. Amos pressed the button without knowing what he intended to say.

'I'm Councillor Cotswold and I've come to see Mr or Mrs Jeremiah . . . er . . . about the stolen drawing.' There was little point in mincing his words and finding himself refused entry or sent to see the housekeeper or the butler; he must strike hard and high. With any luck they might think he'd said Commander or Commissioner or even Constable and assume he was police. Whatever they thought, the gates began to swing open. He drove the Land Rover through and heard them clang shut behind him. He was in.

What he didn't know was just when the police would contact the Jeremiahs to inform them that either their lost drawing was a copy, or it had very implausibly turned up on some long-dead corpse. That's why he'd come straight away, the same afternoon. For his purposes it would be much more useful if the Jeremiahs were to remain unaware of that, at least initially; once they knew they might clam up, people disliked being thought fools.

His mind resumed its gymnastics routine, the warm-up session — so many questions he could ask, so many possibilities of giving offence and failing to get the information he wanted. For instance he could hardly ask their nationality outright but the name was a good indicator. Had they been relatives of the dead man, Schumann? How old were they? What was their story going to be, would they attempt to hide how they'd come by the picture? Sifting fast he reined in the Land Rover just short of the front door and alighted.

From around the far corner of the house came a scuffle and a scream. A small boy emerged — obviously terrified, tripping over his own feet as he tried to escape, hotly pursued by a magnificent cockerel in bright plumage, its outstretched wings dwarfing the child, its blood coloured coxcomb erect. Smelling fear, its cruel curved beak stood open, ready, and its predatory claws danced in anticipation.

Amos hollered at the cockerel. Hobbling as fast as he could towards the boy, he picked stones off the drive and hurled them at the bird to divert its attention to himself. It worked. Seeing him as a competitor for its prey, the cock abandoned the child and launched itself at Amos who waited until it was almost upon him when with one well-practised blow he felled it to the floor. Had it tried again he would have broken its neck without blinking, but it scuttled back whence it had come with its head hung low, mortified.

At the crucial point of the battle, while Amos had been focused solely on the cockerel, a lady had emerged through the front door and was now hugging the boy, pressing a handkerchief to his eyes, issuing soothing words.

'He just went for me Grandma, he's never done that before.'

'Unpredictable things, cockerels, can be very nasty. I'd give him a wide berth in future if I were you son,' Amos said, ambling over to them.

The lady disentangled herself from the child and smiled warmly at Amos. 'I'm very grateful Mr, er, Cotswold was it?' Amos nodded, thinking how fortunate the timing of his arrival had been, for the boy . . . and for him. She went on. 'I wouldn't have known what to do, I'm frightened of them myself. Do come in.'

Amos followed her into the large elegant entrance hall which rose up through two floors like an atrium, its tall windows flooding the walls with light. Walls lined with pictures.

He looked up, turning a complete circle slowly; stunned.

'You know about art, Mr Cotswold. You've come about the stolen picture, you said? Which one?'

He hadn't thought about that and he should have but no matter. 'The Dürer.'

Her face lit up. 'Have you found it?'

'No, Ma'am, I'm sorry to have raised your hopes there for a minute. No, not exactly.'

Why had he come then? How was he going to tell this lovely lady that her painting, which she obviously cherished, was not what she thought it was. She was looking at him curiously. 'You'd better come through and explain. My husband is having his nap but he'll be down presently.'

Ushering the boy towards the back of the house, she led Amos through into what Lord Gray would have called a salon — a large lounge filled with plump sofas and floor to ceiling chintz curtains. A grand piano stood in one corner, its surface covered in silver-framed photographs. Here too the walls were adorned with paintings. He perched on the edge of a delicate chair as directed. She sat facing him.

'I'm not sure where to start, Mrs Jeremiah.' He'd been about to tell her about finding the body, but what if Schumann had been an elder brother or something and she'd never known what had happened to him. He couldn't just go blurting it out. The least he could do would be to work up to it. 'Could I ask, did you by any chance have a relative in the German Luftwaffe who became a prisoner of war here?'

'What a strange question. No, well, I certainly didn't and I don't think Donald did either, in fact I'm sure he didn't.' She didn't blink or bridle or look flustered, simply puzzled. 'It would have been unlikely . . . since we're Jewish.'

Amos breathed a sigh of relief. At least he no longer had to tiptoe through that potential minefield, afraid of upsetting them. So Amos told her about finding Schumann's body and how he'd been shot trying to escape because he was half Jewish and afraid his fellow prisoners would discover his secret.

She listened patiently then asked very sweetly, 'Mr Cotswold, what has this got to do with the Dürer drawing?'

'I'm coming to that. Er, could I ask you how long you'd had it before it was stolen?'

'Not very long. As I mentioned, we lost several pictures that night, all from my husband's study. He's the art connoisseur, Mr Cotswold. I bought the Dürer for his birthday about six months before the burglary.'

181

Amos had failed to notice Donald Jeremiah enter the room but he must have overheard most of the conversation. Now he approached to sit on the arm of his wife's chair, a patrician gentleman in burgundy slippers and yellow waistcoat. He looked coolly at Amos, as if trying to sum him up. 'Do I detect a story of German art treasures someone wants back, Mr Cotswold, is that it? Can I ask where you fit in all this?'

His wife turned to him. 'Mr Cotswold saved Sammy from the cockerel, Donald, it was lucky he arrived when he did. Councillor Cotswold, my husband, Donald Jeremiah.' She introduced them formally. Donald remained impassive.

Amos swallowed. 'A well-preserved Dürer drawing was found on the body of a man called Franz Schumann. The police had it authenticated by the Renaissance art expert at the National Gallery this morning.' Donald nodded, as if to say yes, that's who he would have used. 'He pronounced it as the original.'

'But that's impossible! Found on a body which had been lying there sixty years . . . ?' Mrs Jeremiah stopped mid-sentence, realizing. 'Unless, of course, it had been planted there, stolen from us and left there.'

Amos shook his head. 'The police forensic people are checking that now but it's highly

182

unlikely, isn't it? I can think of better places to hide a picture.'

'What are you saying, Mr Cotswold? Why have you come here?' Jeremiah asked.

'The specialist who authenticated the drawing mentioned that the same Dürer sketch had been stolen two years ago, though he himself had never seen that one.'

'So you came to tell us we had a fake,' Mrs Jeremiah said quietly.

Donald Jeremiah put his arm around his wife. 'I'm not altogether surprised, my dear. I adored it as I know you did, particularly since you gave it to me but I did wonder . . . I mean, it was so rare and so beautiful. Too good to be true, you see?'

'But he seemed so genuine, so knowledgeable. He showed me its old insurance certificate, it had been insured for four million.' She swivelled to look up at her husband. 'I didn't pay nearly that much, of course. He explained how you have to insure these treasures for considerably more than their retail value or the insurers won't pay out. So he charged me a lot less — quite a bargain I thought. He can't have known.'

'Where did you buy it, Mrs Jeremiah?'

'From a very reputable gallery in London. Henry . . . somebody. I can't remember his surname.'

'Fishbroke?' Amos offered, holding his breath.

'Oh, no, I'd have remembered that.' She got up. 'There's a picture of him somewhere, it was in a magazine a few weeks ago. You'll remember Donald, I pointed him out to you, he'd opened a new gallery.'

She went over to a large antique desk in the corner, flicked through a magazine lying on the top and returned to show it to Amos. 'That's funny, you're right Mr Cotswold, but I could have sworn . . . There you are, that's him.'

20

Smiling out from the photograph, framed in the doorway of his renovated gallery in Weston Hathaway, was Henry Fishbroke. But surely that meant he was innocent — those wishing to remain incognito didn't pose for pictures in magazines, did they? And it wasn't a crime to change your name — if that's indeed what he'd done. It could pay off in business, open up new markets. Authors wrote under pseudonyms if they wanted to write different books, reach a separate readership — it caused less confusion, avoided false expectations. So why not art dealers?

It was no good, who was he trying to fool? Henry had at the very least been underhand in not admitting he knew the drawing and had sold the original to Mrs Jeremiah — if that's what he'd believed it to be — and it had subsequently been stolen. He had duped her, but had he done it purposely?

Hell, the Gainsborough! What was that about? The pit of his stomach felt cold and sick. It was he who had introduced Alec Fitzsimmons to Henry Fishbroke. He who, knowing nothing of art, had been brought in to keep Alec company — make it look as though Alec was being offered a special privilege, make Alec feel safe because this wasn't a stranger offering him a dubious opportunity; Alec could trust Henry, he was a friend of Amos's.

Instead of his favourite old road up through Woodstock and Long Compton, Amos took the motorway back from Oxford. He had to see Alec, he couldn't tell him this on the phone.

Alec slid down from his hunter, handing his reins to the groom as Amos swung round in front of the stables. 'Saw you coming up the main road so I cut across country,' he said, catching his breath. Registering Amos's expression he added, 'What's up, you look dreadful?'

'You haven't put the money up for that Gainsborough Henry Fishbroke offered you have you?'

'Well . . . I . . . What's this about Amos?'

'It's complicated — truth is I'm not sure what's real and what's not.' Literally, thought Amos to himself. 'Can you stop the cheque? What about the others?'

Alec patted Amos on the back. 'Don't worry, we haven't paid anything yet — we're due to go over this evening. But we have committed verbally — I don't like going back on my word. What's happened?'

Leaving the groom's stool for his friend, Amos sank down on an upturned bucket outside the tack room and recounted to Alec the developments in the story of the Dürer; beginning with Karl Weiner and the specialist from the National Gallery, and finishing with his trip to Winchester and the photograph Mrs Jeremiah had produced.

'So, what do you make of it, Amos?' Not a man who flustered easily, Alec had remained calm and thoughtful throughout the tale. 'He's done so well — his is just the sort of business Weston Hathaway needs.'

'Not if it's crooked it's not.'

'Do you really think . . . ?'

'I don't know what to think, Alec, but I don't want to be responsible for you losing your money — or worse, your reputation. Bengy and your cousin's husband have said yes I presume, sight unseen?'

'Yes.'

Amos groaned. 'It's not safe, Alec. I never dreamt it wasn't but knowing what we know now . . . Yes it may be a good money-spinner but the risk has suddenly shot up. I feel dreadful about this, it was me who got you into it.'

'Don't worry, Amos, I agree it's too risky. I

can't afford to lose that sort of money. I'll just tell him we've changed our minds.' Alec gave a wry smile. 'I don't mind doing that now you've told me what he's been up to. Whatever it was it was less than straight, wasn't it.'

'It makes me wonder if there really was a stack of pictures brought out of Europe, and it's that which enticed Henry here in the first place?' Amos said, thoughtfully. 'Now we know he can be devious . . . I'd like to find out, you know.'

'What are you saying?'

'Just that if I'm to regain confidence in Henry — or if not in him then anyone else who sets up business in the Weston area, because right now my track record isn't looking so good — then I need to really understand what's going on and I'm blessed if I do at the moment.'

'Go on.'

'Well, I'm not sure how to go about it but if we let on we think Henry isn't being straight with us we may never discover the truth.'

'Oh, yes, I see what you mean.'

'Can you turn him down without making it look as though you suspect him?'

Alec laughed. 'Oh easily, it's almost the truth anyway. I'll tell him some more slates came off the roof in that gale last night so I'm afraid I can't afford to invest in the Gainsborough, and the others won't if I don't. I'll just say I'm so disappointed, I know we're missing a really good opportunity, thank him profusely for allowing us first refusal, say how much I appreciate it and how grateful I'd be if he'd consider us next time. That should do it.'

'Yes! After he's led us to believe anyone in their right mind would jump at the chance, that there are heaps of punters out there dying to take part — he can hardly afford to sound as if he cares that much. He offered it to you first out of friendship for me. He was doing us a favour.'

Amos felt better already. The burden of thinking he might have led Alec into a possibly fraudulent scheme had been lifted, immediate disaster averted — as far as he knew. The trouble was there were many others who knew he supported Henry Fishbroke and his enterprise, who would therefore consider it safe to deal with Henry. If Amos supported it ergo it must be all right. He had to find out what Henry was up to before anyone else suffered or Amos's reputation, his judgement, would be for ever forfeited.

'Talking of art hauls and wartime,' Alec said. 'I was thinking the other day about those

Spitfire noises of yours. And what you said about re-mobilization.' He laughed. 'It reminded me. You do know the special underground forces used something of the sort as an alarm system don't you, for when somebody ventured too near their bunker?'

'Really? No, I didn't know. Can't see it helps us much though, unless you reckon some old system is being triggered by vehicles driving along that road, in which case why does it only sound at night, why not the rest of the time?'

'Mmm, see what you mean.' Alec shrugged. 'Just thought I'd mention it.' He grinned. 'Prefer the ghostly reincarnation theory myself.'

★ ★ ★

Lost for how to tackle Henry, Amos decided to concentrate on the stash of pictures. If he found out more about that, he felt sure he'd find out more about Henry. First thing the next morning he'd go back out to where the Dürer had been found, have a look round, see if he could figure out where this mysterious cache might be hidden . . . if indeed there was one.

In case there was any substance to Alec's suggestion, Amos decided to try and recreate exactly his journey of the night when he'd found the body — only this time in daylight. He'd even take Napoleon, drive up the other way to the army camp, so as to set off from where he'd left the Land Rover that night, and drive back along the perimeter road in the same direction he had before.

Arriving at the place where the corner of the airfield joins the No Man's Land, the area of copse and rough scrubland between the airfield and the army camp, he pulled over. Even at eight in the morning it felt ominous out here. He let Napoleon out though neither of them knew what to do next. Amos wandered idly along the roadside peering into the ditch, detecting nothing. No sign of recent activity, no squashed bracken, exposed soil or strangely arranged vegetation suggested any disturbance, except where he himself had fallen and myriad police vehicles had parked on the verge inconveniently obliterating any previous clues. He retraced his steps between there and the area of scrubland, staring at the ditch, which he doubted the police had ever searched.

Napoleon had been keeping close behind him, but as they approached the scrubland he left Amos and ventured cautiously into the scrub. Amos followed, expecting to be confronted by a barbed wire fence or similar obstruction set inside the undergrowth.

Instead, hidden from the road, the path which Napoleon took exploited a hole in the corner, where the lack of a support post over the stream had left a gap after the county council had demolished the outer defence between the airfield and the road. Was this the way Napoleon had come that night? It certainly appeared to have been trodden before and in various directions, probably by Napoleon in his panic.

Ahead to the right Amos caught a glimpse of bricks, the corner of a building. It must be the shed he'd seen Stanton in, only he'd approached from the other side before, from the army camp where the original path had been laid. Presumably the building had belonged to the army complex, not to the air force, although it had been positioned well away from the main buildings. It sported a matching brick canopy and porch on this side too, a back door.

Napoleon stopped dead, yards from the building, shaking. Amos bent to pat him. 'What's the matter old boy? Is this where you came that night? No nasty noises today, eh? Come on.' The pig refused to move.

Amos had to walk around him and then resume his place on the path which from here to the shed was remarkably clear of vegetation, devoid even of dead leaves

— almost swept. He turned the handle in the porch and pulled. The rusting metal door scraped across the concrete floor revealing a small ante-room, four feet by six, completely enclosed by metal and frosted glass partitioning up to the ceiling, with another metal door opposite. He tried it. Locked. It looked remarkably clean for something so abandoned, no spiders or piles of leaf litter, no discarded rubbish or mud. And it had that smell, the one he'd smelled the day he'd come to see Stanton; he still couldn't identify it.

Amos shut the outer door and stood with his back to it. To his left the undergrowth had encroached on the building, ivy and brambles clambered in profusion over the roof, but he was able to navigate around the end of the building to his right, detouring past the thicker trunks and stamping down the more obstinate barriers until he reached the front entrance. He tried the door, hammered on it. No one answered.

By standing on the gnarled trunk of a tree Amos could just see in through the window next to the door. Hanging on to a branch to keep his balance, he craned his neck to gain more from his vantage point. If the pictures were stored around here they could be anywhere, but surely they'd need to be under cover, perhaps in a store room? Yet from what he remembered from his previous visit the shed looked to be one big open space.

The machines in his line of vision looked as tidy as before, in military rows, silent and obedient, waiting; every conceivable piece of precision engineering equipment — oiled and ready. Amos flashed back to Alec's remark about alarms and thought that if Stanton hadn't got one he ought to seriously consider it, this stuff must be worth a mint even if much of it was obsolete for today's purposes. No sign of him yet this morning, must be a night owl.

Amos had the uncomfortable sensation he was being watched, of eyes boring into the back of his head. It was this abandoned place, secluded, shut up; no wonder he was imagining things, even in broad daylight — must be getting like Napoleon, too sensitive by half. He struggled down from the tree trunk and, as he raised his head, glimpsed a figure surveying him from the path to the army camp, advancing towards him, festooned with greenery and forest camouflage.

A soldier on manoeuvres, a ghost, a trick of the light? The sun sat very low, flickering through the trees with uncertainty, twisting the shapes, catching the angles, reflecting off the dew. Amos decided to stand where he was, fully expecting the apparition to melt back into the copse whence it had come, another disturbed shadow retreating into its cocoon. But the figure continued to advance.

'Wondered who was snooping around, thought I'd best investigate,' George Churchman boomed from a distance of fifty yards and closing fast in his ridiculous disguise.

'I might say the same of you,' retaliated Amos, openly looking Churchman up and down.

'This is a site of special interest, Councillor, designated as such.'

So it seems, thought Amos, I only wish I knew what that interest was. 'Oh?' he said.

'The wildlife. This area has been left as wilderness for fifty years so the wildlife has adopted it as its sanctuary. Now it's been officially protected, it's not supposed to be disturbed.'

That would make sense. That would account for Churchman's skulking habit, his paranoia about immigrants who might trap and stew his linnets like the French did their little songbirds; his camouflage gear a makeshift hide from which to study the fauna, except . . .

Napoleon chose that moment to come crashing through the dead leaves. Pheasants shot up in the air, black birds changed perches squawking their warnings, a veritable bull had upset their china shop, but Churchman said not a word. He failed to even look surprised, presumably having heard about the pig. Most of all, Amos noticed his lack of anger. Other bird watchers he knew would have been furious that their whole day's viewing had been frightened away.

Churchman was too much of a caricature and a bad one at that. Too inept for a spy, too uninterested for an ornithologist, overcostumed for his role unless he imagined himself as part of the Home Guard. What was he doing here? What was he hiding beneath his gross over acting? Was it all a clever ruse to fool people into believing he was the buffoon he portrayed and thus fail to spot his real purpose? If so he'd almost succeeded with Amos who was fast failing to take the man seriously.

'I was looking for Eric Stanton,' Amos explained, not that he needed to.

'Too early for him, he comes about eleven.'

How did Churchman know that? Did he keep tabs on everyone? Whatever the answer this wasn't getting Amos any closer to the hidden paintings, if there were any. The trail was cold. He'd spent a useless morning.

★ ★ ★

'Smells better in here, I must say,' Amos said, tucking his feet under Jack's bar.

'It's the hops.' Jack indicated the vines strung across the beam. 'They give off a special aroma which makes you fancy a drink.'

Amos recounted his visit to the brick shed in the No Man's Land that morning, the overgrown approach from the back, and the smell inside.

Jack roared with laughter. 'That's rich, that is, coming from you two. I'm surprised either you or Napoleon can smell anything beyond your own pong!'

Amos ignored him. 'Napoleon wouldn't go anywhere near the place, just stopped in his tracks, refused to budge.'

'Sounds like that Labrador when they were filming the *Dam Busters* — wouldn't walk across a particular piece near the landing strip, always made a wide detour. Whatever method they tried to coax him failed, he simply refused to walk there.' Jack lowered his voice, affected by the emotion of his tale. 'And do you know why?'

Amos shook his head.

'Well, the reason the Labrador was there was to play the part of Guy Gibson's dog

— Squadron Leader Gibson had owned this hound who always waited there for his master to return from his missions . . . so when the dog died he was buried in that spot.' Jack swallowed. 'This Labrador couldn't possibly have known that, after all this was what — twenty years later? Some long time anyway. But he still wouldn't walk over the other dog's grave.'

21

'I don't think it was a particular spot with Napoleon, I had the feeling it was the building he disliked. He'd walk parallel to it — followed me from that distance when I circumnavigated it — but wouldn't get any closer.'

'Couldn't help overhearing, like, Mr Cotswold.' It was Sid, one of Jack's elderly clientele who had been sitting by the fire with his cronies. 'But it were probably the smell you mentioned that upset you pig.' He pointed in Napoleon's direction with his empty beer mug, as he made his way to the bar.

'You can laugh, Mr Ashley, but pigs is very sensitive to smells, they relies on their nose for their food.'

Marion came bustling into the bar, flustered. 'What took you so long?' Jack asked.

'I took young Susan, Lindsay's girl, to sign on while she looks for work. Anyway, I went in with her and you know how long they can take.' She shuddered. 'I hate that place. I amazed some old girl when I said it smelled like Queen Alexandra's and she said how did I know because it hadn't been used as a hospital since the early 1950s and we weren't around here then! It must be the ether they used . . . gets in the fabric of the place.'

Amos stopped with his beer mug halfway to his mouth. 'That's it, Marion, you've got it! It smells like a hospital!'

'The Work and Pensions place, yes, I know it does. I just said that,' Marion treated him to one of her poor-imbecile looks.

'No, no, I mean that big old brick shed in the scrubland between the airfield and the army camp. You probably didn't know it was there, you can't see it from the road. It's where Stanton has set up his machine shop for mending rolling stock.'

'I'm not surprised it smells,' said Sid turning away from the bar with his refill. 'It were the isolation hospital for the army camp during the war.'

Sid returned to his fire and Marion hurried away. Amos supped some more beer. 'Which reminds me, I bumped into Churchman again over there. Dressed in camouflage, even down to the leaves and twigs sprouting out of his hat.'

Jack nearly choked. 'You're kidding.'

'I wish I were. He gets more strange by the day and I have the oddest feeling he wants us

200

to think he's nuts so we won't notice what he's doing, won't take him seriously. Why else would he go to those bizarre lengths ... unless of course he really is round the bend? What the heck is the man doing over at the army camp all the time?'

Jack must have considered the question in between changing the gin optic and serving another customer because when he returned he suddenly said, 'The disappearances — those immigrant workers who've melted into the countryside.'

'What about them? Churchman hates the immigrants, it was him who told us about the drivers who never turned up. I was convinced at first that he was one of these right-wing extremists, you know, the ones who'll do anything to get rid of foreigners. I still think he could be and what he's doing is preparing for a raid — where he'll get his pals over here to annihilate the people in the camp. He's mapping the territory, finding out who everyone is, watching when they come and go. It fits.' Amos was becoming more certain.

'Unless, as you said a minute ago, it's all a bluff.'

'What?'

Jack explained. 'Well, what if the reverse is true about everything he seems to be or does. Like how come he seems to be a man of leisure? So maybe he's working. Like him loathing the immigrants, when maybe he's the one planning their escape, helping them?'

It was Amos's turn to think. 'For money, you mean? They're paying him to move them on from here.' He chuckled. 'If you're right it's no wonder friend Karloff isn't very keen on him. Do you think he suspects?' Amos remembered the night he'd lain in wait for the phantom speeder which had turned out to be a motorbike . . . followed by Karloff . . . followed, later and much more slowly, by Churchman. 'It's a possibility.'

Jack beamed, praise from Amos was rare, to be savoured while it lasted. Encouraged he said, 'It's not all I'm right about either.' From under the bar he produced a framed colour photograph of an Aquitaine bull entitled 'Burlington Brewster' in gold lettering. 'I've bought a share in it, in this prize bull.'

'I hate to tell you this, Jack, but it doesn't look much of a prize bull to me. It's hindquarters aren't what they should be and I'm not sure of his head either. Nice bull . . . but a prize Aquitaine?' He sucked in his breath and shook his head sceptically.

Jack snatched back the photograph and looked at it again. 'Well, that's where you're wrong, Amos Cotswold. He's won 'Best in class' at several of the major shows, chap showed me the certificates.'

'What are you going to do when it scarpers or gets drowned in the river then? You can't keep him in all the time.'

Jack smiled knowingly. 'He's well insured don't you worry.'

Amos shrugged. 'I've never known you take an interest in champion livestock before, what's brought this on?'

'Oh, chap I know, comes in here about once a month in the summer. We got chatting.' Jack straightened himself and adjusted the bar towel on the counter in front of him. 'So when this opportunity came up he gave me a chance to join in. Told me to keep it to myself otherwise he'd be snowed under with people wanting a slice of the action.'

So that was why Amos hadn't been consulted.

★   ★   ★

Amos heard Linklater's perfunctory tap as he walked in to the cottage. The sun wasn't even up yet but he'd have known Amos would be awake — done his rounds by now, like as not.

'Trust you to smell the tea,' Amos growled, fetching another mug.

'We went to see your friend Karl Weiner.'

'I rather thought you might,' Amos

glowered at Linklater. 'Poor old boy, he's clearly petrified of the police, I told you that.'

'Mmm,' Linklater said helping himself to a biscuit from the tin which stood open on the table. 'You were right — about the models I mean. That's what he makes; got quite a set-up at the back of his place.'

'Did you ask him where he tests them?'

'Yes, wouldn't say a word.' Linklater sank into a chair. 'In fact he wouldn't say a word about anything.'

'What did I tell you?'

Linklater looked at Amos. 'We got on to the Nuremberg authorities about the Schumanns . . . and their paintings. They couldn't turn up any Schumanns who met that description. Said the only Schumanns they could trace were butchers, railway engineers and hospital workers. No one with big houses and priceless art.'

'Maybe they kept it quiet, especially if it raised questions about their race — which it might. Weiner could give you their address before the war. That would help surely?' Linklater continued to study Amos unnervingly. 'What's the matter, Stephen?'

'You don't know, do you.' It was a statement from Linklater not a question. Amos was stumped. 'As well as putting that piece in the paper we've also been asking around, talking to ex-POW's who returned here in the fifties, and to civilians who worked at the camp during the war.' He smiled. 'We do do our job when people let us get on with it, you know.'

'Well?' Amos could see Linklater was enjoying drawing this out.

'They say the dead man can't be Franz Schumann.' Linklater left it hanging there — without support or explanation.

Amos sat down, puzzled. What did that mean? Did it change much . . . except put them back where they'd started? If he wasn't Schumann, how come he had Schumann's Dürer? But Nuremberg denied knowledge of any Schumanns who'd had valuable paintings . . . and Weiner had said the Dürer had been in Schumann's family for centuries. The National Gallery man had been equally discouraging, admitting the records had been in a mess since the war.

'Before you ask, yes, we're fairly sure these other people are right, they volunteered the information. More than one of them said the man we'd found couldn't be Franz Schumann because they'd seen him since . . . over the years. Although they hadn't actually spoken to him.'

'Seen him! Where?'

'Locally from what I can gather, though

not necessarily recently.'

'Did they say who they think the dead man is then?'

'Not a clue, lots of people went missing around the end of the war.' He gave Amos a warning look. 'And yes, of course we're trying to get an identikit picture of Franz Schumann put together. Whoever he is, he should have the answers we need. Let's just hope he's not dead by now as well.'

'But you found Schumann's papers on the skeleton.' Amos remembered what else the police had been looking into. 'And had he been moved?'

'Forensics don't think so. Apparently all the pollen matches the camp and where he was found. We could probably pinpoint which hut he'd lived in if we had time. Oh, and there's something else which might help with identification. Do you remember me mentioning that forensics said he hadn't been in good shape? Well, they're pretty sure he'd lost a kidney before he died — surgically removed.'

What had Weiner said? 'Franz wasn't very well.' But if the body wasn't Schumann's then that wasn't relevant. Amos shook his head to clear it; pieces of the puzzle rattled around the space without resolution. 'Did you tell Weiner it wasn't his friend Schumann after all? What did he say?'

'Of course, that's why we went — to see if he had any other ideas.'

'And?' Amos was fast becoming exasperated.

'I told you, he wouldn't say anything. Not one word.'

Short of getting Weiner to identify the corpse, which was of course impossible because of its state, Amos didn't know what they could do. Just because several people said they'd seen Schumann since, didn't mean they were right. It could easily have been a doppelgänger or even a brother. As for the Nuremberg authorities . . . he wouldn't be surprised if they were less than keen to repatriate drawings which had belonged to Jewish families, it would open the floodgates, resurrect the witch-hunts, create work. No, they might not try very hard.

'And there's something else,' Linklater said, rising to leave. 'Friend Weiner isn't registered in this country.'

'What?'

'No naturalization papers, no work permit, no National Insurance number. He doesn't exist as far as the authorities are concerned.'

'That would explain why he's afraid of you people. Did you ask him about it?'

'I may look dim, Amos, but it did occur to

me that if he is here illegally, and probably has been since the war, he might just run, even at his age. And we may need him yet, so no, I didn't mention it.'

Before Linklater could reach the door there came the sound of pounding footsteps and Jack barged into the kitchen at a gallop. 'It's gone, some blighter's stolen it.' Then he spotted Linklater. 'The prize bull, Burlington Brewster. He's been stolen from his pen during the night, down near Broadway.'

The chief inspector let out a sigh of relief. 'Not my manor, Mr Ashley. Now, if you'll excuse me . . . ' He looked meaningfully over his shoulder at Amos as he left. He would never openly have asked Amos to involve himself in police affairs but somehow Amos felt Linklater wanted him to talk to Weiner again.

'How much were you in for, Jack?'

Jack looked sheepish. 'Ten grand.'

'Ten thousand pounds? And how many shareholders are there, do you know?'

'Oh yes, all our names were on the insurance certificate. There were ten of us.'

'What? All for ten thousand?'

'Oh no, some must have paid a lot more. He was insured for £250,000.' Jack saw the expression of utter disbelief on Amos's face.

'It's the sperm, isn't it? He's worth a fortune in breeding fees.'

'Jack . . . ' Amos said as gently as he could. 'That bull was never a champion in the first place.'

'So you say, and now of course I've no way of proving how wrong you can be, Amos Cotswold.' He stood up, indignation personified. 'If I didn't know you better, I'd think you'd stolen him yourself just so I couldn't show you up! Anyway, what about the prize certificates?'

'Faked. That's not difficult, is it?'

'And the insurance document? I suppose you're going to say that was faked as well!'

'Oh no, that won't be a fake, that's real enough, that's what's so clever about it — seemingly everyone wins. Everyone except the insurance company that is. The bull had to go because you, its new owners, would want to enter it for shows to increase its value and hence the value of its sperm for breeding. But the minute you showed it you would lose value instead because any professional judge of cattle would see immediately that Burlington was no champion Aquitaine. Whoever dreamt up this little charade couldn't afford for that bull to be assessed by experts.'

Jack sat down, looking beaten. 'So, are you saying that chap I bought it off is a crook?'

'It depends whether he was the instigator or not. He may be genuine, may have been given a commission to sell shares in a prize bull and that's all he knew. If you think about it, the people behind the scheme made their money by selling shares in a bull whose price was vastly inflated. Say they paid £10,000 for him, sold £150,000 worth of shares and insured him for £250,000. They'd make a £140,000 on the original sale plus maybe another hundred on the insurance — because the investors won't know the size of one another's individual stakes and at this stage will only expect their stake money back. So, the crooks could easily afford to pay attractive commission to their salesman, no questions asked.' Amos paused for breath. 'Added to which they'll get the net proceeds from the sale of the carcass after they've paid the er, removal men.'

'You make it all sound so good. Who loses?'

'As I said, the insurers of course.' Amos shook his head. 'Oh yes, Jack, very neat is this . . . if you'll excuse the pun. The fraud is never uncovered because the bull is never judged and the shareholders get their money back.'

After Jack had left, Amos continued to sit where he was while the tea stewed in the pot and Napoleon dozed in the corner. The

Dürer, the fake Dürer, what if . . . ? Had the Jeremiahs known it was fake? Had they insured it for the price of the genuine article then had it stolen and pocketed the proceeds? What had it once been insured for, four million? But having met them he didn't believe it. Not that upright couple with the vicious cockerel and the house full of priceless art, not them. No, if anyone had deliberately over-insured the fake Dürer it had been Henry Fishbroke. Mrs Jeremiah said he'd shown her the previous insurance certificate — used it to provide a provenance of sorts, to indicate the drawing's value. In the absence of any other evidence, it seemed the amount for which a picture was insured acted as a rough guide to authenticity. Which would make some sense. Amos could guess insurance premiums were prohibitively expensive; no one was going to pay that kind of money unless they had to . . . normally.

The Gainsborough! Henry had done the same with the Gainsborough. He'd shown Alec the insurance certificate which, coincidentally proclaimed an insured value of £4 million pounds. Amos knew little about insurance, could never afford it himself, but Alec Fitzsimmons did, sat on the board of one of the major companies. Which also meant the certificate for the Gainsborough was genuine or Alec would have noticed. He made a swift phone call and leaving Napoleon to snooze headed for Moreton Hall.

Amos found Alec in the gun room. 'You did tell Henry you'd have to pull out of buying the Gainsborough, didn't you?'

'What? Oh, ah, yes,' Alec said. 'Yes, I did.'

'What did he say?'

'Well, nothing much really, which surprised me, sounded preoccupied.' Alec shrugged. 'And as you said, there's probably no shortage of willing takers who are unacquainted with the Jeremiahs.'

Amos explained the prize bull scheme to Alec. 'Ever since I realized what they'd done with that bull, I can't stop thinking that's what Henry has been doing with pictures; especially since he wrongly said the one on the body was a copy. Why would he do that?' Amos paused. 'I'll tell you what I think: it was in case the Jeremiahs heard about the drawing found on the body, and they easily might sooner or later with the publicity Stephen Linklater is giving it.'

'Oh I see, and Henry didn't want them realizing he'd sold them a dud, so he had to say the one just found was the dud . . . when in actual fact the reverse was true,' Alec scratched his head. 'Well, that's certainly a possibility.'

'No wonder he looked amazed when Linklater first showed him the real Dürer. I mean of all the bad luck! Why should it be that specific drawing which was found on a sixty-years-dead body. Of all the thousands of valuable pictures which exist why did it have to be that one? I bet he couldn't believe it. One might almost forgive him for thinking it was yet another copy.' Amos had grown short of breath in his excitement at deducing what he thought had happened. Amos couldn't be stopped now. The minute he'd turned his mind to believing ill of Henry and had stopped inventing excuses and explanations for his new acquaintance, many little instances stood out which had seemed inconsequential at the time. 'I've just remembered that scene at his gallery opening where he asked you what sort of paintings you liked.'

'Well, surely that was a natural enough question to ask in the circumstances.' Alec frowned. 'I believe I said Stubbs and . . . oh, I see what you mean . . . I also mentioned Gainsborough.' He turned to Amos. 'Are you sure about this? I mean, I just thought he was being a good businessman, researching his clients' tastes in case something juicy came up — which as regards the Gainsborough, it did.'

'I think he used a Gainsborough deliberately. Since you said you liked his work, producing one for sale not only guaranteed your interest but with any luck you would recognize it as a Gainsborough — which you did, straight away. Henry congratulated you on it. The fact that you knew it looked like a Gainsborough made you feel comfortable with its value.'

'You're forgetting one thing, Amos.' Alec looked relieved. 'Unlike animals, with art the insurers would insist a picture insured for that sort of money was kept in their vault — to ensure it couldn't be stolen and that they'd never have to pay out. Look how they vetted Henry's premises for security before they'd let him borrow the Gainsborough. He couldn't possibly have been intending to pull the same stunt as that chappie with the prize bull because if the painting had disappeared during the time it was in Henry's possession the insurers would have held him responsible.'

22

Rather than take the bypass on his way back from Alec's, Amos drove through Stratford and made a detour into the old town, looking for the sign in the garden. He drew up outside and hobbled up the path. There was no answer to his knocking.

Retracing his steps he explored the end of the row. Sure enough an access path led across the back of the terraced properties and, feeling like a trespasser, Amos counted the cottages until he arrived at Weiner's. What had once been a vegetable patch was almost entirely given over to two large cabins, smartly painted and heavily padlocked with blinds drawn down on the inside. Weiner was obviously conscious of his vulnerability, anyone could walk through here with impunity.

Amos hammered on the back door of the cottage — no reply. He wondered how long Weiner had lived here — since the war? The sound of a door opening nearby heralded the head and shoulders of the next door neighbour, an elderly woman. 'He's gone,' she said.

'Gone?'

'Yes, early. He left early this morning, I seen him go down the road.'

Amos employed his most charming smile. 'Lived here long has he?'

'It were hers, left it by her aunt she were.'

'Hers? His wife's?'

'Aye, her died, about a year ago. We hardly sees him now.'

'Any idea where he's gone?'

'No. He were carrying one of them rucksack things over his shoulder.'

Amos thanked her and left. Had Weiner really been frightened away by the police — taken to the road after all these years? Despondency set in. The only person who'd known the dead man had gone . . . no, that wasn't true either. If the dead man wasn't Schumann then he could be anyone — and Weiner may or may not have known him. Which meant Weiner had lost his peace for nothing. If Amos hadn't come across him that day, and told the police what he'd said, then they wouldn't have checked him out, wouldn't have called and he could have gone on living in his cottage. Linklater denied asking Weiner about his lack of proper registration here . . . but the man was intelligent, had probably been fearing exposure most of his adult life. He'd have guessed they'd look into his citizenship.

Weiner was old, lame and had received two shocks in as many days. First he'd read about the dead body and the finding of the Dürer and, thinking it was his old school friend, had gone out to the airfield to pay his respects ... something interrupted Amos's train of thought, something about Weiner going out there, but he couldn't grasp it, never mind ... what had he been thinking? Ah yes, that Weiner had suffered a second shock when Linklater told him the body wasn't Schumann's after all. And then of course he must have felt for his friend because if the body wasn't Schumann's then had someone else, the dead man presumably, stolen the Dürer off him? Or had he bought it?

Amos drove back slowly, thinking and keeping a careful watch for an elderly figure trudging along the road. His phone rang: 'News desk at the *Gazette*,' said the voice. 'Anything for us this week, Councillor?' It was a regular call.

'No, I don't think so.' The *Gazette*, that's what had been nagging at him. Weiner had said: 'They said it was here,' yet Linklater had promised to keep the location of the find quiet. 'While you're on, you remember the story of the body I came across and the drawing which was found on him? Have you

217

people told anyone where it was found?'

'Certainly not, Councillor.'

'You sound very sure.'

'I am. We wanted to know ourselves and Chief Inspector Linklater wouldn't tell us.' The voice sounded miffed. 'Said if we didn't know we couldn't accidentally let it slip.' The voice was lowered confidentially. 'We suspected it might be up by the old airfield because the police have been up there a few times lately, but the chief inspector said that was about some car accidents.'

'Did you tell anyone about your, er . . . suspicions?'

'No!' Again the indignation, then it softened. 'Besides, nobody has asked that I'm aware of.'

So how had Weiner known of the location? Perhaps it was obvious. He'd known where Schumann had escaped from, had helped him escape. So it had been an easy guess. Even so, Amos had found Weiner very close to the exact spot when there had been a couple of miles of perimeter road from which to choose. Amos caught his breath; had 'They said it was here', referred to some other people — the killers?

He met Lindsay coming down the path having finished her chores in his cottage. 'Thank goodness you're back. I've left him in the kitchen, looks worn out, poor soul, said he'd come specially. Napoleon's keeping him company.'

Karl Weiner started to his feet as Amos came through the door but Amos waved him back. He looked troubled, yes, but much more in command of himself than he had been before, less vacant. Good, now perhaps Amos could finally discover the truth about the dead man and those paintings. Amos took the other chair.

'The police told you, didn't they? The man whose body I found, it wasn't your friend. It's not Franz Schumann.'

Weiner's pale eyes clouded. He opened his mouth to speak then closed it again. He seemed quite calm, held his hands together on the table in front of him, their long slim fingers loosely intertwined. What was going on behind that rigid German façade? Was he translating what he wanted to say into English, was that what was taking the time? Because he obviously did want to say something otherwise why come all the way out here. Or was he figuring out just how little he need reveal?

'Why have you come?'

Still the man said nothing. Whatever turmoil was going on inside was not being transmitted to the outside. If that's how controlled he could be, it showed how enormously disturbed he must have been the day Amos had found him out on the road.

'You knew where the body was, didn't you?' Amos prompted, getting up to put the kettle on. Perhaps if he lightened the atmosphere the man might feel more encouraged to talk.

The eyes flickered. Finally he said, '*I* am Franz Schumann.'

Amos sat down abruptly. 'Then who? Why . . . ?' He wasn't sure what he wanted to know first. He had realized the man knew more about this than had at first been apparent but even then . . . thinking back, Weiner's behaviour had been very odd from the start. Amos had attributed it to his wartime experiences and his age. 'Then who was the dead man?' he asked. Was he going to shrug and say he'd no idea? Why had he changed his own name? Why complicate things by saying the dead man was him? Had Schumann committed some crime and seen this as a way of passing it on to someone else? Someone who would be difficult to identify? Had he killed the man himself? No, he couldn't have, the man had been shot from above, by an aeroplane. Amos went cold. Could this man in front of him, this model maker, the real Schumann, if indeed he was now telling the truth, could he have used one of his models to shoot his friend? For the first time Amos glanced down at the rucksack on the floor and felt uneasy. Only Amos had seen him looking for the body, now he'd volunteered his identity — what had this cold-eyed man come for? Did he intend to kill Amos too?

'Mr Cotswold, even now this is very painful for me. I never realized, never knew . . . ' The coldness went when he spoke and humanity returned, as if he had been encased in a tough shield through which no heat could pass. Only words could break through the rigidity of that constrained exterior, that carapace. Amos kept perfectly still, subconsciously empathizing through his mirrored posture. The man sighed and opened his hands in a small gesture, a shrug with hands instead of shoulders. 'We had to try and escape. We knew we might be shot, but well . . . we didn't have any choice.'

'You mean it was your turn to try — for the honour of the corps, that sort of pressure?'

He laughed, a dry racking laugh. 'Oh no, nothing like that. What I told you the other day was true. My friend was half Jewish and was being blackmailed over it — in a most horrible way. When they realized I knew he was Jewish they threatened to do the same to me for keeping quiet about it and not reporting him, which by law we were meant to do. As I said, we had no choice but to run. What's that saying of yours: 'between the devil and the deep blue sea'? Well, that's where we were.'

'We had reached the corner of the airfield when the planes saw us. They strafed the road hitting us both.' He looked down at his leg. 'But Karl was hurt much worse than me. I stayed with him until the planes had gone then he begged me to go quickly, before they sent the foot patrols to pick us up. He knew he was dying.' Schumann lifted those icy eyes to Amos. 'I left him there to die, Mr Cotswold. To my eternal shame, I left him there to die.'

'Doesn't sound as if you could have done much else,' Amos said gruffly, affected by the man's obvious grief, yet now even more curious to understand what it was Schumann 'never knew'.

'Then we heard the sirens and the aircraft scrambling and that's what gave me the chance — while the search parties were preoccupied.'

'So how come he had your papers?'

'That was Karl's idea. He had family in London. That had been our plan, to get to them and claim asylum if we could. He knew

I had no one in this country and they hadn't seen him since he was a child. We weren't dissimilar in appearance, so he thought if I pretended to be him . . . ' He trailed off. 'I was desperate, Mr Cotswold, it made sense then. There was no time to argue; Franz said: 'Go as me, as Karl Weiner. Then they'll help you.' So we swapped papers.

Amos could picture these two lads in a dark cold field, shot up, one of them dying. He said thickly, 'And did his relatives help you?'

'I never got that far. My leg was a mess, so I crawled as far as I could and hid out in some farm buildings. I don't think they're there any more. A girl found me and felt sorry for me. She used the farm's tractor to smuggle me into her aunt's house in Stratford at night and they looked after me.' He looked up sadly. 'The war was nearly over, she said there'd been enough killing.'

'And you married her and stayed here?'

'We stayed together yes, we daren't marry in case they found out I wasn't Karl Weiner. Having started with a lie, I didn't know how to get out of it. And I didn't want to be sent back to Germany, not after what they'd done to people like Karl.'

'What about the picture, the Dürer drawing?'

223

'What about it?'

'Why didn't you take that too?'

'I didn't think. I was far too scared to worry about that. Of course later, well, I never knew . . . never dreamt Franz's body would still be there, so it didn't occur to me to go back for the drawing.'

Unlike the other day, thought Amos. For the second time in their short acquaintance Amos heard himself ask: 'Were there any more paintings? Did Karl Weiner have more than one valuable — '

Amos was interrupted by a sharp knock at the front door. Silent throughout, peacefully accepting of Schumann, Napoleon now growled forcefully.

'Come in,' Amos bellowed without getting up. He looked over his shoulder to see through the sitting-room. The front door opened and Eric Stanton came as far as the edge of the carpet. His eyes on Stanton, Amos heard only the bang of Schumann's chair as it toppled when he leapt up. By the time he'd turned, Schumann was staring as if his eyes would start out of his head. He said nothing, just stared hard, transfixed. Amos looked at him, wondering if he'd been hurt by the chair but he seemed all right physically, except . . . Amos couldn't find the word to describe the look on Schumann's face

224

— horror, revulsion?

Grabbing the rucksack the German turned and fled out of the back door. Had he been frightened by Napoleon's abrupt change in temper or mistaken Stanton in his trench coat for the police?

Stanton advanced to the next floorboard, lining up his toecaps against the gap. Napoleon stood his ground, growling, until Amos moved through into the front room, shutting the door on him. For some reason the pig seemed to share Amos's view of Stanton.

'You were looking for me.' It was a statement.

'Was I?' Amos scratched his head, he didn't recollect such a thing.

'You were up at the shed. Where you came before — about the railway. You must have been looking for me. Why else would you be there?' Stanton appeared to be struggling with his temper.

'Oh yes, yesterday. So I was, there I mean.' Churchman must have told him. The creep, tip-toeing everywhere, spying on everyone and giving out carefully guaged information, weighted to bring most advantage to himself — like the things he'd volunteered about Karloff. He was obviously still trying to get in with Stanton — Amos only wished he knew why. 'I wasn't looking for you, no. But it's nice of you to call all the same. How's it going up there?' Amos assumed his most amiable attitude in an attempt to cover his actions with the appearance of idiocy, a ploy he'd witnessed over the years of his acquaintance with Bengy Pargetter. Bengy was the buffoon's buffoon — and as sharp as a billhook.

Stanton looked at him quizzically, clearly doubtful, yet presumably unwilling to reveal his own hand unnecessarily — that is if Councillor Cotswold really were as stupid as he seemed. 'Oh, er fine. Everything's fine.' He turned smartly on the spot and left.

Amos breathed a sigh of relief, as no doubt did Napoleon. What was the matter with that man? He'd seemed upset about Amos visiting the shed — what was he hiding? Did he think Amos was going to muscle in on his operation, bring in hordes of local railway enthusiasts? If the man weren't so unpleasant it would be funny. Amos sat down again. Or was Stanton concealing something much more interesting? Amos had gone up there with some half-baked idea about a hidden art cache. Was it so implausible that Stanton had found it, found the store of pictures left behind after the war? Perhaps he'd had to dig out foundations for his machines and had come across the pictures by accident, buried under the floor.

And what about Schumann? He'd left in such a hurry anyone would have thought he'd seen a ghost. Perhaps he'd simply seized his opportunity to escape — flight had become a way of life for him. Pity he hadn't had time to answer the question about the number of drawings Weiner had. Was that why he'd wanted to make a speedy exit? Had Stanton's interruption actually been convenient for him?

Amos felt guilty, he'd have given the old man a lift home. Hoping he might yet catch him, he went to the front window and peered up the lane in time to see Franz Schumann climbing awkwardly into the passenger seat of Henry Fishbroke's Jaguar.

23

Amos blinked and looked again, believing he'd imagined it. But as he watched, the old Mark II Jaguar backed round the corner by the gallery and set off up the Stratford Road, Henry driving, Schumann's silver head easily discernible beside him. So Schumann hadn't come to Weston Hathaway solely to see Amos.

Who had approached whom or were they old acquaintances? Amos tried to make logical sense of what he'd just seen. Could Henry and Schumann have business interests in common? Was Henry a closet radio-controlled model fan, was that the connection? He didn't look it.

Art had to be the link. Amos hadn't asked Schumann if the Dürer had been his or Weiner's but from the flow of the conversation they'd had he thought it must belong to the dead man — Karl Weiner. Which would also explain why the police had failed to discover a likely Dürer-owning Schumann family in Nuremberg. What had Linklater said they'd found? Butchers, railway engineers and hospital workers.

But Schumann could still have known what

else his friend Weiner had managed to smuggle into Britain, that night they'd been fortunately captured by the British. Now he thought about it, if they had indeed engineered their own detention then one of the questions he and Linklater had posed was answered — how come a prisoner of war could bring in such valuables without them being found and confiscated? If they'd planned to be held they could also have planned to surrender themselves near to a POW camp, and have allowed time for hiding the pictures. Was that why they'd been discovered the night they'd tried to escape — because Weiner had stopped to retrieve a drawing with which to pay their way?

It still didn't explain why Schumann had never returned to the site. Maybe he had and had lied about it. Maybe he only knew roughly where Weiner had hidden the rest of the haul or couldn't find it, things might have changed.

Then Amos realized something and, suddenly unsteady, sat down. The conversation he'd had with Henry flooded back into his mind. 'How would you sell priceless art, Henry?'

'Well, you'd have to find a crooked art dealer, I suppose.' How nonchalant he'd been, appearing to pay the question little attention, when all the time . . .

That was it, it had to be. Schumann may well have had a fair idea where the rest of those pictures were stashed but either he'd never plucked up the courage to return to the scene or he knew he couldn't realize their value anyway. That's why he needed Henry.

But why now, after all these years? Presumably he'd been telling the truth about never dreaming Weiner's body would still be where he'd left him, which explained why he'd never tried to recover the Dürer. But it didn't account for his not unearthing the rest before now — if indeed there were any — unless, as with the body, he'd not unnaturally assumed the authorities had found the stash and removed it. Amos supposed it was the finding of the Dürer which had worried Schumann — made him anxious that someone else would find the remaining paintings if he didn't recover them.

And of course his 'wife' had died. Amos understood now. Schumann's wife, his saviour, his partner all those years, the woman who'd shared his pain, risked her own liberty, nursed him back to health . . . either he'd never told her about the pictures or, more likely, she'd forbidden him ever to touch them, probably fearing he'd be caught and imprisoned again . . . or deported. That would be it, he felt certain. But with her gone and the Dürer splashed across the *Gazette* . . . the temptation had proved irresistible.

How had he met Henry? Had he looked him up in the *Yellow Pages* or visited the gallery? However they'd met, knowing what he now did about Henry, Amos considered Schumann may well have selected wisely.

Oblivious to the dusk which was falling fast, Amos continued to sit where he was without turning on the lights or drawing the curtains. He knew he ought to ring Linklater and explain that Schumann was Weiner and vice versa, but it could wait; what difference did it make? Should he tell him what he thought about the pictures and that Henry Fishbroke might be involved in handling stolen property? Whose property was it anyway? What if the Weiner family had since died out?

He wasn't aware he'd been waiting for Henry's return but was pleased he'd remained well placed to observe it. This time without a passenger, the Jaguar made its stately way back down the Stratford Road. But instead of turning straight into the lane leading to his garage, as he usually did, Henry parked the car in the street outside the gallery.

Where had they been? Finally Amos remembered the rucksack. Whatever it contained had been bulky without being heavy. A new model perhaps? A new transmitter? Equipment for changing the function, tools? What for? So it was Schumann, and now Henry, who wished to deter folks from using the perimeter road after all. Not because they cared about any army camp development but because they needed to keep people away from the paintings.

He thought it an idea which could easily backfire — conversely draw attention to the place — but then he remembered Jack's tale about the cemetery and the coach and four and how even Jack hadn't dared use that road ever again after dark. The strategy had been proven to be effective. That is if you were oblivious to the number of innocent people you killed in car accidents before the message became sufficiently well broadcast.

Uneasy in his mind, Amos set about his chores. What if Henry and Schumann had rigged up a more effective Spitfire strafing or other lethal deterrent and someone drove along that road later on? What could he do? Linklater would probably laugh at him — just how dangerous could an eighty-year-old model maker and a flamboyant, if suspect, art historian be?

Amos couldn't concentrate while his mind ploughed up and down the same furrow, repeatedly turning over what could happen out on that road. He gave the cattle two loads of hay instead of one, fed the sheep the wrong nuts and would have forgotten to close the gate on Horace if the bull hadn't decided to make his bid for freedom that fraction too early, allowing Amos to rectify his mistake before disaster struck.

That's what he must do about the Spitfire model or whatever trap those two had set. He must close the gate on it, prevent it happening. He turned slowly towards the Land Rover, and was holding the door open for Napoleon when the silence of the early evening was blasted with a raucous two-tone hooter as Karloff raced past in his truck, horns blaring. Where was he going in such a tearing hurry anyway? He must have been doing over a 100 mph — burning up the tarmac between Lower Farthing and Weston in his haste. Had his immigrants staged a break-out?

Amos drove slowly back towards the village, still cogitating. Why had Henry mentioned the immigrants when he'd first heard about the Dürer? He now realized the two events may not have been simultaneous. And why had Schumann seemed so scared at the mention of Romanians? It wasn't as if these people here now could possibly have any connection with what Schumann and Weiner had been forced to do during the war.

He coasted past the gallery and drifted to a halt beside Henry who was examining the offside wing mirror of his car with great concern. 'Maniac, I saw him! Came past here like a bat out of hell. I'm sure he's clouted my Jag.'

Amos assumed Henry was referring to Karloff. 'Yes, he's just done the same to me up towards Lower Farthing — he's probably afraid some of his internees might be escaping again. Can't think why else he'd be tearing along like that . . . not at this hour.' Though Amos did recall the gang master travelling at that speed once before, in the early hours of the morning, trailing in the wake of an even faster motorcycle.

He couldn't help himself, something had to give and he was going to help it do so. Besides, he knew no other way of stopping those road accidents, linked as they must be to the hidden cache.

'Maybe this is the night they plan to dig up that art haul and disappear into the English countryside so no one will ever be any the wiser.' Although it was dark Amos could have sworn he saw a shadow cross Henry's face: concern, curiosity? He was unsure which. Then Henry asked a strange question.

'Oh? Where do you reckon it is then?'

It was Amos's turn to let shadows cross his face, until he realized Henry was only trying to make sure he and Schumann had positioned the Spitfire machine in the best place. If, for instance, Amos were to say, 'Just inside the army camp gates, the haul is meant to be underneath one of the old bunkhouses,' then presumably Henry would rest easy.

But because Amos now felt convinced the pictures must be in the No Man's Land between the airfield and the army camp, near where he and the other unfortunates had heard the Spitfire strafing, close to where he'd discovered Weiner's body, and where Schumann had been wandering in the road — then he knew what he must say.

'I reckon it's somewhere in that No Man's Land between the airfield and the army camp. There's a big brick shed there which Eric Stanton . . . ' He'd suddenly remembered Schumann's reaction to him. What had that been about?

'Brick shed?' Henry prompted.

'Oh yes, the brick shed, well, it's in that piece of scrubland . . . and if you think about it, the POW's were in the army camp and it's right on the edge of there, tucked out of sight. I know the immigrants are on the airfield these days but you can access it just as easily from that end too, via the road. Did it myself the other day.'

Amos had said enough, too much maybe but he wanted Henry to take the bait. The haul must be roughly in that area because that's where he and Schumann had positioned the Spitfire machine before — and if Henry thought the immigrants were going to steal the pictures tonight then he would want to prevent them.

Amos made his excuses for not going for a drink, bade Henry goodnight and pulled the Land Rover up outside his cottage.

He didn't have to wait too long. At 11.30, presumably after conferring with Schumann by telephone, Henry went out in his car, heading west along the road to Lower Farthing.

Amos was able to follow at a distance because he knew where Henry was going. But in case he had misread the situation, not wanting to lose sight of Henry entirely he left immediately, driving without lights — the road was very familiar and the moon half full. He could switch them on if anything came the other way. Nothing did.

Not until he was through Lower Farthing and approaching the first part of the airfield did he sense he had company. It wasn't the smell, his Land Rover always smelled so ripe he didn't notice. He could have sworn something moved in the back. Keeping one eye on Henry way in front of him he slowed and felt around behind him with his free hand to be rewarded with a grunt and a rough lick — Napoleon. In all the excitement he'd forgotten the old boy, assumed he'd gone walkabout around the village for supper as he often did; whereas he obviously hadn't budged from the car since they'd returned from feeding the livestock. Damn, Napoleon was the last thing he needed on this trip.

It was too late to turn back now. If Henry wasn't going where he thought then Amos certainly wanted to know where he was off to at this time of night. And if he was going to the shed, then Amos wanted to witness what happened. If he took Napoleon back now he'd miss everything and he wouldn't get another chance.

Admittedly he was curious but the pressing need was to stop these two and their killing machine. That's what came of obsession. He'd like to bet Henry wasn't normally a violent man but faced with the opportunity of laying his hands on millions of pound's worth of artwork, he must have lost touch with morality. He couldn't speak for Schumann — he'd had his own living hell by the sound of it.

Amos had no alternative. He hoped Napoleon would go back to sleep but he'd have to leave the door open otherwise the pig would make a fearful row if he wanted to get out. And if Amos were discovered because of him, then he'd just have to use Napoleon as the excuse — say he'd been driving by and Napoleon got caught short.

Henry must be close to the scrubland by now, as he'd slowed down. The lights ahead went out. Amos stopped so Henry wouldn't hear him once he'd turned off his own engine. Amos held his breath, he could just discern the large figure in front making his way across the road with the aid of a torch and walking along by the ditch towards the gap in the fence over the stream. Henry moved slowly, looking over his shoulder every now and again. Could he sense he was being watched or was it that he expected the immigrants to be headed in the same direction — as Amos had suggested they would be?

Amos got out of the car and followed Henry, wanting to keep him in sight. He'd already assumed the cache must be around this area. Find the cache and he'd find the Spitfire strafing machine. Or rather it would find him, or Henry, the moment they got too close. But this time he wouldn't fear the bullets, he knew they weren't real.

It was Alec who'd said the Spitfire noise had been used before. Not in models but as alarms to protect the special operations bunkers, the hideouts of the underground movement Amos would have to be part of if there ever were an invasion. The organization set up when Hitler's hordes had been expected any day.

An unwelcome thought stabbed him. Is that how Churchman had interpreted what he'd seen at the army camp . . . as an invasion? So could it be he who had resurrected the Spitfire alarms; desperate hours requiring desperate remedies? Amos dismissed the possibility as being ridiculous, even for Churchman.

He approached the gap in the fence very quietly. Henry would be alert to someone else possibly being around, and he didn't want to interrupt him at this juncture. He could just make him out ahead, keeping in the shadows, skirting the path. Predictably however, Napoleon chose that moment to come crashing through the undergrowth. Having almost reached the back entrance to the shed, Henry turned, stepped into the path and triggered the sound of the Merlin engines followed by the firing — which came as a shock even though Amos had

239

been expecting it.

'Desperate remedies . . . ' At that instant he remembered how the special operations people had solved the problem of their interlopers — not just with alarms.

Henry stood with his back to the building, tall, silhouetted, as Amos, who had no chance of reaching him, threw himself to one side yelling at Napoleon. 'Get Henry, knock him down!'

24

Amos held his breath. Only the day before, Napoleon had refused point blank to approach the building. How could Amos hope the animal would obey and deliberately advance towards the cacophany emitting from it now? But tonight, his master's cries resounding in his ears, Napoleon charged at the man full tilt — a hundredweight of adult black boar with its prey in sight. Henry went down.

Had Napoleon been too late? The Spitfires swooped and circled, the relentless aerial bombardment ricocheting through the trees, the sound of their bullets dancing through the leaf mould throwing up dusty pellets in their wake, deceiving his eyes. Amos lay transfixed. He dare not look, refused to acknowledge that he'd lured a man to his death. Then as if in slow motion, the soundtrack out of kilter with the action, he heard the bullet imbed itself in the tree beside him.

The night fog drifted like gun smoke across his vision. From somewhere further off, behind Henry's body, he thought he heard something, sensed another presence, but could see no one. Napoleon ran back to him for reassurance, or to make sure he was all right, then on, out of the wood — like Amos so wanted to do. Amos shook his head, still he dared not move.

He'd lost his string. He felt around, his jacket flapping open, letting in the cold. That's why he was shivering, he must find the string, do his jacket up properly, keep himself together. He'd got some more string in his pocket which might be long enough but that wouldn't do. Even though it was a very similar piece of string it still wouldn't do. He must find the piece he'd lost, his lucky piece. He cast around feebly in the undergrowth . . . anything so as not to think.

The Spitfire noise stopped abruptly. The silence felt eerie, as though it had all been a bad dream from which he'd woken too soon and been left on the wrong side of the door, in limbo, neither in one world nor the other — no man's land.

Henry rose slowly to his feet. Had they both been shot and landed in this other world? Had they been trying to escape? Who were they? Or was he simply seeing what he desperately wanted to see. Amos shook his head to try and clear the fog as Napoleon came trotting back through the trees, emboldened now the noise had stopped.

Glancing just once in their direction, Henry took off, running through the scrub towards the army camp and the railway — running away.

Thank God. That's all he could think for a minute, thank God Henry had survived. And thank God Napoleon had stowed away in the Land Rover when by rights he should have been left at home. He must have winded Henry, keeping him down for those few crucial seconds. Henry may be a crook, but Amos hadn't wanted to be responsible for the man's death. He struggled on to his knees, grasping the nearest sapling with which to haul himself upright, thinking.

Henry hadn't moved when the Spitfire noise started so, like Amos, he must have been expecting it. Amos couldn't separate his thoughts; parts of sentences whirred around inside his head, the shrapnel of logic smashed into pieces. If Henry and Schumann had set up the trap then they'd deliberately set out to kill — not just warn. Was that the lethal addition Schumann had had in his bag? Could Henry be that evil? Was beauty worth that much? That ethereal image of Dürer as Christ, the King of Peace, flashed ironically in front of him.

Amos trod through the brambles to the willow which had taken the bullet, running his hands over the gnarled surface, realizing it was hopeless to look for it in the dark, but knowing it would be there.

Until Napoleon had disturbed things, Henry had kept carefully to the side of the path, so as not to set off the alarm. But never having actually experienced it before had he then been mesmerized by the sound and forgotten about the bullets? Or hadn't he known? Other than Amos, the only person likely to have known Henry intended to go out there that night was Schumann. Had Schumann double-crossed him — decided to go it alone?

His senses were returning. Keeping his eyes on the building he dialled Linklater, whose number was engaged.

Napoleon was walking down the path towards the back entrance, Amos daren't yell, didn't want to advertise his position — in all the commotion he may not yet have been spotted, any eyes would have been on Henry, not him. And Napoleon being black might not have been seen. If they had been, Amos was a dead man — he already knew too much.

It was difficult to tell from this angle but Amos would have sworn Napoleon must have reached the position where Henry had been when it started up before. He put his hands over his ears, the Spitfires would scramble again any moment. Is that what had frightened the animal that very first night? Had it been Napoleon rather than Amos who had triggered the alarm — and that's why he'd refused to go past the spot in daylight, instead keeping parallel to the building, his porcine mind perceiving the alarm as some kind of ring defence? And was he now in protection mode, his duty overcoming his fear?

And if it had been Napoleon who'd triggered the alarm that night, who or what had set it off on the other occasions — when the young couple had heard it and the two men who'd been playing bowls? None of them had mentioned wandering around in the undergrowth — but had they been and not wanted to admit it?

The Spitfires remained grounded. This time Amos fervently wished they wouldn't. The alarm's absence meant someone had switched it off — while they reloaded the rifle. Napoleon reached the door which must have been ajar because, using the same technique he used at home, the pig leaned on it heavily forcing it inwards. That grating sound where it snagged on the concrete was what Amos thought he'd heard during the shooting. Had someone come out of there?

Napoleon disappeared inside. Amos confidently expected him to re-emerge in seconds having inspected that small unattractive ante-room, and failed to find a way through the metal barriers. He waited, but Napoleon failed to return.

If he was going in, then the quicker the better. Even if he could contact them, the police might take ages to arrive and whoever had nearly killed Henry, whether by accident or design, would get away. He must try and prevent that — how many others might not be so lucky if this were allowed to continue? He need not tackle them on his own but he must discover their identity. Unless . . .

Oh no! He'd thought the bullet had proved it, proved Henry wasn't the culprit. But had it? Is that why Henry hadn't moved, because he knew exactly where the shot would come and by remaining stationary was making sure he wouldn't trigger it? Had it been Napoleon's action in knocking him down, throwing him sideways, which had caused it to be loosed — the binary decision of an unfeeling machine? One side of a line it shoots, the other side it doesn't.

Henry had run off, he'd seen him. So where was Napoleon now? Amos made his way towards the door, skirting the path. Reaching the wall he flattened himself against it, catching his breath. This was madness but he had to find out. He peered around the door post into a well of darkness. Putting one foot on the step, he dislodged a weighty object which rolled heavily on to his other foot. His imagination threw revolting alternatives around his mind. Had they killed Napoleon? But he knew that couldn't have happened quietly and that they'd be even less likely to then waste time making bacon joints out of him — but logic was struggling to assert itself right now. He bent to touch the object but mercifully instead of warm flesh his hand connected with cold hard rubber — cylindrical rubber. Henry's torch, tossed this way when he'd fallen.

Amos found the on button, it still worked. If there was someone here they weren't by the door or surely they'd have come for him by now, so with renewed determination he aimed the beam and entered. He'd guessed as much, the inner door was also open. He pushed it gently and played the light well ahead, following it in. Shrouded guillotines and borers lined the room at this end too. Who knew what was under all those winding sheets; shapes, shadows, imagined movement.

He walked up the aisle with a confidence he didn't feel — the dictum: 'If in danger show no fear' rattling like a litany around his brain. He wanted to turn and run, or in his case hobble quickly, get the hell out of here. What was he doing creeping around this godforsaken place after midnight? No wonder he felt all those sepulchral spectres were watching him.

Suddenly, close by, he heard Napoleon whimper. Without stopping to consider the foolhardiness of his action Amos swung the light in the direction of the sound. Napoleon was sitting beside a bench . . . from which hung a lifeless hand open in supplication; the rest of the body sprawled backwards across its length.

25

Amos literally froze, not knowing how many seconds, if any, he had left. His own pulse beat inexorably in his ears, marking the time, highlighting each instant which might be his last. He couldn't see how the man had died. Was a gun now trained on him? What was Henry waiting for? Nothing happened.

He moved a step closer, still no other sound. Then another step. With bewildered eyes Napoleon turned tiny circles in his own space but gave no indication of another's presence as he surely would, had the murderer still lurked. Amos looked down on the body of Franz Schumann.

Henry must have killed him when he'd brought Schumann up here earlier. Had he come back tonight, not so much to safeguard the pictures but to hide the body in case the immigrants broke in? But the doors had been open and Amos knew positively that Henry had never reached the porch. And if he'd come back since, through the front while Amos had been still outside, Henry wouldn't have had time to walk through and unlock the back, and it would have made that scraping sound. No, Henry must have left the door open earlier, been disturbed perhaps and got out fast.

Had Schumann developed cold feet, was that it? He'd kept quiet all these years and been safe. Maybe here, at the last minute, he'd heard his wife's voice warning him not to do it, not to unleash the greed and set off a chain of events that would lead maybe to someone's death, to his own detention by the authorities, to his trial for war crimes.

Amos felt unbearably guilty. Why hadn't he helped the old man more? If only he'd spent more time with him . . . maybe all he'd needed was someone he could confide in, someone to guide him. Instead Schumann must have played into the hands of the devil and when he'd changed his mind, Henry had lost his temper and murdered him in frustration and disappointment.

Or was there a much simpler explanation, a much more likely reason why Henry would kill Schumann? Never mind about why the door was open or other technicalities. Why was Amos trying to complicate things? Wasn't it obvious? Having led Henry to the hidden cache of pictures, Schumann was dispensible. Henry couldn't trust him to keep quiet — and didn't want to share the proceeds — so he'd killed him. Simple. Except

. . . Amos twisted his face in reluctance. Had he so misjudged Henry? Greedy, yes. Blinded by beauty, yes. But a killer of old men?

It was Schumann who'd told Amos the Dürer was real. He hadn't exactly come forward with the information but in the emotional state in which Amos had come across him, had volunteered it. Would he have done that if he'd wanted to keep the haul a secret? Or had the finding of the Dürer only slowly awoken his desire to possess the rest and he'd sought out Henry later?

Amos bent over the old man, touched his papery, stiff hand. His eyes were open, terrified . . . as they had been at the cottage earlier, when Stanton had called. Stanton! Amos whirled round but Napoleon remained beside the body, unmoving, and with relief Amos realized the animal wouldn't do that if Stanton were here — he hated the man.

But then Schumann had been frightened of his own shadow. Amos recalled that first day he'd met him, on the perimeter road, how scared he'd been at the mention of Romanians. Amos gasped aloud. Could they have exacted this dreadful revenge for some past atrocities committed against their grandfathers? Had they really done this? After all this time? And how had they known who he was?

He leaned closer to see if he could see how Schumann had died. After all this anxiety had he simply had a heart attack and collapsed — on his own?

Schumann's body, splayed unnaturally across the bench as if tossed there, suggested he'd been killed. As Amos discovered when he looked, half-buried in congealed blood he could see the wound where the garrotte had sliced through Schumann's neck.

Amos's mobile rang, shrilling through the silence, sounding profane beside the corpse. 'We're out on the perimeter road. Where are you?' He'd never been so pleased to hear Linklater's voice.

Suddenly reluctant to remain in that shed a moment longer, Amos retreated the way he'd come. Irrationally, perhaps even more fearful than when he'd entered, knowing salvation was at hand but realizing the murderer would know that too and choose to strike while he could. Amos swung the torch from side to side as he went, not to catch a glimpse but to ward off the darkness, hoping to illuminate those shrouds but actually creating more shadows, more unknowns, more questions — much like the turmoil in his head. The more he discovered, the less he knew.

He imagined he could hear the sound of

men approaching through the trees — perhaps distantly. But first another sound, by the door, a slight sound like a sniff or a snuffle yet Napoleon was behind him. It was probably a label or a piece of paper flapping in the draught. He stopped in the gangway. Ahead of him, in darkness, lay the open door.

The alarm had been switched off. The Spitfires hadn't started up when he and Napoleon had come down the path. So between Henry tripping and now . . . Of course, Henry could have done it, the switch could be at the front of the building. Who was he kidding? The rifle hadn't been at the front. Was there then a third conspirator? Or a Romanian assassin? How much danger was Amos in? Whoever had done this was no random psychopath, he'd had a reason to murder Schumann. And Amos hadn't seen him, so why . . . ? But he had seen Henry Fishbroke, it kept coming back to that man.

'Henry? Is that you?'

No reply, except for another infinitesimal sound, which this time appeared to come from outside the door, in the foyer. Galvanized by fear, Amos snapped off the torch and ducked behind the nearest machine. Footsteps advanced up the room very softly. Napoleon growled, giving away their position. Amos could have wept.

He cast around for a weapon, no hand tools had been left lying about in Stanton's pristine shop, no convenient wrench or spanner with which to defend himself. Amos had only the torch. The footsteps stopped, shuffled — as if casting around, unsure. In different circumstances he'd have said they were idling, waiting. Amos imagined the man's hands, the wire twisted across his fingers, ready. Without making a sound, could Amos reach the shroud of the next machine, pull it to divert attention then attack the killer from behind? One thing was certain — he couldn't hope to outrun him.

Too late. Quietly, very quietly the footsteps resumed, coming to a halt beside Amos's hiding place.

26

In that same instant the noise from outside grew louder as he tensed ready for a last-minute attack in the only moment his would-be killer had left in which to strike and escape. Amos then realized he hadn't warned Linklater. Now he could only pray the alarm had not been reset since he and Napoleon had last come down the path; or that trained policemen would instinctively dive for cover, rather than stand around wondering who might be shooting at them, endangering their lives through indecision.

He took a breath, clenching his fists, swaying with anticipation, his shoulders hunched to protect his neck, wondering how much longer he had to hold out and where the blow would fall . . . when the police with powerful torches and restrained Alsatians burst through the door.

'Just making sure you were all right, Councillor . . . until the police got here.' Now exposed, Churchman stood in the aisle facing him, with less of his false grin — but more unconvincing than ever.

Linklater strode up the gangway with two

other plain clothes men, while the entourage fanned out across the room. Churchman turned to him. 'I'm George Churchman, Chief Inspector, the man who rang you.'

Where had Churchman secreted the wire? Amos had read somewhere that the person who reports a crime is frequently the one who carried it out. Clever though — murder Schumann, make the call, then murder Amos before they arrive. Who would suspect Churchman of a murder committed after he'd rung the police? He must have heard about the art cache from the immigrants and it wasn't the first time he'd been hanging around the shed; Amos had come across him before. It also explained why Churchman had been so keen to help Eric Stanton with the railway work. It would have given him the excuse he needed for being in the building where he must have guessed the pictures were hidden. But when that had failed, he had hung around awaiting his opportunity, which Schumann and Henry eventually provided. After Henry had left, Churchman must have forced Schumann to reveal the hiding place and then murdered him. But why not take the paintings and run? Was he hoping to use Henry for the same purpose as Schumann had — as the expert, the go-between? Who had he fingered for Schumann's murder

— the immigrants . . . or Amos?

'Over here, sir.' They'd found Schumann. 'Garrotted by the looks of it.'

'Karl Weiner,' sighed Linklater.

Reluctantly Amos joined them. 'I'm afraid not, Chief Inspector, this is Franz Schumann. Things moved so fast I didn't have time to tell you — they swapped identities when Weiner was fatally wounded but believed Schumann would still need the help of Weiner's English relatives. The man I found in the ditch was Karl Weiner.' Amos turned to Linklater. 'How come you got here so fast?' Then he realized someone must have reported another Spitfire incident. 'Did someone get hurt because of the siren?'

'No, at least, not that I know of. We received a call from Mr Churchman . . . wasn't he around here somewhere a moment ago?' Linklater twisted his head and shoulders in both directions without moving his feet, clearly expecting Churchman to appear at his elbow which, unusually for the perennial jack-in-a-box, he didn't. Linklater shrugged, unconcerned. So that's why Amos hadn't been able to get through to Linklater's phone when he'd needed to.

'Mr Churchman apparently overheard a group of the immigrants at the airfield plotting to break in here to look for that art cache you and I talked about before. Seems we weren't the only ones with that idea. He said that they planned to disappear into the countryside without proper entry permits.'

'Never mind about them now. He's probably the murderer. Someone tried to kill Henry. There's a booby trap, a rifle, the shot is disguised by the Spitfire noise.' Amos blurted out the events of the last hour as quickly and succinctly as he could, brooking no interruptions — they hadn't time for detours. 'Whoever set it could have re-armed it by now. Tell your men not to go down that back path and, if they do hear the Spitfire strafing, to hit the deck fast — if the bullet I heard is typical it's aimed at chest height for a man. You've got to find that box of tricks before someone else gets hurt.'

Linklater beckoned his second in command, relayed the warning and gave instructions to find the alarm device. Someone found the switches and lights went up across the building like dawn breasting the horizon. From the awful quiet which had greeted Amos, the place was transformed into a bustle of fevered activity.

'Churchman's got a thing about those immigrants,' Amos continued when Linklater returned to him. 'Hates foreigners.' He rested against the edge of a machine table, weary now the adrenalin had ceased to pump so fast. 'He was creeping up on me in the dark

258

in here before you arrived, but of course I didn't know it was him then.'

Linklater considered Amos quietly, probably thinking he'd been through a lot of stress hearing the Spitfires again and finding Schumann murdered; which Amos would admit he had.

'We have to find Henry, Stephen. He's the key. I saw Schumann in his car this afternoon, so that's probably how Schumann got here.' Amos realized he hadn't seen Napoleon since the arrival of the police. 'Have you seen Napoleon?'

'No, probably gone back to your Land Rover. That's how I knew you must be here, saw it parked on the road out there.' He smiled for the first time tonight. 'Thought you might be holding a debate with the immigrants, trying to turn them back through persuasion.'

'You know, it's funny, but that tale about the immigrants being about to seize the paintings and make off is the same one I told Henry to get him out here.' Amos saw Linklater's expression. 'I know, I know, but having seen Henry and Schumann together — Schumann with a rucksack — I thought they were rigging an even more frightening aircraft model which would lead to someone else swerving off the road, this time with fatal consequences. I had to try and stop them. I thought if I could get Henry out here then I could . . . '

'Why didn't you call me? You could have been killed,' Linklater frowned, puzzled. 'So when did you realize it wasn't an aircraft model at all? More to the point . . . how did you know it was a booby trap?'

From the far end of the shed the Alsatians started barking. 'Sounds as if they've found Napoleon.' Linklater said drily. 'They always bark at bad smells, even I can tell he's been around.'

'That's not Napoleon, it always smells like this in here — used to be a hospital during the war. They never lose that smell.'

The barking continued, together with shouts from the men. Amos and Linklater were moving towards the commotion as one of Linklater's men came hurrying back towards them. 'I'm sorry, sir, but there's this enormous pot-bellied pig sitting in the gangway, he won't move and now the dogs won't either. The handlers think maybe his scent's so strong they're confused.'

Linklater gave Amos an exasperated look as if to say: 'Haven't we got enough to cope with here without your damned pig upsetting the sniffer dogs?' But he must have decided against saying it. Instead he explained, 'I want to find those pictures while we're here, that's why I brought the crew — but I wasn't expecting a murder scene. The sooner we find that damned haul the sooner we prevent any more crimes. It's time to take temptation out of harm's way.'

'We don't know there are any pictures.' It was Amos's turn to be dry.

'On the basis that everyone seems to think so — and because we have found an extremely valuable drawing on a skeleton in the ditch — there's no smoke without fire is what I say.' Linklater stopped as the thought struck him. 'And now we can have another go at Germany. It sounds as though we'll have a much better response if we ask them to check out the Weiner family.'

Amos could still picture the wire in Churchman's pocket . . . or Henry's, or, implausible as it sounded, the Romanians'. 'You know Schumann was petrified of Romanians, don't you?'

'As well as of us, you mean?'

Linklater had a point, Schumann had been nervous of everyone. As it turned out — with good cause. He must have considered his escape in 1945 to have been a mistake, a fluke. Schumann was meant to have died then; as far as the authorities were concerned, he had.

'He and Weiner were ordered to carry out reprisals on some Romanian dissidents, those who didn't fancy the Führer.' Amos looked at Linklater. 'All this seems to stem from the war, doesn't it. In the heart of the English countryside — where God knows we've battles enough of our own — here we are, beseiged by other people's.'

'I don't know about Schumann, though he seemed a decent enough man, intelligent . . . but I'm definitely being beseiged by your blasted pig. From what you say, if he hadn't wandered into the scrubland to do his business that night none of this would have happened.'

'Not true, Chief Inspector. All this would have transpired under your nose and you'd never have known.'

With that they proceeded silently up the gangway in single file. Trained in obedience, the Alsatians had quietened; though Amos thought they looked extremely agitated — and not because of Napoleon.

'Come on, old boy, you can't sit there.' Amos approached the pig who growled from deep down in his immense stomach. He looked fine, not ill or especially tired. Amos changed his tone and placing his boot behind the pig's rear end gave him a hefty shove. 'Enough, now move it.' The pig remained where he was and started to howl. The men muttered and shuffled, showing their impatience.

Amos stooped down and the pig nuzzled him but stayed where it was. Amos straightened. 'He's not a mule, not stubborn in that way. He'll be doing this for a reason. He doesn't seem to be injured so your guess is as good as mine.' Amos cast around, addressing the assembled faces. 'He won't bite, not with me here, so can four of you just lift him up and move him aside.' He didn't tell them what Napoleon weighed but by the look on their faces he had no need to. Linklater indicated four or five men who wrinkled their noses in disgust but took off their coats while everyone else bar Amos stood back.

As Amos had predicted, apart from growling loudly and ominously, Napoleon made no other move whatsoever; presumably assuming his weight would win the day. It did not. With a final heave five policemen and Amos hauled the beast aside.

Necks craned to examine the area where he'd lain, and as they shrugged and turned away, tugging at the dogs, putting the episode down to animal fallibility, Linklater's assistant, crawling around on all fours, discovered that the floorboards, though smooth and well fitting, displayed telltale signs of wear around the edges — revealing a very well camouflaged trap door. Though, if he'd been hiding priceless art, Amos thought he'd have hauled one of the larger machines over the top rather than indulge in this degree of skilled carpentry.

The door was large, spanning seven or eight six-inch boards — its very size assisting its disguise. The detective tried lifting it with his fingernails but it was obviously mechanically operated and wouldn't budge. Deciding against wasting further time and effort in trying to locate the mechanism or the switch, they fittingly adopted a military solution. Producing a crowbar, a police constable levered at the edges until, bent and splintered, the door parted from its brackets and swung back with a crash, landing the priser on his back.

Amos was expecting a floor cavity probably a foot or so deep since the shed floor was raised that much above the ground. Space enough to store some canvases which, considering how they'd been imported — clandestinely by aeroplane — were unlikely to be large. Though he wondered fleetingly why the trap door should be so wide if the canvases were out of their frames. Had the hiding place originally been designed for some other purpose and simply hijacked for hiding the pictures?

When they released the door, the smell grew stronger, if anything more chemical, filling the air around them. Had they set up a picture cleaning facility, was that it? The police shone their lights into the hole revealing not a recess or even a large hole . . . but an underground room — or rooms — complete with what appeared to be a serviceable flight of stairs leading down. They all fell silent.

'Did you know this was here?' Linklater asked Amos, his voice edged with accusation.

Amos scoured his brain. 'No, no I didn't, but if you think about it — a field hospital next to an active airfield in wartime — they could well have had an underground section, their own built-in air-raid shelter so they didn't have to move the patients every time the siren went.' He grew more confident in his explanation as he worked fervently to convince himself this could not be the hidden bunker — the headquarters of the under-ground movement which to this day must still remain a secret — which, with the booby trap, was feasible. Why had he never bothered to find out where it was? 'I wouldn't be surprised if the operating theatre was down there too and there's probably a lift

265

somewhere,' he continued, hoping that was the case.

Linklater looked puzzled. 'Not a good place to hide pictures in then — at the time. Unless of course they were moved in here later.' He nodded at the men poised to go down and Linklater, his assistant and two constables, descended into the depths, followed with far less agility and huge foreboding by Amos.

The cold seeped into his flesh; Amos pulled his jacket about him, remembering that string again, the one he'd lost, the one he wished he had now. He stopped, searching in his pockets, giving all his concentration to that length of red twine, seeing it in his mind's eye, wondering how it had come adrift, thinking how to tie it next time to make sure it would stay put, keep him together.

He should have felt relieved. From the torch beams he could see that the space down here mirrored the large shed except this was divided into a number of rooms and ante-rooms. He'd been right. Clearly the nearest had been the hospital ward. Bed frames still lined each side, ante-rooms leading off in the gloom were likely to have been toilets, washrooms, dispensaries. The space echoed with the long-gone sound of nurses footsteps, the rustle of starched aprons, the moans of wounded soldiers and the whispers of hushed discussions. Horrified, he began to suspect more recent occupation judging by the clothes and boots heaped haphazardly on the last bed.

He followed in a daze as Linklater and the others led the way through various smaller rooms into what must have been the operating theatre. Their torches lit up an impressive array of overhead lighting trained on a spotless stainless steel table which took centre stage, surrounded by numerous pieces of expensive-looking equipment, trolleys, and sets of operating instruments neatly arrayed in rows. Could all this have been left? No one said anything, just looked at one another, stupefied.

The next complex of rooms was the worst. Huge cabinets lined the walls, white with big metal handles applied horizontally to the drawers. Shelves full of what looked like pickling jars were displayed in glass cabinets, their contents all too obvious even in the gloom. The room was colder than the others and a motor whirred quietly in the background, like a fan.

Nearest to the operating theatre stood a polished slab surrounded by instruments whose dials and screens registered unintelligible readings, numbers, lines, colours — monitoring every function; while what looked like a set of rubber bellows rose and fell in time with the man's chest, forcing oxygen into him.

Linklater sprinted back to the staircase and shouted up it, 'Get an ambulance and come and get these lights down here switched on — quickly.'

27

They were pulling open the heavy drawers, the ones with the big metal handles. Some were empty. Others contained cadavers cut open, their organs removed, their eyes gouged out. Shocking though it would be, Amos wanted to believe them remnants from the war . . . that these atrocities had been perpetrated by a foreign enemy and the men brought back home. Is that why they'd never disconnected the electricity from here but left it on to keep the air conditioning functioning; then simply forgotten the men were there? He knew it couldn't be true.

'What's going on here? Who are all these people?' Linklater asked of no one in particular, all thought of pictures obviously forgotten in the repulsive turn events had taken — this stumbling into Frankenstein's workshop. 'And who's this poor devil?' He indicated the man on the life support machine. 'Why keep this one alive? Is this that chap who runs the machine shop? Did he find out so they had to murder him as well?'

Apart from the instant when he'd found Schumann's body and remembered whose workshop he was in, Amos hadn't given Stanton a thought. After what had nearly happened to Henry, whether or not through his own fault, together with Amos's recent uncanny knack of causing grief for others — like Bill Thomas — Amos had been grateful to have one less liability to worry about.

Being the only one present who knew Stanton by sight, very reluctantly he forced himself to take a proper look at the man's face, to literally look on death warmed up. 'No, it's not Stanton, too young.'

So that's what Churchman had been up to. He'd hated the immigrants so much he'd been murdering them — wholesale. Perhaps he'd known about the pictures and found this place while searching for them? No wonder he'd been miffed when Stanton had set up his workshop above — must have given him a headache or two. Amos couldn't begin to understand.

'I think you'll find they're all immigrants from the processing plant. I wouldn't mind betting one of them is a man known as Stephan, one of their leaders who was about to shop Karloff for fraud,' Amos said, answering Linklater's earlier question.

It was Churchman who had first told him the immigrants were continually going

missing. Clever bastard. He'd figured someone would mention it sooner or later, when
enough of them had gone to make it
noticeable — so he'd made sure he said it
first. That way, if searches were made and the
whole set-up discovered, people would be
much less likely to suspect him — the
whistle-blower.

'This is Karloff's work?' exclaimed Linklater, incredulous. 'Graham Carlton's not
capable of all this!'

'No, but George Churchman might be. We
don't know anything about him except the
man's a fraud. He could be capable of
anything.'

'Over here, sir,' called one of the detectives,
trying not to gag. In front of him were rows of
businesslike containers with sprung hinges
and inner liners like those in a thermos flask.
'It looks like . . . an eye.'

Linklater opened up another box and
hastily replaced the lid. 'We sent for the
pathologist when we found the man upstairs.
The speed that chap drives he should be here
soon, rides a motorbike.' Amos noticed that
casual reference to the mundane, the
irrelevant, anything to lighten the atmosphere
of horror down here.

Motorbike — he remembered the man
careering through Weston Hathaway in the

early hours, followed by Karloff and Churchman . . . and who may have stopped at
Henry's. 'That's what he was doing! Transporting body parts. He had body parts in
those paniers, not pictures. That's why he was
going so fast.'

'The pathologist?'

'No no, the courier I saw.' Amos explained
about the survey and how he'd lain in wait.
'And Karloff. Karloff sped through the village
earlier tonight like a cow with a firework in its
tail, headed up here. I joked with Henry, said
Karloff must have heard his immigrants were
staging a break-out.' Amos remembered
Henry had been cross, said Karloff may have
hit the Jaguar . . . but what if that had been a
blind . . . that instead Henry had been telling
Karloff where he'd left Schumann?

Was Henry a middle man? Did the same
underworld who dealt in stolen art also
trade in kidneys and corneas? Did that
explain why Henry never seemed to be
around after dark? And what had that to do
with Schumann?

A shout came from upstairs and an officer
ran halfway down the stairs then tilted his
head over the bannisters to address the chief
inspector. 'We've found it, sir. The recording
equipment . . . and the rifle. They were both
inside, up in the roof space over the front

272

entrance with speakers mounted under the eaves.'

Amos couldn't imagine why he'd gone down into the pit in the first place, this hell he was in. Had these people been alive when they'd had their parts removed? Had they felt the pain? He couldn't get back up those stairs to life fast enough.

'What sort of rifle is it?' Amos knew he should have waited and hoped Linklater would mention it in passing, but he had to know. One of the policemen in the loft appeared at the opening with it in a gloved hand. 'A hunting rifle, Councillor, is that what you meant?'

Amos felt relieved — too soon.

The policeman was examining the gun in the light from the main room. 'Mind you, I'd say it's an old one, pre-war.'

What had the underground movement used? He'd assumed it would have been an army rifle as they'd been issued with those . . . but it could have been a hunting rifle. So, had this alarm come from the special operations bunker or been found elsewhere, or even copied? Was the hideaway compromised? Just because the murderer had used an old gun didn't necessarily mean he'd found the original trap, perhaps an old rifle was all he'd had to hand.

Linklater was eyeing him thoughtfully. 'What do you know about this, Councillor?' Unsaid but plainly intended was the rider ' . . . that you're not telling me.'

Amos wandered out through the still open door, Linklater close behind him. 'During the war the Ministry of Defence recruited whizz kid civilians, gave them army commissions and used them as problem-solvers. For instance, if a specific part failed to arrive in time for a spy's radio pack, they'd invent a substitute on the spot.'

'So these whizz kids invented an alarm . . . that sounded like Spitfires strafing?' said Linklater.

'Mmm, something like that.'

'So you knew all along . . . so why all this nonsense about radio-controlled models then?' Linklater looked exasperated. Downstairs he'd managed to contain his revulsion which now manifested itself in short temper.

'No. That is, I haven't known long. Someone else mentioned it but I didn't think it fitted this case.' Amos glanced at Linklater, the man who missed nothing, but he was not about to betray Alec Fitzsimmons or the underground movement, not even now. He continued. 'What threw me was the fact that the alarm here didn't always go off.' Linklater cocked an eyebrow. 'What I mean is, the device invented during the war was more or less a permanent fixture.' He and Alec had considered it might be one of the old bunker protectors accidentally left in situ which was still being triggered but if so, it wouldn't have been intermittent. And anyway, they'd only considered the alarm function.

Amos went on. 'I came out here several times during the day and evening. Once I approached along the army camp path to the front door, so it wouldn't have worked then, I understand that. But the other times I was either out on the perimeter road where I'd been that first night . . . ' He stopped abruptly, puzzled.

'Go on.'

'I was about to say it didn't go off those other times when I was out on the road, but I remember realizing earlier tonight that it must have been Napoleon who triggered it that night, nosing round here looking for a suitable lavatory. In other words — it never was triggered from the road. But then . . . how come those other motorists heard it too?'

'Because they must have been going past on the road when the alarm happened to go off — triggered by something or someone else,' Linklater said slowly, feeling his way. He and Amos looked at each other.

'It didn't go off that day I came here with Napoleon, early in the morning. I came down that back path, through the gap in the fence off the road. Straight down it I came.' Then he remembered. 'Mind you, Napoleon wouldn't. He came so far and no further, stopped short. He knew, didn't he? He knew just where he'd been before when the Spitfire strafing started.' Amos thought for a moment. 'Then of course tonight, I made him jump through it to knock Henry down and he must have realized it didn't hurt him — all that strafing I mean. After that he was OK with it.'

'So somebody, whoever rigged it up here in the first place, switched it on and off at will, whenever they wanted to prevent people from approaching the shed,' surmised Linklater. 'Do you reckon they could hear it down in that cellar?'

Amos was glad Linklater had chosen that innocuous word, cellar. He preferred not to dwell on what was there. 'Ask your men but I expect there's a link into the cellar, a flashing light or something to tell of visitors.'

'So how did you know there'd be a real bullet too? How did you know about the rifle, Amos?'

28

There, he'd known Linklater would come back to that eventually. Amos supposed it was due solely to their long association that Linklater wasn't saying it with more menace, suspecting Amos of having set it up himself — since he appeared to know what no one else did.

'How did you know the Spitfire strafing was a booby trap? And how come Napoleon didn't get shot?' Was there a trace of regret in that last sentence? 'Having said that, it's a funny kind of booby trap — most people would avoid the strafing if they could,' Linklater added, doubtfully.

'It's very disorientating. When it first happens, you're mesmerized — unless you're trained for that sort of thing.' Had Amos said that too quickly?

'And why a combined booby trap and alarm? Come on, Amos, this is far too serious for playing mind games.'

Linklater was right. Amos looked straight at him, decision made. 'I can't tell you how I know, just take that as read, will you?' He paused, not to allow for acquiescence or debate, but to gather his thoughts. Swallowing, he went on. 'I was following Henry along the path when the Spitfire strafing started and I began to think about how close our country had come to disaster . . . and for some reason I started to think about Churchman and his hatred of immigrants. I knew he was hiding something, what with all those ridiculous disguises — pretending to be a bird-watcher when he clearly knows nothing about birds. He was using that as a cover. Then it struck me, right there on the path, almost too late.'

Linklater said nothing.

'You see, in its original incarnation the Spitfire strafing wasn't really an alarm, it was cover for a booby trap — there to hide the location of the rifle so people wouldn't be able to tell from exactly where the shot had been fired.' He glanced at Linklater and went on. 'So when I heard it tonight and realized this wasn't a model aircraft but more akin to what . . . I'd heard about — regardless of whether it was functional all the time or not — I remembered what else it might have.' He paused. 'I was about to add, 'Thank heavens I did . . . and managed to save Henry', but if he's the one behind, or has even been involved in, you know, downstairs . . . ' Amos found it hard to conceive of anyone perpetrating what he'd seen. 'Then maybe I should have let him take that bullet after all.'

'Napoleon saved his life, you know.' Amos wanted to defend the pig. 'To answer your other question, Napoleon escaped being shot that other night because the bullet is at chest height for a man. Napoleon's much shorter.'

'Did you know that when you sent Napoleon to knock Fishbroke down?'

'No, of course not, I just knew there'd be a shot. But I'll show you the tree the bullet's imbedded in, you can see for yourself then.' They walked along the path together, Linklater still looking puzzled.

'Why this side and not the main entrance? Why wasn't it rigged to cover the path coming from the army camp, the way most people would approach this place?'

'It's the way I first came, yes . . . but who was our killer aiming at?'

'Immigrants by the looks of those poor bastards below,' Linklater answered.

'Exactly — and where are they? On the old airfield.' Amos's knowledge of the local geography gave him the advantage.

'So you reckon our killer deliberately set the booby trap to kill these poor sods and then carve them up for his own sadistic pleasure? But why aim at their chest? From what I saw downstairs . . . ' Linklater gulped, 'I'd have thought he'd want to preserve the

279

heart or the lungs maybe.'

'Let's see what your pathologist says but that's my theory, yes.'

'So he wouldn't need the flashing light for the alarm downstairs if all it was was a death trap, not an alarm?' Linklater mused.

'Oh yes, he would. He'd want to come straight away, see what he'd caught, like tonight. Only this time he comes up, sees he's failed to catch his prey so switches off the alarm before anyone suspects it exists. That's what was so devilishly clever about it — anyone who heard it refused to believe their ears. As I did. You think you've imagined it — especially if you then retrace your steps and deliberately repeat what you did, where you went, and nothing happens. As I did. Anyway, he was probably in the process of escaping when he saw me out there or sensed someone was there and decided to get the hell out fast without locking the door, for fear he'd be spotted.'

'Surely he could have gone out the front way?'

'No time, not if he was here switching off the alarm. Remember, his one thought was not to be found in that building . . . especially since Schumann's body was still on display.' It was becoming clearer to Amos. 'And he didn't go far. Just far enough to call you people and thereby make himself appear innocent. Have your men found him yet? Churchman?'

'No, he was last seen headed towards the army camp.'

Amos looked alarmed.

'Don't worry, no one's going to escape from here; we'd already blocked the roads to prevent the supposed immigrant break-out.'

29

Then they heard it, the motorbike in the distance. Amos could see why the pathologist chose that mode of transport, no leaving the car up the road and walking, no making his way through forests or down hillsides with his equipment to examine bodies deposited in the wilderness. This man rode straight to the scene, through the wire, across the stream and down the path, slowing where the police tape fluttered across the track and drawing to a noisy, fume-laden, halt beside Linklater and Amos.

Fresh-faced from his exhilarating ride and revealing a mop of carrot-coloured hair when he removed his helmet, the pathologist exhibited the traditional bonhomie of the caring professions.

'They said you had a cache of bodies for me, Chief Inspector. Been saving them up have you? Thought you'd get a better service for volume?' Then he saw their faces and fell silent, wheeling his bike up to the shed where Linklater handed him over to his deputy.

'I'll be out here, Derek. I'd like a preliminary view in the next ten minutes but

the urgent one is the man on the life supp — '
Linklater was interrupted by the sound of the
ambulance wheeling in through the camp
gates as the area around the shed errupted
into a frenzy of activity with ambulance men,
paramedics, police, and more technicians
running up the path.

Amos found a tree trunk near the entrance
and sat down on it, overcome by nausea at
what he'd seen. Those had been vibrant
young men killed like so many sheep, as if
their lives had been worthless. What sort of
person could treat life, anyone's life, so
cheaply? And what for — money, hatred? To
prevent the immigrants taking over? Were the
body parts a sideline to make a living? Is that
why Henry had been needed, to sell them?
He shuddered. He knew these people, had
stood beside them, talked to them . . .

Napoleon emerged from the bushes and lay
down beside him. It was cold out here, but
much cleaner, fresher — the killing fields
compared with the morgue. Linklater came
across. 'Give me your keys Amos.' He
surrendered them without question. Linklater
handed them to one of the newly arrived
officers. 'Fetch the councillor's Land Rover
up to the army camp entrance, constable,
you'll find it half a mile down the perimeter
road.' To Amos he said, 'At least that'll save

you the walk,' and disappeared back inside the shed.

Funny choice of words that young pathologist had used, cache of bodies — instead of paintings. The body that was not part of the hoard was Schumann's, hastily garrotted . . . why? If it were for the obvious reason, that he'd shown Henry and Church-man where the paintings were and outlived his usefulness then why hadn't they planned to kill him like the rest?

Or had he unexpectedly tried to double-cross them . . . or changed his mind and threatened to go to the police so they'd killed him to stop him or keep him quiet? Maybe at the last minute he had refused to tell them where the paintings were hidden and they'd tried to torture it out of him with the garrotte. If so, had they succeeded, or had he died with his secret intact?

Amos patted Napoleon's head, they were both tired. None of this felt right, none of it felt likely. The more he thought about Schumann the harder it became to picture him as a dishonest man. Introverted, frightened, clever . . . but a villain? Was it those damned radio-controlled models which had given him the sinister connotation? But that had turned out to be a complete coincidence. The noise had not come from models at all, they knew that for a fact now. So why should Schumann's trade have any bearing on this — unless it had indeed been Schumann, with his knowledge of gadgetry, who had built the booby trap? Amos stood up and paced to encourage his brain.

Schumann had been a prisoner of war here. Had he heard about the special operations bunker, known about its protection system? Was that the connection? Could they possibly have hidden the paintings there?

Paintings, paintings. Were there any? Were they at all relevant now? Think. Amos paced. Policemen came and went. The constable who had been sent for the Land Rover returned his keys.

The ambulance crew re-emerged carrying on a stretcher the man who'd been on life support — disconnected from his machines, his face covered. Although Amos had feared the worst it was still a sight he'd had no wish to see. Linklater and the pathologist followed them out. Linklater watched the stretcher-bearers manoeuvre their burden through the copse. 'We found the lift — all in perfect working order. It's obviously how they got all that spanking new equipment down there — and probably the bodies. It's at this end, looks like part of the ante-room walls.'

With the most urgent task attended to,

Linklater brought the pathologist out to show him the booby trap and where the men had been shot.

'Were they killed outright, Derek?' Amos heard himself ask.

'Oh, I should say so. Difficult to tell until I open them up, but yes. I don't think they suffered.'

'So, having a lift nearby would have been handy — not having to manhandle the bodies too far.' Now Amos appreciated why this area around the back entrance had struck him as being well swept. He'd thought nothing of it, put it down to Stanton's fastidiousness when all the time Henry and Churchman were . . .

'One thing that puzzles me is if the rifle could only shoot one at a time, what happened if two or more men approached together — they can't all have been loners.' Linklater said.

'I imagine when they saw their mate fall they'd leap for cover, believing he'd been hit by aircraft fire. If they hung around long enough to see the body being taken in they'd either be even more frightened and flee for their life . . . or the congenitally brave would have come back another night to find their friend and get killed themselves.' Amos sighed. Then went on. 'It's only an assumption but it must have been something like that. The last thing these people felt they could do was approach the police. For all they knew it could well be the police who were shooting at them for trespassing.'

'Our killer would have waited until he thought their friends, if any, had gone. And then when they returned with help or to collect the body, and couldn't find it, they'd have assumed the man had not been killed after all but had escaped,' added Linklater.

'You're probably right but he wouldn't have been best pleased when that happened.' Amos and Linklater looked at the pathologist who was now speaking. 'The killer, I mean, having to wait.' They looked at him blankly. 'The sooner he got them on the life support machine the better.'

30

'I don't understand,' Amos admitted. 'If they were already dead? You just said you thought they had died instantly, didn't suffer.'

'Most people don't realize. But this man knows what he's doing, whether through trial and error, couldn't sell his wares so he learned on the job as they say, or whether he knew to begin with . . . ' He shrugged. 'Who knows? But if first impressions are anything to go by he seems reasonably skilled as a surgeon.' Derek paused then shrugged again. 'But then, anyone would be with the practice he seems to have had here.'

He ran his fingers through his shock of hair. 'You hear really tragic tales of poor buggers in the Far East, in India, Africa . . . where they're so desperate for money they try and sell their own kidneys. Gangs of highway robbers kill people for them. The tragedy is that in most of these instances, by the time they get to the buyer they're useless — and therefore valueless. But our man here obviously understands that. Kidneys can, very rarely, be removed up to an hour after heart death but it's essential for the heart, lungs and liver and usually the kidneys, to be removed from someone who, although brain dead, has had their breathing maintained — hence the ventilator you saw.'

Amos had another thought. 'All this equipment upstairs, it is for engineering, renovating the train and the tracks isn't it?'

'What I've seen of it I'd say so, yes. Not that I'm an expert on trains, more of a bike man myself. I imagine the workshop is just that, an engineering workshop. By the way, the old man upstairs was indeed garrotted.'

But Amos was still wondering. 'Is that what he actually died of?' Out of the corner of his eye he caught the expression of exasperation which crossed Linklater's face. 'Only it occurred to me they might have been threatening him with that — to get information out of him — and, well, he could have died of a heart attack. After all he was an old man.'

'I don't think so, Councillor, all the signs point to his having been throttled.'

There, it had gone. That last vestige of hope he'd held out for Henry. That maybe he and Churchman hadn't meant to kill Schumann . . . and that maybe Henry hadn't realized about how the body parts were being supplied.

Impatiently Linklater went on. 'So why

shoot them in the heart if that's what you're selling? Doesn't make sense.'

'Do you think a booby trap rifle shot to the head would bring such good results Chief Inspector? The chances of a hit on that size and level of target are much less than hitting a man in the chest.' He put out a hand towards Linklater apologetically. 'What I haven't mentioned is that other things like corneas can be removed up to twenty-four hours after death. Given his resources and expertise, he was going for the things easiest to supply.'

'The eyes in the jars,' Linklater whispered. 'The bodies, with their eyes missing — I thought it was some kind of — '

'No,' said Derek. 'I suspect he was selling corneas as well as kidneys. He only had the one life support machine — that I could find anyway.'

Is that why he'd left Schumann where he was? wondered Amos. Because the machine was already occupied? 'So that's why he used nothing more powerful or that would splatter the body with shot — he needed a weapon which would kill without destroying the organs he wanted.' Amos said.

'Precisely.'

Linklater was pacing up and down, hands behind his back. 'But why did they keep coming here? Surely word must have got out that it was a death trap?'

'Not necessarily. These were desperate men don't forget. How many people would you tell if you thought you knew where to find a load of priceless art?' Amos snapped.

'And don't forget this isn't your normal village, not Weston Hathaway or Lower Farthing where everyone knows everyone else. None of us knew these people, we didn't realize anything untoward was happening. And like the POW's before them, those who knew they'd gone other than Churchman that is, said nothing, covered up for them even. So nobody reported these poor blighters missing.'

'And do you think Karloff knew?' Linklater asked.

'Knew! I expect he was paid to provide the raw materials, don't you? And he had an easy solution to his problem when one of the ring leaders happened to discover his National Insurance scam. Maybe Karloff feared he'd discover this little lot next.' Amos rubbed his chin, thinking back to the motorbike rider. 'And I reckon the biker I saw that night must have been a courier.' He looked to the pathologist for confirmation.

'Parts are very often transported by bike, or train, or plane. Whichever method is fastest depending on where they have to go,' Derek answered.

'He could just possibly have used all three from here,' Linklater said.

So why had Karloff been following the bike, Amos wondered? Maybe he was unaware exactly what went on and was trying to find out — in order to get a bigger slice of the profit? Or, ignorant of Henry's involvement but suspecting a middle man existed, wanted to know who it was? And, of course, Churchman had simply been returning home after his night's work.

'And what about this railway fanatic, Eric Stanton? Do you think he realized what was going on?' Linklater asked.

Amos thought. 'Lives in a world of his own.' He'd examined only the body attached to the machine, what if one of the others had been Stanton? 'It might explain why he was so adamantly against anyone helping him in here, particularly Churchman. He must have realized Churchman was up to something, saw things out of place sometimes, smelt that smell . . . and was determined not to let Churchman in if he could help it. It might even explain why the trap door wasn't covered by one of his machines. It would have upset Stanton's orderly line so he'd have moved it back.'

Amos turned to Linklater. 'It took us long enough to realize there was a trap door there even when Napoleon and your dogs were doing their damnedest to tell us.'

'So where are the paintings?' Linklater could have been relied on to return to that subject sooner or later. 'What's the link between the paintings and what happened here?'

Amos tried to put himself in Weiner and Schumann's cockpit. They had chosen the area near the POW camp deliberately, purposely ditching their plane nearby, pretending to be shot down, out of fuel . . . whatever. They knew they wouldn't have long because the aircraft spotters would have already reported the sighting. Even if all the canvases were relatively small, like the Dürer, and if there were only say, half a dozen of them at most . . . they still had to find somewhere dry, safe from being eaten by animals, or insects, and safe from being discovered accidentally. If they'd left themselves enough time they need not worry about the pictures being discovered through a formal search because no one would have suspected they'd been smuggled into England in the first place.

Schumann had not only left the Dürer behind and never returned for it — but as far as Amos knew, neither had Schumann ever attempted to recover the other pictures in all that time. He may have done, but the state in which Amos had found him suggested otherwise. His wife, the possible steadying influence, had since died but even so — Amos wasn't satisfied. Was Schumann really likely to have gone after those pictures now?

Something else had happened, or someone else had. It was there, back in something Schumann had said, if only Amos could get hold of it. Where did Schumann come into this?

'Sir, they're ready to start moving the bodies.' Linklater and the pathologist were called back in.

Reasoning that he could do no more here, Amos started up the path to the army camp, Napoleon at his heels. The police would pick up Churchman and Henry sooner or later and he didn't want to be the one to have to tell Stanton he wouldn't be able to use the shed any more — not for a while at least. No doubt alerted by the heavy police activity in the area, Karloff would have already made off.

Bodies, mutilated bodies — he didn't want to think about them, or remember what he'd seen and smelled and sensed — all those parts, as if a human being amounted to some fleshy Meccano set, nothing more. When he'd set out to follow Henry little had he expected . . . He swallowed hard and took a deep breath as he walked. He wanted to feel all right, be the same as before, to turn the clock back. This time yesterday . . . no, even earlier this evening, it hadn't happened. Yes it had, but he Amos Cotswold hadn't seen it. He'd seen worse done to animals, alive, but men . . . He fought down the bile which rose in his throat.

Halfway along the path his ears picked up a strange sound. Strange for here, but unmistakeable: the sound of a steam engine starting up. For a second he couldn't comprehend it, must be mistaken. Could anything else make that noise, a truck, a police helicopter? His certainty grew along with the strength of that engine.

31

That's where they'd disappeared to — they must have been stoking the boiler and preparing all this time. How could he have forgotten? Churchman liked trains, didn't he? It was one of the few things which had rung true about him when he'd begged Amos to help him get a job with the renovation team. No wonder the police had failed to catch them, they weren't going by road! They were going by rail.

The track down to Honeybourne and the lines to Oxford or west to Worcester were all open; the whole of the British rail network formed their getaway tunnel. What could he do? Amos cast around, no sign of any police — they were all busy bringing up the bodies and manning useless roadblocks. His mind focused on action, he fumbled for his phone but in his hurry, couldn't find it. It was down to him to stop Henry and Churchman escaping.

Sighting the Land Rover through the trees he stumbled forward, heedless of the surface roots and the overgrown vegetation hanging low across the path, swishing in his face, wiping away his doubts.

As he gained the cab, he heard the train move off, its steam rising visibly across the acres of old carriages and dilapidated huts between him and the main line, the smoke coursing through his nostrils drawing him on. He could try and follow it but he couldn't see much of the track; how wide it was on either side, how unobstructed. Clearing the land around wouldn't have been their priority, the train needed only the rails. No, foolhardy enough as he was to attempt it, determination to succeed rather than common sense told him that route was a non-starter.

He gunned the Land Rover into action, wheeled it around and drove at breakneck speed out of the main gates, turning towards Evesham. To his right he could see the grey smoke streaming along the track which ran parallel with the road half a mile away across the fields. Ahead of him in the distance he could see the flashing blue lights of the police roadblock. Surely they must realize something was up, had they no eyes?

He had no time to stop and explain, whereas if they followed him so much the better, as long as they didn't catch him before he could stop the train. Though quite how he was going to do that he didn't know yet. Adrenalin fuelled his body, his mind was in overdrive. He had three options, stop and explain; crash through the roadblock and pray the Land Rover survived well enough to continue driving across the field just beyond it or divert off the road before the junction and hope he could get from there into the meadowland for which he was aiming. The quickest way was to branch off here and hope they followed him.

As he turned at ninety degrees into the field — thanking God the gate was open — he strained his eyes across the rutted acres to spot the easiest way of entering the next field, the one he knew. Keeping his foot to the floor the Land Rover pitched and tossed, groaned and rattled beneath him but kept on, relentlessly.

The train lay just to his right but he knew the track snaked after this field, giving them much further to travel than he and forcing them to slow for the bends. Amos also knew that where the track turned away from the road and headed towards Honeybourne, the field there, the one he'd rented years ago, had a crossing place for cattle — or used to have.

He glanced in his mirror, no sign of the police yet, probably just as well. If there were a gate he'd no time to find it, but ahead in the blackness he saw what he was looking for — a thinning in the hedge. On arable land there'd have been no need to plug the hole to keep the livestock from straying.

Amos aimed the Land Rover at the hedge, put his foot down and prayed. The sturdy off-roader roared through the gap, snagging hawthorn and ivy, snapping branches in two and knocked sideways by the ground-level trunks it encountered — but he was through, unfettered and gathering speed on the other side.

Now he had to gain more time, give distance to his lead. The field had been ploughed end on to the track so he could drive along the furrows which made the going much quicker. The crossing was about a half a mile ahead of him; he could have found it blindfolded the number of times he'd worked this land as a young man.

For the first time he wondered if they'd seen him from the train yet. Maybe, maybe not. Glancing to his right he could see they'd slowed round the bends as he'd guessed they'd have to. The track couldn't be that good, used only occasionally for storing all those wagons up on the army camp, and always driven along very slowly. Even if they'd been using it for transporting their 'goods', he'd like to bet it hadn't been often — trial runs in daylight so no one would make anything of it, and again, never at top speed. So goodness knew what an eighty mile an hour dash would rattle out of it.

Snatches of conversation whipped past him, like wisps of steam from the train — things Schumann had said: 'Franz wasn't very well', and then later: 'He was being blackmailed in a most horrible way'. Presumably no one had known about Weiner's Dürer as he still had it. So what could they have been demanding? What was it they'd wanted?

And how was Amos going to stop the train on his own? Would the Land Rover parked across the track be enough? The trouble was they wouldn't care about the damage or whether the train would be wrecked, they'd risk it.

One thing was certain. Unless the police moved fast, Churchman and Fishbrooke would reach Honeybourne and then they'd be free. Free to go on treating people like insects, crushing them underfoot and recycling their parts — indulging in some cannibalistic green policy.

Behind him, way back across the previous field came a single wavering light. To his right the train was labouring up the incline towards the crossing. And in front of him lay the long decayed fencing which prevented the cattle from crossing the line at whim, inside of which was the shingle ramp up to the track and the horizontal boards which comprised the crossing.

As the engine breasted the incline and rounded the last bend, poised to gather speed, Amos drove up the slope on to the crossing at an angle and pointed the Land Rover towards the oncoming train, headlights blazing. He wanted them to see him, didn't want it to be an accident. They'd time to avoid the crash. Which was more than he had.

An agile man could have done it; scrambled out and back across the line before the train hit, but Amos knew he hadn't an earthly chance of achieving it. Even if he hadn't been dog tired, even if his legs hadn't turned to jelly from the night's experiences and this headlong rush into oblivion — even without those, he doubted he could have got out quickly enough.

Yet he had to stop the train. Had to try his best to avenge all those men, the ones he'd seen . . . as well as Weiner. Oh yes, he knew now. Flashed up on that inner screen of his, amidst the smoke, the smell, the fear, amidst the paintings and the search for wealth — amidst survival — was the piece of the puzzle he'd ignored. On it he was staking his life.

If he was right, the train would stop. If not, it wouldn't.

32

The small single light bounced towards him across the field he'd just traversed. Almost homely in its seeming insignificance . . . and too late. It couldn't stop the train and the roadblockers wouldn't make it to Honeybourne in time even if they knew where the line came out — and few but the railway enthusiasts would know that. The police would wait, assuming the track would come to a dead end. The helicopter would take too long. Amos's was the only way.

He felt cold, freezing. Where was that string he'd lost? If only he could pull his coat together he'd feel warmer. He'd had that red twine for years. Sometimes he had to retwist it, retie it, but this week he'd ignored it and now look what had happened. He tried to snuggle down away from the night air coming through the open window but the cold issued from inside those lights which were trained on him. White light surrounded him, getting closer and closer, blinding him, engulfing him.

Then came the high pitched, long drawn

out scream, the belching smoke. Amos began to choke.

★   ★   ★

Strong hands pulled him from the Land Rover, helped him on to the side of the track, gently eased him to the ground. A face surrounded by a shock of ginger hair studied him with grave concern.

'Are you all right, Councillor?'

'The screaming? Who was screaming?' Amos asked.

The pathologist paused, puzzled. 'The train brakes I expect. Had to stop in a hurry — thanks to you.'

Amos struggled to rise. 'They'll get away, we must go after them.' Then in the background he overheard the familiar voice of Stephen Linklater.

'You have the right to . . . '

'The chief inspector was on your bike?'

'Yes, we heard the train and, well, it seemed the quickest way so he leapt on the back and as I drove out into the army camp we saw you disappearing fast up the road. The chief inspector instructed me to follow you, otherwise we'd have done the obvious and gone along the track.'

'I didn't know what state it was in.' Amos

swung an arm wide. 'I used to rent these fields.'

Linklater came striding over. 'He's hand-cuffed to the guard rail, he's not going anywhere. There's no sign of the others.' He surveyed Amos. 'What the bloody hell do you think you were doing? It's a miracle you weren't killed.'

'I thought he'd stop. It's the *Pride of Dundee*, isn't it?' Etched in gold and green against a black engine, Amos could just make out the gleaming name plate on the side of the beast. 'He wouldn't risk damaging that, it's the last of its class. I knew he wouldn't hurt that.'

Amos felt better, the warmth seeping back. He looked down and caught on an inside button, hung a piece of red twine. Absent-mindedly he unhooked it, rolled it, looped it through the button-holes in his jacket and did himself up.

'How did you know who it was?' Linklater demanded.

'I didn't until I was crossing the field, then I realized. It had been bugging me all night, especially when we discovered the Spitfire strafing had nothing to do with model aircraft. I kept wondering how Schumann fitted in to all this. Yes, I'd found him wandering around on the perimeter road near where I'd found Weiner's body. Yes, he'd known about the Dürer . . . but don't forget it was he who told me it was real. If he'd been trying to keep people away from a hoard of paintings he'd not have volunteered that information would he? It would have been in his interest for us to keep thinking it a fake. Yes, he lied to me when he referred to the dead man as Franz Schumann . . . knowing all along it was Karl Weiner and yes, I'd seen him go off in Henry's car and he may have known where Weiner might have stashed some paintings during the war. All very circumstantial. But what has any of that to do with those corpses who've been cold-bloodedly killed and butchered?'

Neither Linklater nor the pathologist moved.

'But I'd forgotten what else he'd said. That first time I found him, he'd said his friend had been ill. And later, when he confessed to swapping identities he'd said they'd had to escape because Karl was being blackmailed for being Jewish and their so-called comrades were threatening to do the same to him, Schumann, for harbouring a Jew — for not betraying his friend.'

'I began to wonder what they could possibly have hoped to extort from men like that, fellow prisoners of war in a foreign

305

country. They wouldn't have had any money would they? If Weiner had paintings and they'd known that, then yes, they could have been demanding those. But my guess is that either he'd already handed them over, the Dürer being the last one, or there never were any more because I'm certain he'd have given them willingly rather than have to pay the price he did.'

Linklater looked puzzled. 'And what was that?'

'It was you who told me, Chief Inspector. When we were talking about Weiner's identity you mentioned something the forensic people had come up with — that Weiner had been in a bad way healthwise before he was killed . . . and that he'd had a kidney surgically removed. They'd said it might help towards identifying him.' Amos shrugged. 'Which of course it wouldn't have done because it wasn't done officially.'

'I don't understand . . . ' Linklater said.

'Neither do I entirely but it seems to tie in with those men we found tonight.'

'Except it's sixty years on.' Linklater was visibly trying to nail the connection, willing but as yet unable.

'Those men have been dead only a few months at most,' the pathologist added.

'I know that. But you didn't see Schumann's face in my cottage this afternoon.' Had it really been only that afternoon? It felt like weeks ago. 'Schumann came to see me — after you'd called on him.' Amos stood up, finding it easier to talk on the same level as his listeners.

'What did he want?'

'I never found out — but I think he wanted to confess to someone, explain why he'd swapped identities, gain absolution through it . . . I don't know.' Amos went on. 'But while he was there I had another visitor and Schumann knocked over the chair in his rush to be gone. Grabbed his rucksack and fled. He looked ghastly . . . as though he'd come face to face with his own murderer.' Amos stepped back, reaching for the hedge to steady himself, thrown by his own statement. 'Which of course he had. It was Eric Stanton who murdered Franz Schumann wasn't it?'

With both hands chained to a rail in the cab of the engine, his feet perfectly aligned with the plate, leering down at them from his elevated position, Stanton raised his voice to attract their attention. 'The man was stupid! Mistook me for my father. Said I'd killed his friend. How dare he endanger my enterprise when I was so close to breaking my father's record? He would have been so proud of me.'

'Oh yes,' Linklater said. 'Why was that?'

Stanton looked down on him as though addressing a particularly dim child. 'He was heartbroken when they wouldn't give me a place at medical school, but I said to him, 'I'll show them. You wait, Dad, I'll show them.''

'Was your father here during the war then?' Linklater prompted.

Stanton straightened his back, throwing his chin even further in the air with that arrogant twist he had. 'They didn't appreciate him. Thought he wasn't good enough, wouldn't let him do the surgery. But he was going to show them, after the war, he was going to show them. That's why he had to bribe the POW's with cigarettes and money.'

Linklater exchanged puzzled glances with the pathologist, but Amos had had longer to digest what Schumann had told him. 'Your Dad wanted to practise, didn't he?'

That toss of the head again. 'Practise! He didn't need to practise. He was an artist — experimenting with new ideas. He knew much more than all those so-called doctors with their degrees and diplomas. Anyway, they were all far too busy to notice what he was doing. Nobody found out.'

'So your father paid the POW's for supplying human guinea pigs,' Amos prompted.

'Well, who cared? They were our prisoners

anyway, our enemies; they'd been trying to kill us! Why shouldn't he use them for his experiments?' So that was it. Franz Schumann and Karl Weiner, through no fault of their own except for Karl's genetic make-up, had been offered up as a human sacrifice to a butcher; an unqualified quack who had extracted one of Karl's kidneys rendering the man seriously ill, and who was proposing to do the same to Schumann. Amos felt an overwhelming feeling of failure. Even after sixty years they'd failed to protect Franz Schumann. And now here was the butcher's son, inheritor of the same madness.

'So you decided to carry on where your father left off?' Linklater asked.

Amos looked back in the direction of the army camp and thought to himself, Yes, literally.

Stanton treated Linklater to another of his withering looks. 'Of course not. The world had moved on, hadn't it? My father showed the way but of course they never admitted that. Instead they locked him up so they could claim the credit.' With great concentration he realigned his feet by a fraction of an inch. 'That's why they wouldn't let me into medical school, I know it was. I was too clever for them, they were afraid of me.'

'Too right,' muttered Derek the pathologist behind Amos.

'People are crying out for kidneys and skin and heart valves . . . all sorts of things. Soon they'll realize they can make them using plastic resins and metal alloys.' He puffed out his chest. 'I've started a production line, moulding them from real ones. I'll be trying them out on my volunteers soon.' Amos almost choked. Those rows of machines in the workshop weren't all for machining railway parts after all. No wonder Stanton hadn't wanted any help. 'The so-called surgeons are so slow, they're not up to that yet. Meanwhile someone has to supply human ones.'

The colour drained from his listeners' faces.

'It was up to me. No one cared about those people anyway, nobody valued them, certainly not their employer, that thug Karloff, and not their compatriots it seemed: no one ever reported them missing. If someone had to exploit them why not me? For the good of mankind.'

Stanton stood aloft, high on the gleaming locomotive, delivering his speech to the audience, playing God. Amos remembered his own shock when he'd seen the Dürer, a portrait of the artist metamorphosed into

Christ. What had Henry said . . . that Dürer didn't exactly think he was God but 'liked to imagine himself in the role'.

Recovering first Linklater said, 'How did you get them to the shed?'

'Oh, that was easy.' Stanton preened. 'I simply spread a story about buried treasure, in this case art confiscated by the Germans and brought over here later by the American airmen.' There it was again, that echo from Henry — it had been the German hordes who'd destroyed the ancient Greek culture. 'After the discovery of the Dürer sketch was reported in the local paper, I had difficulty coping with the numbers who came.' If only Amos hadn't found that body, some of those poor blighters would still be alive today. Stanton had manipulated the immigrants in the same way he'd manipulated the villagers when he'd wanted to block the army camp development — by spreading stories to the gullible.

'I only had one ventilator, I'd been wanting to get a second and even maybe a third so I could do more — maybe livers and hearts eventually — but you held me up.' He turned on Amos. 'You and your army camp plans, which meant more prying eyes up here! I had to apply for change of use so you wouldn't have an excuse to sniff about, but still you came snooping around with your harebrained scheme to reopen the railway. I couldn't bring in more machines while you were hanging around, so I had to work quickly in between arrivals; shipping the kidneys out fast so I could free up the machine for the next donor.'

Amos experienced a second's relief, he may after all have played a small part in reducing the number of murders.

Linklater scratched his head. 'So there never were any hidden pictures, no hoard of stolen art?'

'Not that I know of. I told you, I made it up.' By his tone the last thing Stanton wanted was to lose the credit for his clever ruse.

'And you used the booby trap to kill the immigrants?' Linklater prompted.

'I found it.'

'Where?' demanded Amos before he could stop himself.

Unfazed, Stanton replied, 'In the hospital of course. It was ingenious. My father had obviously made it for when he couldn't get enough . . . patients.'

'You found the whole thing in the hospital, the rifle as well?' Amos demanded before Linklater could continue.

'Yes, thrown in a corner.'

Amos breathed out. It sounded as though

the underground operations people had dismantled the trap after the war and left it in the old hospital, out of harm's way as they must have believed. Since Stanton had been taking the credit for everything, Amos needn't fear he'd found the underground operations bunker. If he had he'd have claimed it as his own . . . or his father's.

Amos had to ask. 'What about Henry Fishbroke?'

33

Stanton's eyes narrowed then he tossed his head and said nothing. Linklater and Amos exchanged puzzled glances. Linklater tried himself. 'Henry Fishbroke, the man who has the art gallery in Weston. He was out here tonight, did you see him?'

Still no reply. Why couldn't he simply say no? He'd admitted everything else, was proud of it. What had happened to Henry? Had he been an accomplice? Why had he brought Schumann out here — which Amos felt sure he had? Amos began to pray the answer to Stanton's reticence lay in his refusal to admit failure. If he had killed Henry surely he'd be claiming the scalp, wouldn't he?

'But you did kill Franz Schumann?' Amos needed to test his theory, see if Stanton had suddenly realized it was a bad idea to admit guilt and had switched from pride to denial.

'He came to see me. He knew too much and would soon have guessed the rest so I had to kill him.' Stanton sneered. 'Not that he was any use to me, too old.'

Suddenly there were sirens, motors, flashing lights, the whirr of helicopter blades

. . . had the apocalypse arrived to support its envoy of death and depravity? Mercifully not, though nothing would have surprised Amos tonight. The police Land Rovers from the roadblocks together with the dog handlers who'd been in the shed came streaming across the field towards the train. Amos moved aside, all attention focused on Stanton.

Linklater and the pathologist were engaged in directing operations so Amos stood in the dark by the hedge, out of the glare of the police arc lights, away from the ordered formalities of Stanton's arrest. The flickering scene coupled with the night's events exerted a mesmerizing effect, like a strobe light, dimming his senses, confusing his thoughts.

At first he thought he must be watching an old film. He could almost hear the rattle of the reel as the jerky pictures bounced up on the screen in shades of grey and black, the action taking place in the shadows so he couldn't make out what was happening or who was who. He saw a man leap off the rear of the tender on to the track and another man come up the track and attack him. The two men were on the ground fighting. It was a silent film. The sound had been bled out, siphoned into the background noise surrounding the train.

Amos glanced towards the knot of police fifty yards away, then back to the film. He rubbed his eyes. The younger man, the one who'd been on the train, was sitting astride the older one, hammering his head against the rail. Amos didn't think. He snatched the red twine from his coat and hobbling silently the few feet to the fight, whipped it round the younger one's neck and pulled hard . . . until the sniffing stopped. The older one struggled from underneath and clouted his assailant hard on the jaw who, released by Amos, fell back stunned.

Alerted by the action the dogs were there in seconds, grasping the older man by the sleeve. He subsided peacefully on to the ground holding his head . . . a few yards from Karloff. The police came running.

George Churchman looked up at Amos. 'Thanks for the assistance Councillor, but I got him, didn't I? It was me, I got him!'

Karloff was being hauled to his feet by three policemen and led away. Others hovered at Amos's elbow uncertain, confused by this latest development. Linklater strode up. 'I turn my back for one minute and you get yourself into a fight!'

Thank God for Linklater's humour is all Amos could think, he'd just about had enough hell for one night. Apparently none the worse for its excursion, he threaded his twine back through its buttonholes and retied his jacket.

Linklater turned to Churchman. 'I think you've got some explaining to do Churchman . . . down at the station.' He glanced to where Karloff was being led away. 'Friend of yours?'

'You can charge him with importing workers illegally and defrauding the inland revenue for starters,' Churchman said with authority. Still markedly shaken from his rough encounter, Churchman fumbled in an inside pocket. The police looked wary, distrustful of their own shadows and about to stop him but Amos, having realized his identity, looked on placidly. From the ineptitude with which he'd handled himself with Karloff, Amos had ruled out Special Branch or MI5. Churchman produced an identity card which he handed to Linklater. 'Geoffrey T. Periwinkle, Senior Immigration Officer.'

As they helped Churchman away, limping, Linklater turned to Amos. 'Rather than guess, it's quicker to ask you. How did you know?'

'Once I started thinking straight about Schumann and remembered that look on his face, which I will never ever forget, and realized Stanton must be the perpetrator of all that . . . I began to ask myself whether

Churchman was his accomplice. OK, Churchman had asked me to intercede with Stanton on his behalf, to ask Stanton if he, Churchman, could come and help with the railway project, and I supposed that could have been a clever way of deflecting me . . . the same as I'd thought about him calling you tonight. But I doubted he had that brand of cleverness. That's why none of it fitted.'

'If Stanton and Churchman had been in it together would Churchman have always been hanging around that shed as he seemed to be? Would he really have brought you people in? Would he have constantly drawn as much attention as he did to the immigrants? Don't forget it was he who first told me they were disappearing. No, his obsession was with the immigrants. That's why he wanted to help with the railway project — it would have given him a cast-iron excuse for being up here near the airfield all day, instead of having to skulk around being a bad bird-watcher.'

'Then the day I went to enlist his help with Stanton — get him to support the commercial reopening of the old rail network — he sided with Stanton! But that was because he still hoped to be taken on to the project and saw publicly supporting Stanton as a way of ingratiating himself with the man.'

'But you said he'd been stalking you in that hell-hole before we arrived?'

'As he had been,' Amos answered indignantly. 'Bloody fool! He must have got wind of that story I put about, may even have overheard me telling Henry in the street that a number of the immigrants were planning to snatch the paintings and make off tonight. Churchman thought they were still hiding in the shed, and actually I think Karloff might have been, so that's why Churchman was creeping about in there.'

'After you arrived and turned on the lights and he saw the shed was empty, my bet is, still convinced they were hiding somewhere, he went to look in the army camp. Hearing noises he went to investigate and saw Stanton getting into the train. After the Spitfire strafing tonight I'd sensed someone leaving the shed behind Henry's body and now I realize it was Stanton.'

'So how come Churchman was here — fighting with Graham Carlton?'

'Oh, I expect Karloff, or Carlton, saw the place crawling with police, knew you'd find far more immigrants than he has official papers for — by the way, look in the army camp too — and we know he's been pocketing the National Insurance money, so he decided it was time to go. He had spotted the roadblock but seeing the train begin to move he stowed away on it.' Amos stroked his chin. 'I don't know, I'm only guessing, but it will have been something like that.'

'Friend Churchman — Periwinkle, is it?' Amos chuckled for the first time that night. 'He probably saw Karloff board the tender and jogged along behind assuming, as I believe some of your police did, that the track would peter out.'

'But he was in luck anyway because you stopped the train.'

'Yes, and when you arrived, Karloff daren't move, he'd have been too obvious. But as soon as your reinforcements came racketing across he thought he could slip away unnoticed.'

'Meanwhile Churchman had had time to catch up.' Linklater finished for him.

'Exactly. And well . . . you know the rest.'

Linklater frowned 'But why didn't Church . . . Periwinkle tell us who he was and let us help him? Especially when he rang us tonight?'

'Well, I don't suppose it occurred to him that he'd be a prime suspect in a mass murder enquiry; sees himself as a model citizen.' Amos looked at Linklater. 'But I suspect the real answer to your question lies in what he said just after the fight. He thanked me for helping him but was desperate to prove that it was him who caught Karloff!'

'You mean he was determined to get the credit for perhaps stopping a people smuggling ring?'

'His promotion probably depends on it — didn't want you or me or anyone else muscling in and taking over or beating him to it. It's probably the biggest coup he's ever had in his life. As I said, he was obsessed with those immigrants . . . and their guilt. So much so it blinded him to the truth.' Amos paused for breath and looked at Linklater. 'The tragedy is, if he hadn't been so convinced they were melting into the countryside illegally, he could have suspected what was really happening to them and been able to save some lives.' Amos shrugged. 'But I daresay they don't promote you for that.'

He climbed wearily into his Land Rover, reversed it off the track and followed Linklater's police car back down the road to the army camp, keeping an eye out for Napoleon whom he'd not seen since the train started off.

The little convoy pulled up in the corner of the parade ground by the entrance to the No Man's Land and the path to the shed. At Amos's insistence, Linklater had sent his men on ahead to search for Henry.

Linklater strode over to Amos. 'His Jaguar's still on the perimeter road so he can't have gone far.'

That was Amos's concern . . . and it was all his fault. What on earth had possessed him to lure Henry out here in the first place, what did he think he'd been trying to prove . . . that Henry had been creating Spitfire strafing noises which might kill some unsuspecting motorist? Still, it hadn't been difficult, had it? Henry had taken the bait instantly. That made Amos feel even worse because of course now he knew the whole art cache thing had been a hoax; a cruel hoax deliberately devised by Stanton to entice his victims to the shed. And Stanton had probably killed Henry too. Encountered him in his flight and killed him because he was in the way . . . or in case he gave the game away. Just what had been Henry's connection with Schumann . . . and with Councillor Bill Thomas, the man whose last words had been 'Henry said?'

'By the way, did you say Schumann was carrying a rucksack when he came to see you? A large rucksack?' asked Linklater.

'Yes, why?'

'My men say there's one in the boot of Henry Fishbroke's car.'

Before Amos could give this new discovery any thought, he was greeted by a rustling and grunting behind him where an agitated Napoleon was struggling out of the undergrowth. Head down he ran towards them but a few yards short turned abruptly and ran back whence he'd come, his message clear.

The dog handlers were busy searching on the airfield side, so Linklater beckoned a constable and the three of them set off through the scrub, shining torches into the clumps of bracken and calling. After about a hundred yards the vegetation changed, saplings, brambles and decaying branches giving way to grass and moss in a small area near the brook ... as if once cleared deliberately. At the edge of which, propped against a tree trunk and holding a voluminous silk handkerchief to a nasty cut on his head, sat Henry Fishbroke.

He blinked in the torchlight looking utterly bewildered. 'Amos ... Chief Inspector ... What's going on?' He inched away from Napoleon who sat commandingly beside him. 'Your pig attacked me. I remember now. There was a lot of noise and he attacked me.'

'And then you ran off, I saw you.' Amos said.

'Wouldn't you?' Henry answered, indignation returning with his strength. 'With the hound of the Baskervilles after you?'

'Did Stanton do that?' Amos asked, nodding towards Henry's head wound.

'Who?'

'Stanton, Eric Stanton. The man working here . . . on the railway.'

'No of course not. I'd lost my torch and I was running, trying to get back to the car.' He looked around for the culprit. 'I don't remember, must have stumbled and pitched forward into this tree.' Using the trunk as a back stop he stumbled to his feet and shivered.

'I'll call an ambulance,' Linklater said.

'No, no. Can't abide hospitals,' Henry replied. 'I'll be all right.'

'Let's go back to my cottage, the police will bring your car,' Amos said taking command. Certain he knew what the clearing had been used for, he was anxious for them all to be gone from it — especially Linklater.

34

Amos coaxed the fire back to life and settled himself and Henry beside it, scotch in hand, still feeling guilty yet overwhelmingly relieved that Henry had survived relatively unscathed. But for Napoleon, Amos would undeniably have led Henry to his death. He needed to explain, justify his actions.

Haltingly he told Henry about Stanton, how he'd lured the immigrants to the shed with stories of a hoard of pictures in order to kill them for their body parts. He didn't dwell on it, it still seemed too macabre to be real.

'The shooting you heard was the same Spitfire strafing which scared the wits out of me the night I found the skeleton. It was a booby trap — amongst other things the noise served to disorientate the victim.

'I'd seen the old man getting into your car earlier and I thought the pair of you knew where the pictures were, which he and his friend had hidden during the war, and that you were using the noise to frighten people away. It could have caused no end of car accidents on the perimeter road. I had to stop you.' Amos glanced at Henry who was gaping at him open-mouthed, uncomprehending. Amos looked him in the eye. 'I know about the Jeremiahs, Henry. I know you sold Mrs Jeremiah the same Dürer we found on the German POW and that you told her it was real when it wasn't. And I don't suppose that Gainsborough you tried to interest Lord Gray in was genuine either, was it?'

Henry buried his face in his hands and moaned. 'I had no choice. You don't understand, there was nothing else I could do.'

They were interrupted by the scuffing and barging of someone manoeuvering a burden inside the narrow porch, as Schumann's rucksack preceded Linklater through the door. He dumped the bag unceremoniously in the centre of the room where Napoleon sniffed it thoroughly.

'Oh hell. That belongs to that old boy. He got out so quickly I forgot I'd stowed it in the boot for him,' Henry exclaimed.

'You mean Franz Schumann?' Amos asked.

'Is that his name?' Henry looked confused. 'But wasn't that the man you found in the ditch . . . ?'

Helping himself to Amos's whisky, Linklater showed distinct signs of irritation. He was in no mood for playing games after the gruesome night he'd experienced.

'You were with him earlier today . . . '
Amos glanced at the clock and corrected
himself, ' . . . yesterday.' Was Henry con-
cussed or did he think he could lie his way
out even now?

'What?' Henry looked genuinely perplexed,
but then he *was* a confidence trickster. Amos
had seen him do it, with Alec; he'd been
convincing then too.

Amos wondered if Linklater had already
checked the rucksack, surely it was standard
procedure — in case it contained a bomb or
something. But with it being so late and after
what they'd all seen tonight maybe he hadn't.
Why had he brought it in here? To test
Henry's reaction?

'You mean the old man I found collapsed
outside my gallery?' Henry's face relaxed when
he realized to whom they referred. 'I'd been
into Stratford and I was just turning into the
lane when I saw him. He looked so dreadful. I
couldn't just leave him there, could I? Had to
offer to take him home. I picked up the rucksack for him and stowed it in the boot. Never
gave it another thought until now.'

'So you went back into Stratford?' pursued
Amos.

'Stratford? No. He said he lived up on the
airfield, got me to drop him up there. He had
a bit of an accent, I assumed he had

something to do with that immigrant community.' Henry frowned, remembering. 'I must say, I was worried about him, but for all his frailty he was determined to be dropped on the perimeter road, wouldn't let me take him right in. I didn't want to push it, he was scared enough as it was.'

'You're saying you don't know him?' Amos persisted, disbelieving.

Henry looked directly at him and shuffled forward in his chair. He glanced at Linklater, obviously wondering how much he knew. 'Look, I know you think I'm a charlatan but I can explain that . . . ' He stopped, presumably debating whether to do that first. 'I had never seen that old man before — ever.'

So far having remained quietly in the background, sipping his whisky, Linklater now interjected. 'That's funny, because he obviously knew you.'

Both Henry and Amos turned to stare at Linklater. 'He's written you a note.' So Linklater *had* looked inside the bag. 'Why don't you read it?' He indicated the rucksack with his foot.

Bewildered, Henry opened the bag. On top of several cylindrical metal containers sat an envelope addressed to Henry Fishbroke. Henry extracted the letter gingerly and read it aloud.

Dear Henry,

It wasn't until recently, when they found your uncle's body and the Dürer sketch was still with him, and intact, that I realized these too might still be where we'd left them.

I'm more sorry than I can ever express that he did not live, but there again, he'd been ill ever since they took his kidney so maybe it was for the best.

After the war I contacted your grandmother's family in London who told me your father, my friend Karl's younger brother, was the only one of the family in Germany who had escaped the Nazis and had himself settled in England; however I believe he too died when you were very young.

Perhaps for reasons of guilt that I was the one who survived, I made it my business to always know where you were . . . in case I could ever help.

I'm so glad you inherited your family's love of art. Your father and uncle would be pleased to know you will appreciate what they left you.

Yours in memory,
Franz Schumann

Henry was crying. He sat hunched in the middle of the room sobbing into his handkerchief. Amos couldn't move. In between the sobs Henry said, 'I knew Uncle Karl had brought the paintings over here, my mother said Dad was always on about it — reckoned the other Germans had stolen them from him.' He looked round at Amos. 'So when I heard the stories which were circulating, I had to look; I'd already been looking for weeks when you found that body, Amos . . . and the drawing.'

'Where did Bill Thomas fit into all this?' Amos asked gently. 'You were the Henry he meant, weren't you?'

Henry nodded into his handkerchief. 'Yes, yes I was.' He turned to look at Amos. 'I needed time, you see.' Henry got to his feet, ran his fingers through his shock of hair, mopped his brow and stowed his silk handkerchief in its top pocket. More composed, he sat on an upright chair across the table from Linklater.

'I've always loved beautiful things — being surrounded by paintings and sculptures and well-proportioned buildings.' He sighed. 'But I've never been rich and somehow I always owed more than I made.' He paused. 'Then I'd spend again to try and recoup.'

'As a gambler does?' Amos enquired.

'Much the same I suppose, though half the time I didn't want to sell my treasures — which didn't help.'

Jack's words echoed ominously in Amos's mind about Henry not being much of a businessman. Why had he, Amos, been so blind? Because he'd wanted Henry's enterprise in Weston Hathaway to be a success — that's why.

Henry looked across at Amos. 'So I started selling copies of good paintings as though they were the real thing. I'd been told that Uncle Karl had brought the real Dürer with him to this country. But, like my father, I thought it had made its way into some private collection after the war, either back in Germany or in South America with the officers who escaped. No one was ever likely to admit to owning the original they'd stolen — and there were good engravings of it which could be copied. It was the perfect drawing to choose . . . or so I thought!' He turned to Amos. 'You know about Mrs Jeremiah.' He shrugged. 'Even when theirs was stolen there wasn't much risk I'd be found out. No one was going to discover the Jeremiah's Dürer was a fake . . . not when the chances of the original turning up had been a million to one! I took a risk having my picture in the papers over the gallery opening — using a different name. My real name is Werner, as you now know of course, but what's so unusual in changing your name? Even if they saw the photograph, I reckoned the Jeremiahs would think nothing of it.'

And neither had they, thought Amos, until he arrived on their doorstep.

Henry turned to the chief inspector. 'I couldn't believe it that day when you brought the drawing in and there it was, the genuine article . . . my Dürer!'

Amos could contain himself no longer. 'But why didn't you tell us then? Why didn't you come forward and tell us the dead POW was your uncle and the drawing belonged to your family?'

'Because you told me the man was Franz Schumann.' He paused, confused again. 'So I assumed this Schumann character had stolen the picture from my uncle. I had no proof those paintings had belonged to my family, the Nazis wiped them all out so it's unlikely the police would have believed me anyway. And because of the Jeremiahs. How could I tell you the Dürer was mine — and original — without it getting in the papers? The Jeremiahs would then have gone to the police.'

'You could have told us the copy was yours though,' Amos said, thinking out loud.

'Don't you think the Jeremiahs would find that odd? My photograph had already been in the paper over the gallery opening — then the same man recovers his family's Dürer copy! I thought it would make them question the provenance of their own Dürer . . . or think I was the thief who had stolen it. I didn't know what to do.' He turned to Linklater. 'So I told you it was a fake and hoped I could buy it back when the police were done with it.'

Linklater and Amos nodded. 'Franz Schumann and Karl Weiner swapped papers, the dead POW was Karl Weiner . . . your uncle. The old man, Schumann, told me himself yesterday.' Amos watched as Henry stared intently at the bag. 'And the Gainsborough?'

'Well, once you've sold a painting you've sold it — so I began to wonder, what if I could keep selling the same painting?' He looked to see how Linklater was taking his confession, but the chief inspector's face remained expressionless. 'Which meant, either I'd have to steal them back or . . . I could buy a good painting, say school of Gainsborough — a painting by one of his pupils or followers — for£100,000 or so, authenticate it myself as original and then insure it as though it were. By selling shares in the painting on the strength of its certificate of authenticity as backed up by its insurance value, I could make twentyfold what it was worth.' Just like the Burlington Brewster trickster, thought Amos

'But the insurers would have insisted on keeping the painting in their vault, wouldn't they? Amos was sure Alec FitzSimmons had been right about that.'

'Absolutely right but they don't care if it's authentic or not. Not whilst they're holding the painting and the premium has been paid. Because as long as it's not stolen they won't have to pay out.' Henry looked down. 'After I'd sold all the shares, I cancelled the insurance, removed the painting from the insurers and disappeared before the investors discovered it was a fake. That's why I changed my name. Funny thing was, when the investors eventually learned of this and the fraud was exposed, they were too ashamed to report it. Shrewd businessmen don't like to admit they've been duped, it can wreck their reputation.'

Henry kept glancing at the rucksack. 'Have you looked at them, Chief Inspector?'

'Only one or two, that's your subject, not mine. There are seven of them, that's all I can tell you.'

Henry was stunned. 'I never believed, I can't . . . ' He stopped, lost for words. 'That's all of them then, Dad said there were eight

— including the Dürer.'

So Amos had been wrong — had underestimated Karl Weiner's loyalty to his family. He had indeed been prepared to risk his life rather than surrender their inheritance to blackmailers.

'Before I lose you to your paintings — tell me about Bill Thomas,' Amos asked.

'Oh yes, yes.' Henry sat back. 'The debt collectors are after me. That's why I never open the door after dark — I daren't. I live in constant fear . . . they say they'll kill me if I don't pay up.' He sighed. 'As I told you, I'd heard stories about an art cache up near the army camp and knowing Uncle Karl had been imprisoned here . . . call it a desperate man clutching at straws, if you like, but I thought that, given enough time, if it was there I could find it — which would solve all my money problems. So I desperately needed a delay in the development project.'

He looked apologetically at Amos. 'I didn't approach you because I'd heard how keen you were for the development to go ahead so I went to Bill and pleaded. I told him about the men out to kill me. I didn't tell him what the army camp had to do with it but just said I needed the project to stall for as long as he could hold it up. He could see how scared I was.'

'What I still don't understand is why you say you didn't know who Franz Schumann was? He obviously came to see you — to bring you these,' Linklater asked, nodding at the paintings.

'Perhaps I can help there, Chief Inspector,' Amos answered. 'I suspect what happened is that Schumann, probably days ago, retrieved the paintings from wherever he and Weiner had buried them. He packed them into the bag and set off yesterday morning to bring them here to Henry. Henry was out, as he just said, and the gallery closed. Who knows, by the looks of that note maybe he couldn't face you, and had only ever intended to deposit the paintings safely at the gallery. Anyway, Schumann comes to see me while he's waiting.' Amos shook his head. 'Or rather he'd intended to visit me all along because he wanted to tell me who he really was. I believe he was an honourable man who felt ashamed at having been less than honest.

'While he was here Stanton called and that's when Schumann, well . . . flipped. As Stanton said, Schumann thought Stanton was Stanton's father, the butcher who'd extracted a kidney from Karl Weiner and had been threatening to do the same to Schumann. I'm guessing now but I think he was so thrown by seeing Stanton he lost all thought of why he'd come or who he'd come to see. All he could think was he had to confront Stanton.'

Amos looked at Henry. 'He'd never met you before had he? The state he was in he didn't realize you were the gallery proprietor returned, he probably wasn't even aware it was the gallery he'd collapsed beside. It was pure chance, call it serendipity in this case, that it was you who happened by and gave him a lift and that he didn't take the paintings into the shed — because if Stanton had hidden them, we'd never have known they were there. No, all Schumann could think about was Stanton's father. And he knew where to find him — at the old isolation hospital. He knew he had to stop Stanton and his evil.'

'I'm sorry, Henry, but Franz Schumann is dead. Stanton killed him. But it was he who pointed the way right from that day when I met him out on the perimeter road — Franz led us all to Stanton. It's taken sixty years but he has avenged your uncle's death and returned your family's property. He didn't die in vain.'

Epilogue

Taking a deep breath, Amos announced: 'The ministry have sold the old airfield to the rural co-operative set up between the government and local farmers, and the council have passed the plans to allow the building of a modern processing plant on the site.' He beamed. 'So we've finally got what we wanted!'

After news of Stanton's activities had spread, no one had wanted to work up there so the remaining immigrants had been helped to return to their own countries or found legitimate work elsewhere in Britain. With that and Karloff's arrest for fraud and the illegal importation of labour, the makeshift plant at the airfield had closed down overnight.

'And the army camp?' Jack asked quietly, but a hush fell all the same. The development proposals had been widely reported in the local press but three weeks ago Leamington had received the go-ahead for development of its latest industrial park.

'They passed the plans,' Amos said simply, holding his breath. 'We're to have the National Railway Museum over at Lower Farthing and the rail link reopened through to Oxford.' Much to his surprise this met with a huge cheer.

'There's only one thing left we don't know about then,' Jack said later in the evening as he straightened the cloth on the bar between him and Amos.

'I wish you wouldn't do that Jack,' Amos nodded towards the towel. 'It reminds me of Stanton, always lining things up. Gives me the creeps.'

'You're the one who lines things up I think,' said a voice behind Amos. 'Two pints of your best, landlord, if you please. And you, Amos, will you have a drink?'

'Henry!' Amos felt awkward, didn't know how to ask.

Henry rescued him. 'As you can see, the jails were all full.' Linklater came down the steps and Henry handed him a pint. 'Thanks for sending me a minder.'

Amos had simply asked Linklater to do what he could. Henry had been prepared to make reparations and compensate those from whom he had stolen. Putting him in jail would serve no purpose except to teach the criminal fraternity more about art so they could improve their game. Much better to have Henry back here, running his gallery.

Henry took a sip of his beer. 'Ahh . . . I wondered how long . . . But never mind, here I am. Sentence suspended for three years.

Oh, and Mrs Jeremiah sends her regards.'

'I bet she couldn't believe it.' Amos said, pleased his representations and those of Lord Gray, his friends and the police, had served to keep Henry out of prison. To make amends, Henry had loaned the Jeremiahs his Dürer sketch for their lifetimes with only one condition — unlimited visiting rights for himself and Amos.

Linklater drew Amos to one side. 'I hear they've ruled on the army camp.' He looked down at those faultlessly polished shoes of his. 'What'll happen to the No Man's Land — I hear they favoured a garden of remembrance?'

Amos eyed his friend. 'They've decided on a wildlife area. They'll pull down the shed and fill in what was the underground hospital. And they'll put up nesting boxes and coppice some of the perimeter trees but otherwise it'll be left as a haven for nature.' Amos, ably abetted by Lord Gray, had worked hard to ensure the secret underground bunker would be neither discovered, nor disturbed — just in case.

'We won't be hearing the ghostly Spitfires any more then?' Linklater said pointedly.

Amos smiled. 'Let's just say, if we do, we've a suspected invasion on our hands — and it would be best to make yourself scarce.'